BOND DADDY

John P. Bott
&
Jason L. Fowell

iUniverse, Inc.
New York   Bloomington

This is a work of fiction. All of the characters, names, incidents, organizations, and dialogue in this novel are either the products of the author's imagination or are used fictitiously.

iUniverse books may be ordered through booksellers or by contacting:

iUniverse
1663 Liberty Drive
Bloomington, IN 47403
www.iuniverse.com
1-800-Authors (1-800-288-4677)

ISBN: 978-1-4502-1361-5 (sc)
ISBN: 978-1-4502-1363-9 (dj)
ISBN: 978-1-4502-1362-2 (ebook)

Printed in the United States of America

iUniverse rev. date: 03 / 15 / 10

To Laura and Debbie, our loving wives.

Inspired from actual events.

PROLOGUE

▼

1986

They watched him walk across the street towards the front steps of the church. He wore a faded charcoal suit with a plain gray tie. It was an automated reflex as they immediately looked back to the car from which he had just exited.

He always owned the newest and most elegant cars. Owning many of them at the same time, often for less than a few months—unless he just had not driven it yet. Occasionally, he owned a car for just a day. Price was never an issue. And no one ever knew what he was going to pull up in until he arrived.

Their eyes fell upon the car and they turned to walk towards the car he had been driving. Surely their eyes deceived them. They blinked repeatedly, not believing what they were seeing, but nothing changed. The car was an unassuming and unimpressive two-door hatchback—a faded green color, and with several small dents.

His name was Dan Manikan or, as they called him, "Cadillac Dan."

When they had worked with him he was in his prime and it didn't matter what car he owned or even how many cars he had. It was known that he never met a Cadillac he didn't like. There was a running joke that he had a Cadillac buying disorder. Or maybe he just did not know what to do with all the money he had made back then. But Cadillac Dan was now driving a car that would have gotten any broker at the firm fired. This couldn't be his car. Or could it?

Cadillac Dan must have noticed the obvious look of disbelief on their faces as he approached them but gave no answer to their questioning looks. He merely glanced at them. "Gentlemen," he whispered. He tipped his head as he walked by.

They were there to pay their final respects to Jordan S. Strong, who had died of a heart attack. From the moment they started working for him he was only known as Strong. He was their boss, the firm's boss. And everyone who ever interviewed for a job with him was excited to be able to work for the man. However, from the day they began to work for the firm they soon learned to become terrified of Strong. He had no patience for anyone who could not sell. He had even less tolerance for those who could sell, but failed to do so. His words rang in their ears as they remembered his most notable line. "Shove the bonds down their throats or up their asses. I don't care, just make it happen!"

Strong could find a salesman who was a diamond in the rough and make that guy a millionaire. He made both of them millionaires. His corner office was like a luxury apartment. Its arrangements included an incredibly large desk, two oversized Italian leather couches with complimenting leather chairs, and exquisite artwork on every wall. The office also had a private bathroom with a shower, specifically made for two. A wet bar was hidden behind massive bookshelves. He owned the building and it showed.

Strong also knew how to throw a party. Whether at a restaurant, a bar, or his own home, he celebrated somewhere at least once a week. Nothing, however, compared to the clandestine parties held in the Emperor's Lounge on the top floor. The Emperor's Lounge was the most lavishly decorated room in the building and showcased Strong's fondness for mahogany and leather. The room was also furnished with numerous antiques from around the world. Gaming tables lined part of one wall of the room, which was also complete with an unbelievable bar stocked with the finest libations money could buy.

The parties, also known as "Zeros," kept secret from the trainees, rookies, and junior brokers, were by invitation only. However, a party after work in The Emperor's Lounge did not stay secret for long. Every rookie who eventually heard of it could not wait for the exclusive privilege of being invited. But the doors to the Emperor's Lounge only opened when there were enough zeros in a broker's paycheck. It was also an informal passage into the fraternal order of the firm. The Zeros had rules—rules that could not be broken.

They felt that the least they could do was attend Strong's funeral. Neither of them had really anticipated running into anyone else who had worked for the firm. So far, with the exception of seeing Cadillac Dan, they were right. And all of the firm's partners were either dead, in hiding, or eking out a living in other states after being released from prison.

When Cadillac Dan opened the door to the small church they saw Strong's casket from where they were standing on the steps. Hesitating to enter, one simple question made them stop. It brought to mind how their own lives almost became a part of the tragedy that unfolded within the firm.

Aaron asked a single question. "Hey Jack, do you remember the first time you met Jordan Strong?"

Jack lit his cigarette. "I sure do. What about you?"

"Are you kidding me? Of course I do. I sold him a backyard pool."

CHAPTER ONE

▼

1974

For Aaron, it began many years ago, in the early spring of 1974. Aaron was working for A Plus Lawn and Water Works. The company was a combination business of lawn care, installation of sprinkler systems, and everything regarding swimming pools. The company serviced a wide range of clients, from those who just needed their lawns mowed, to others who wanted extravagant pools and the finest landscaping.

Aaron started out as a pool cleaner while just in junior-high school. After a few years of working there he sometimes would, ever so subtly, make suggestions to homeowners regarding their landscaping. By the time Aaron was a senior in high school he eventually added part-time sales to what he did for the company, and once he graduated high school, began working for the company full time.

Aaron had a special talent. He was good at identifying with people. He was especially good at mimicking anyone's voice, style, and mannerisms. If the customer talked in a deep voice, he talked in a deep voice. If they talked fast, he would also talk fast. If they said "um" a lot, he said "um" a lot. He could tell the difference between someone who knew what they wanted, someone who needed to be told what to buy, and someone who just wanted to be sold anything. The owner of the company barely recognized Aaron's talent. It was likely the owner did not even know what hit him when Aaron made the pitch and closed the deal to move himself from pool boy and part-time sales to being in full-time sales, and the company's service manager.

As it turned out, working as a pool boy for so long gave him some early training and an advantage when dealing with the wealthier clients. As a full-time salesman for the company, Aaron spent a great deal of his time in the better neighborhoods in and around Houston. He also made many service calls, and for various reasons. A client wanted more landscaping. The pump in the pool needed to be replaced. The light in the pool burned out. Whatever it was, or whatever was needed, Aaron made sure that he was there, since he usually ended up selling something else to the homeowner.

There was one neighborhood Aaron particularly enjoyed. Every time he made a call to this area he made money. One thing, though, that Aaron always found odd was a particular house towards the entrance of the subdivision, as it always had water running down the driveway, over the curb, and into the street. The house was a large mansion next to a golf course. The house also had an incredibly large front yard edged by large and established oak trees. Aaron had played the golf course once or twice and remembered that this house also had a very large backyard. Surprisingly, there was very little landscaping, and what was there was far from manicured.

One day, after a service call to another client, he slowed down as he passed this house. He was coasting past when he looked up the driveway. What he witnessed was interesting. A middle-aged man was ranting and raving, pacing back and forth, and yelling about the yard and the water. Sensing an opportunity, Aaron pulled over, stepped out of his truck, and started walking up the driveway to introduce himself.

As Aaron was walking up the driveway he witnessed the man picking up his water-sprinkler and slamming it on to the ground. The man then picked it up again and dropkicked it. The man became even more enraged when the sprinkler sprayed him, soaking the lower half of his pants. He was fuming and cussing up a storm. As Aaron approached, the man looked up, saw the logo on Aaron's shirt, and then stared at Aaron intensely. He suddenly started screaming, "I hate this water sprinkler and I fucking hate watering the lawn!"

The man had cussed, so Aaron cussed, too. "I wouldn't hand water this fucking lawn either! Why don't you quit wasting your time and install an automatic water sprinkler system?"

It was either luck or Aaron's God-given talent to recognize that this stranger hated wasting time. He was not really an impatient person, but he hated wasting time that could be better used. In his business time was definitely money. Regardless, Aaron now had his full attention.

"My name's Jordan Strong," he said as he calmly extended his hand to Aaron.

"Hello, I'm Aaron Graham, and it's a pleasure to meet you."

Before Aaron knew it, he had sold Strong a new water sprinkler system, a koi pond, and a backyard pool, complete with waterfalls for both the pool and the Jacuzzi. Of course, as Aaron pointed out, it would not be complete unless the entire backyard was fully landscaped. Fifteen-foot-tall palm trees were to be planted. Aaron sold sandstone rock steps that wound around the yard and between the palm trees. He also sold the latest in pool lighting and a backyard barbeque pit kitchen. With, of course, a complete patio set, including a wet bar and an outdoor pool table, which were to be placed inside an elaborately planned gazebo. Aaron sold products his company didn't even supply.

But the front yard needed to be done as well, so Aaron and Strong walked around the property while Aaron pitched different ideas on what would look good and what would work with everything Strong was going to install in the backyard. After all was said and done, Strong, appearing pleased, coolly asked how much it was all going to cost.

After a couple of minutes of calculating, Aaron had an estimated cost. On the inside, Aaron was excited, terrified, and anxious. He didn't know how Strong would react. Was this the sale of his life? Or was it overkill? And if this was the sale of his life he wished his commission percentage were higher. Mimicking Strong's cool attitude Aaron quoted him the total. "One hundred and fifty thousand dollars."

Without any hesitation, Strong simply responded, "That's fine. Is a check okay?"

Aaron was floored. He had done business in this exclusive part of town for the past few years and nobody had ever written just one check, and even before any work had begun, for such a job.

Aaron was quiet for a minute, and then totally lost the cool composure that he had been mirroring from Strong. All at once Aaron rapid-fired out a series of questions. "I have to know what in the world you do for a living! What kind of degree do you have? Are you a doctor? Where did you go to college?"

Strong laughed. "I don't have a college degree. I only lasted one semester." Strong paused, and then looked Aaron right in the eye. "I move money around in the financial markets."

From Strong's viewpoint, Aaron's salesmanship did not go unrecognized. Aaron never realized that after a few minutes of conversation, Strong was recruiting him. Aaron had sold and sold to Strong, and there was nothing Strong liked more than being "sold." Strong wanted Aaron to come in for an interview at the firm.

Aaron really didn't understand what Strong did for a living. He wondered if maybe Strong was hustling him. Strong, however, was ten times the salesman Aaron was, and immediately recognized Aaron's hesitation. He could also sense Aaron's desire to make more money than he did now, and felt Aaron's craving to impress upon others his stature in life. Working for the lawn care company was not going to satisfy Aaron's dreams of fast cars, expensive homes, and exotic vacations. Nor would it satisfy the sinful pleasures that accompany such a lifestyle.

Furthermore, Strong knew when to push a sale. He also knew when to pull the sale—or at least give the impression he was pulling the offer off the table. As he turned and began walking back to his house, Strong spoke over his shoulder to Aaron. "I make more money than God, and my change goes to Jesus." There was a slight smirk on his face. "Oh, by the way, if you happen to know anyone who can sell half as good as you do, then send him to me. I'll make him a millionaire. Strong could still sense Aaron's hesitation so went in for the kill. "Otherwise, I'll just see you around now and then when you get the work started on my yard."

Aaron agreed to go to Strong's office the following Monday for an interview. He also immediately thought of his best friend Jack. Aaron called Jack right away for two reasons. The first, to tell him about the fantastic opportunity he had received to interview with Strong. Second, to "order" Jack to interview with Strong as well.

*   *   *   *

Aaron and Jack had been best friends since they were in grade school. Aaron also knew that Jack would be reluctant to take off from work to be interviewed by someone he knew nothing about. He also knew Jack would be suspicious since Aaron did not really know what Strong did for a living and would not be able to answer any of Jack's questions.

Aaron had already approached Jack with countless get-rich schemes that would make them, according to Aaron, instant millionaires. When they were kids they both decided that they were going to get rich together.

Jack was just as ambitious. But he knew he was not the salesman that Aaron was. However, he was extremely smart, dedicated, and hard-working.

Jack had graduated from college with double degrees in finance and economics, and immediately upon graduation had obtained a job for a large insurance company. Jack's theory of getting rich was to work for a large company, bust his butt, and then get promoted up the ladder until he was making the "big bucks."

Jack did not work in the sales division of the insurance business. He was a number cruncher and rarely met with clients, but he felt he had the kind of education that would eventually get him where he wanted to be in life. With this attitude, combined with the fact that Jack was not afraid of any amount of work, he thought he was on the right path. It was a slow one, but the right one.

Jack had been working since he was in grade school. He had started his first paper route on his ninth birthday, waking up every morning at 4:30 a.m. to deliver papers. This job opened other doors for him. He knew everyone very well on his route and would suggest extra jobs he could do for them. Before he knew it, shop owners were asking him to make deliveries for them—Christmas cards, birdseed, diapers, and various groceries. Even neighbors would give him a couple of dollars to return a borrowed tool to another neighbor who lived a few blocks away.

Jack, being quite the entrepreneur, soon hired his friends to make some of the deliveries and gave them a cut of the money. He started mowing lawns on the weekends as well. When he got too busy, he hired a crew of his friends and classmates to work for him.

The only thing Jack enjoyed more than making money was playing sports. All sports—basketball, baseball, football—it didn't matter. He especially loved the feeling of winning. By the time Jack was in high school he spent most of his time either practicing one sport or another or working, saving every penny from his various entrepreneurships.

One thing he did not excel in was school, because getting to bed after 11:00 p.m. and then rising at 4:30 a.m. did not leave much time for sleep, or studying. So everyday, without fault, he was ready for a nap after lunch.

Mrs. Cobb had the frustrating task of teaching Jack math, which was right after lunch, and during this nap time. Fortunately for Jack, math was his easiest subject and he always scored high grades. This fact irritated Mrs. Cobb even more. Despite Jack discreetly sleeping in class, Mrs. Cobb started paying particular attention to him. She always felt the need to try to embarrass him in class, but Jack, being good-natured, just took it all in stride.

Because of Jack's sleeping habits, eventually Mrs. Cobb started sending him to the principal's office. The principal would give Jack an option—suspension or "pops." But after delivering newspapers for years, Jack had developed a cast-iron butt from the bicycle seat. He chose pops every time.

Jack also had a tendency to joke around on the football field at the wrong times and piss-off the coaches. This, of course, never went unpunished. The coaches, unlike the principal, truly knew how to deliver pops. The principal never learned the strategy and dynamics of putting his whole body into the swing, shifting his weight, and following through.

As the principal became increasingly frustrated with Jack's non-responsiveness to the spankings, he just started sending him back to class. So Mrs. Cobb was forced to try a new tactic. The ringing of the bell when class was over sometimes did not awaken Jack, so Mrs. Cobb decided she would just let him sleep if he didn't wake up. Because she did not have a fifth-period class, it was fairly quiet and Jack could get in a good nap. Twice in a row he slept so long that he was late for football practice. After a one-game suspension, and a phone call to his parents, things changed. Jack's dad was a retired military officer and knew exactly how to adjust someone's attitude.

Afterward, Jack was wide-awake in class, every day. Mrs. Cobb was soon agitated again as Jack would now not stop asking questions. Even worse, Jack's understanding of math and numbers was overwhelmingly advanced. In his free time he would spend hours going over financial books with complicated math, and he would then ask Mrs. Cobb questions related to these books. Questions she could not answer. Mrs. Cobb was an excellent teacher, but her expertise was not in the advanced subjects Jack was asking about. What she especially hated was when Jack would challenge theorems. One day Mrs. Cobb was so frustrated with Jack that she screamed at him during her lecture. "Please just go back to sleep and let me teach!"

Aaron knew Jack's way of thinking and his workaholic attitude. Aaron also knew that Jack was always chasing pennies when he was quite capable of making dollars. Aaron turned from best friend to salesman and started selling Jack on Jordan S. Strong's Company.

And Jack knew that Aaron was prone to exaggeration, so he was skeptical when Aaron started telling him about Strong. He also knew that Aaron usually didn't know what he was talking about, even if he was selling it.

Jack had goals and Aaron knew which buttons to push to get Jack going. Jack had always envisioned himself driving a Rolls Royce to his ten-year high-school reunion. He wanted to be a millionaire by the time he was thirty. And he wanted his own jet for his fortieth birthday.

These goals seemed so far away though. He knew that working at his current job would never get him there in such a short timeframe. Aaron kept pushing until Jack realized that one interview could do no harm.

Before he knew it, Jack was on his way to interview with the bond daddy of all bond daddies. Jack was ready to make the sales pitch of his life.

The address Aaron had given Jack led to a three-story building with reserved parking underneath. The security guard directed Jack to park in an uncovered area that was behind the building. As Jack drove underneath, and through the entrance of the parking garage, he could not help but stare at all the cars parked neatly in a row. Every single one was brand new. Each was expensive and luxurious. A few Rolls Royces, Bentleys, a Jaguar, some Porsches, and the list kept going. At the very end was an all-American Shelby Cobra.

As Jack parked his car he noticed Aaron's truck was already there. Even though no one told Jack what time to show up he suddenly felt a surge of panic. It was only 9:00 in the morning, but Aaron was already there, and in Aaron's world the clock didn't start until almost noon. Jack started to run to the front door, but stopped when he noticed he was already breaking into a sweat and it was not even hot outside.

Jack exited the elevator onto the first floor of the building. The building's exquisite marble floors led him to a receptionist's desk in what Jack could only describe as lush. Ornate shelves filled the wall to the right of her desk. Fine artwork lined the wall on the left. A gold-leaf mirror hung behind the receptionist.

This was all forgotten when Jack saw the beautiful blonde receptionist who sat behind the desk. Then the sweetest voice rang in his ears. "Good morning. How may I help you?"

Jack was cordial on the outside, but his mind was drifting into the gutter as he stared at the woman. He could not stand it, but managed to keep his cool as he struggled to look at her eyes rather than her low-cut blouse. "I'm here for an interview with Mr. Jordan Strong."

The receptionist checked her appointment book then looked calmly back at Jack, obviously waiting for him to say something.

"I don't actually have an appointment to see him, but I was told to show up this morning."

She smiled in her response. "Don't worry about it. Half the young men who walk into this office for the first time say that. Have a seat and he'll be right with you. He's with someone right now." Jack went to sit down, and after a minute she asked him, "Can I get you something to drink?"

On the inside, Jack thought he was about to die. Her beauty was killing him and the stress of the interview made him feel like he was in a sauna. He wanted to scream, "For God's sake lady, can't you see the bullets of sweat running down my face? Get me some water!" But on the outside he kept his cool. "If it's not too much trouble, some water would be nice. Thank you."

He watched her flawless body glide down the hall beyond her desk. She quickly reappeared with a crystal glass containing perfectly round ice cubes and the clearest water he had ever seen. Jack took a sip and placed the glass on the table next to an ashtray. He picked up The Wall Street Journal and tried to read the headlines while he waited.

For the next ten minutes, which felt like hours, Jack sat there trying to read the Journal. He could not help but fight his wandering eyes as he kept stealing looks at the receptionist. Sometimes she saw him sneaking looks at her, and sometimes she did not. Jack kept turning and folding the pages back and forth, looking and reading without comprehending a thing.

Suddenly, as he watched in what seemed to be slow motion, one of the double doors began to swing open in front of him. Jack quickly began to dry the palm of his right hand for the first handshake and nervously waited to see what Jordan Strong looked like.

But it was only Aaron walking through the door. Jack quietly let out a sigh of relief, but quickly stood up from his seat with a barrage of questions. "What was the interview like? What does he look like? Did you get the job? Are there other positions? Can you give me any advice? How long was the interview? What did he ask you? What did he say?" Jack was too nervous to remember where he was and that this was all business.

Aaron turned and winked at the receptionist. He then looked back at Jack and whispered, "If you think she's hot, wait until you see his secretary! In fact, I think every girl working here is some sort of model or something. It's unbelievable! I can't wait to start working here!"

Jack wasn't quite listening and started asking his questions again. "Pay attention to me. I'm going to kick your ass. Focus. What's the deal? Did you get the job?"

"Practically. I just have to interview with a few more people. I don't really understand what they do here though. He mostly talked about money, and something about bonds. I thought he was in investments, but I guess he gets people out of jail or something."

"Not bail bonds you prick. He's talking about fixed-income securities."

"What?"

"They're kind of like stocks. You know, the stock market?"

"Yea, whatever. As long as I can write hundred-thousand-dollar checks like him, I don't care. Gotta run, I need to get to work and give my notice that I'm quitting."

"But you haven't been hired yet."

"I will be. Plus I need time to schedule my other interviews."

Jack was not fully paying attention again. "What? What other interviews?" Aaron just rolled his eyes as he walked away.

Aaron wasn't kidding about the girls in the office. Jack barely had sat back down when the most stunning brunette he'd ever laid his eyes on opened the double doors and asked him to follow her to Mr. Strong's office. She took him all the way to the back, and then to a corner of the building on the second floor. Passing along the way was one beautiful woman after another.

Despite the attention-grabbing women, Jack could not help but notice the elegance of the office building. There were beautiful, dark-colored wooden floors and rich paneling halfway up the walls. A deep-red rough silk fabric began where the wood stopped, ending at the ceiling, which was adorned with numerous crystal chandeliers.

The secretary offered him a seat in her office, which he quickly noticed was larger than his own office at the insurance company. Her desk was bigger than his, too. And the visitor's chairs were upholstered in leather. Jack made note that he didn't even have any chairs in his office for guests. She spoke softly. "Mr. Strong is on the phone right now, but he'll be right with you. Can I offer you anything, a smoke perhaps?"

Jack shook his head and quietly replied, "No. I don't smoke, but thank you." He sat there crossing and uncrossing his legs and trying not to stare at the secretary while he waited. Her name was Kate. He watched as she put a cigarette between her lips and lit it. It was not long before she called Strong to inform him that his newest recruit was waiting. "Mr. Strong will see you now." To Jack, everything she did was sensual.

As he followed her into Mr. Strong's office Jack could not help but be intimidated by the room's size and splendor. Fabulous artwork that even an amateur would appreciate decorated the walls. Strong had an enormous mahogany desk with massive chairs scattered in front of it. The panoramic view of downtown Houston was perfect.

As Jack walked towards the desk, the strong smell of cologne slapped him in the face. As if in slow motion, Jack watched Strong raise his right hand to introduce himself. Jack's eyes momentarily fixated on Strong's fingernails. The man was wearing clear nail polish and his nails were trimmed to an exact length and precise curve.

Jack extended his hand to introduce himself as Strong began to speak.

"I'm Jordan Strong. Please have a seat," he said as he motioned to one of the Italian leather chairs. Jack somehow could not get his mind off the fact that the man wore nail polish.

"What do you know about bonds, Jack?"

The smell of cologne was overwhelming and causing Jack to get a little dizzy. And what was the deal with the nail polish? Jack began to feel a little faint. He thought of all the fancy cars parked below. And what was the deal with all these beautiful women in the office? And hundred-thousand-dollar checks? What about all this money Aaron mentioned that everyone was making? He was suddenly confused. He didn't know what was going on, but what he did know was that he wanted this job, whatever it was. Jack was stressing himself out, and mustered a response without even thinking. "Not very much, sir. I've never been to jail."

Mr. Strong almost fell out of his chair laughing. "No, not those kinds of bonds. Do you know how roads and bridges get built, Jack? Do you know what happens to a home mortgage?"

"I'm sorry Mr. Strong, I don't know why I said that. I do know a little bit about what you're talking about."

"Good, then let me tell you what we do here instead of wasting more time. Can I offer you a smoke?"

"No thank you, I don't smoke."

"You don't mind if I do?" Strong asked as he lit one up. It was not a question, but more of a cordial response.

For the next half hour Strong gave Jack a sales pitch on the company. Strong told him what they did and explained that it was the best and easiest way to make money. All anyone had to do was come in early every morning with a good attitude, a smile, pick up the phone, and then make about a hundred to a hundred and fifty calls each day. All of the calls were to bankers, insurance companies, and state government agencies and municipalities.

"If I hire you and you're not making more than the President of the United States by the end of the year, I'm going to fire you. It's as simple as that. No one here makes less than that. Our motto is 'smile and dial.' If you can't do that, then you can't work here."

While Jack sat listening, he was thinking that for 200K a year he would pick up any phone, even if an elephant with diarrhea had sat on it. Jack also knew that with his level of determination and his education that he would be far superior compared to most anyone he knew, especially when it came to dedication to his work. He was going to make a fortune here. He couldn't stop thinking about the money. It was very enticing.

Then the room seemed suddenly silent. Jack mentally pinched himself and starting paying attention again. "Excuse me, sir?"

"I said, are you married Jack?"

"Yes, sir," he replied. "To my high-school sweetheart." Jack tried to answer as enthusiastically as he could, since deep down he knew that his marriage was on the rocks.

"That's great, a family man. We need more of you around here. There's nothing more important than family. You need to take care of your family in the best possible way. I promise you, they deserve what you can give them by working here. Luxury. It's my favorite word. It's not the money we crave Jack, it's the luxury and the lifestyle that money can get you." Strong paused for a second, staring off into space. "I love the smell of hundred-dollar bills." He sat for another moment then resumed his speech.

"I can give you all the tools you will ever need to make more money than you will know what to do with. All I ask for is loyalty, Jack. Especially once you are a success. Money changes everything. I want your loyalty now, and I want it after. Do you have a problem with that, Jack?"

Jack thought, loyalty? What does he exactly mean by being loyal? And he wants it after what? A hesitant Jack finally responded. "What kind of loyalty and what do I have to do to prove my loyalty?"

Mr. Strong laughed again. "If I hire you and you start making a million dollars a year, I want your word that you will stay here with me at HAYNES, OLIVE, GAGE & STRONG. I don't want you to leave me and go to another company, no matter what they promise you. Can I have your word on that?"

Jack paused and quickly thought for a moment. If he received the raise he was hoping for at the end of the month, he would make twenty-three-thousand dollars a year. But there was a difference between twenty-three-thousand dollars and the million Mr. Strong was saying Jack could earn, and that was what Jack wanted. A million.

In a straightforward and deep voice, Jack responded. "Mr. Strong, if you do what you just said you can do, I will sign, along with any other document you want me to sign, an agreement allowing you to commit me to an insane asylum should I ever come to you and say that I am quitting."

"Good answer. I think you can work here. In order to get this job, though, you first need to interview with the other three partners and a few junior partners. My secretary will tell you who they are. And it is your responsibility to get the interviews." Strong was firm when he made this last statement.

"The next training class starts in three-and-a-half weeks. If you get the same approval from each of those interviews, then you will be hired and can start with the new class. We run a tight ship here and it has proven to be very successful. We will teach you to be a professional in this business. We will not teach used-car salesman skills. And we are not here to churn accounts or lose client's money. Remember, the pigs get fat and the hogs get slaughtered. I am talking true professionalism and sophistication."

Jack thought that there would be more, or that Strong would ask him more questions about his professional background, but finally realized that the interview was over when Strong turned his chair around, looked out the window, and said, "Now if you will excuse me, I need to make some phone calls." One look over his shoulder told Jack that it was time to leave, and if he wanted to make a good impression, he had better leave, and quickly. Jack left the office as fast as he could.

CHAPTER TWO

▼

The hardest part of breaking into this business was making enough phone calls to succeed. Most rookie brokers would not make their first sale for weeks, or even months. Generally speaking, it was very intimidating to some poor little rookie who did not know too much about bonds to call a bank president, chief executive, treasurer of an insurance company, or comptroller of a governmental entity. Many rookies could never quite overcome the intimidation and fear they felt and would quit within a month.

The first sale usually would not happen until an average rookie grew some "alligator skin" and was either too angry or too hungry to care who was on the other end of the phone. It was at that moment that a rookie broker truly believed he could do this job. When the rookie realized that he had something that others needed to buy, and finally made that first sale, was when he became a junior associate.

However, no one ever spoke of this during the interviews. The potential employee had no clue and the partners intentionally omitted mentioning this for a number of reasons. Half of the interview was to motivate the potential broker by talking about how much money he could earn. The other half was to assess whether or not the person had the determination to make it in the business.

Despite all the talk about working hard and making lots of money, Strong never mentioned what it was like to make a hundred cold calls everyday. He also never mentioned that most bankers did not want to talk to cold callers. In fact, many bankers were very rude to bond salesmen. They did not want to be called and often let it be known to the pitiful young rookie on the other end of the line. That was only if a rookie was lucky enough to get through to them in the first place.

Most secretaries at the target companies were well trained to smoke out cold callers. They also discouraged prospective cold callers from ever calling back again. The repertoire went something like this: "He's not in." "He's in a meeting." "He's on the phone." "Give me your name and number and I will have him call you back." "Who is this again? He doesn't know you."

If a rookie happened to get past the secretary, cold callers were then blown off as quickly as possible. "Call me tomorrow." "I don't have any money." "I just bought some bonds yesterday." "If you had only called me this morning." "I have a client coming into the office so I can't talk with you now." "Send me the information in the mail." "I already have a broker." The average rookie accepted the lines and moved on.

Every rookie looked for the chance for someone to respond, "I'm kind of busy right now, but tell me what you've got." Those people were whores, not that a broker cared since it meant a sale. These bankers and chief executives would buy from anyone who called as long as they thought the bond was good and would make their company some money.

Most rookies did not realize that quite a few bankers and executives actually knew very little about bonds, other than some key phrases or words. These were bank presidents or some other executive, not bond brokers. For banks, most were loan officers who had moved up the corporate ladder to the top. They knew about loans, not about bonds. Even once they became bank presidents buying bonds was secondary to originating loans. It seemed, however, that these people knew just enough about bonds to shake off the rookies to get them off the phone, "I need more spread." "What's the yield to maturity?" "Is it callable?" "Sorry, that's not what I am looking for." "It doesn't fit my portfolio."

The firm's preferred method of weeding out the prospective brokers was to begin their training before they were even hired, and did so when the prospective employees were scheduling interviews with the other partners. One of the means to the firm's success was that an interviewee never knew this information in advance, as it was a well-kept secret. It was what the partners called "running the gauntlet." This meant that the prospective broker could not take "no" for an answer if they were going to survive. Successful salesmen had to pursue a sale to the "ends of the earth," so the firm had developed the best way to see if each potential salesman had what it took. Each partner would treat each interviewee as a cold caller. This served to weed out those who would surely fail. It also substituted as an early training ground for those who would succeed.

Over the next few weeks Jack tried to obtain the required interviews with the other partners at the firm. This proved to be much more of a challenge than he originally anticipated. Jack repeatedly called to schedule appointments.

Both the partners and the secretaries were rude when he called. Jack often received the same responses. "He's busy." "He has no time." "He's not here." Several times Jack did manage to schedule an interview and he arrived only to be disappointed by a no-show because the partner was "busy," "in a meeting," "not there," or "he just interviewed somebody else and had just left."

On the off chance that Jack finally obtained an interview, he would walk into the office only to hear, "I'm busy right now, whatcha got?" At this point, it was up to Jack to pursue and develop a positive relationship with the partner.

For every ten or so potential trainees that went through this ordeal only a few made it to the training class. And every day before a new training class was to begin at least one guy would be at the firm trying to obtain an interview.

Like every other future trainee, Jack did not know about the particular routine the partners put all prospective employees through, and he soon became increasingly frustrated trying to get the interviews. His frustration slowly turned to anger towards some of the partners.

Jack slowly, but surely, had obtained every interview he needed, except for one, "Mean" Dean Davidson, a junior partner with the firm. In the preceding three weeks, Jack had called Dean at least once a day and had scheduled five interviews with him. Dean especially made Jack angry because it took valuable time away from his job at the insurance company. Jack would schedule an interview; drive down to HAYNES, OLIVE, GAGE & STRONG, only to arrive and discover that Dean was "busy," "in a meeting," "not there," or something else.

On the Friday before the training class was to begin, Jack called Dean's secretary in the middle of the day. She informed him that Dean was leaving at 3:30 that afternoon and would be gone for two weeks. Despite how busy Jack was that day, he dropped everything and said he would be there in half an hour. If Jack wanted to be in the next training class he would have to get this interview with Dean, and he had to do it that day.

Jack arrived at the firm and exited the elevator into the lobby in a near panic. By this time he knew the receptionist who sat in the lobby fairly well. Jack smiled at her. "Hi, Samantha. I'm here to see Dean Davidson. Again."

Samantha was just as friendly. "I thought you were done with your interviews."

"This is my last one."

"Haven't you said that before Jack?"

"Yea, and I'm at my wit's end about what to do about this, too, as he keeps blowing me off."

"Just hang in there, Jack. I promise everything will work out fine."

Samantha's cute little smile when she bit her lower lip had a calming affect on Jack. Jack trusted her and had confided in her how frustrated he was with Dean and all the canceled interviews. And Samantha had more respect for Jack than she did for the other interviewees. He was the only one who did not make rude comments to her, or even flirt with her.

"I'll tell you a little secret, Jack," Samantha whispered.

Jack leaned in closely. "I'm listening."

"Dean is leaving the office today at 2:00. It's Friday and he does not like to work past 2:00 on Fridays." She looked around the lobby quickly. "And I shouldn't even be telling you this, but he has made it a point to make sure you never get an interview with him either."

Jack looked at his watch. It was ten minutes to two, so it was now or never. "Which office is his?" Jack blurted out.

"Take the elevator to the top floor. His office is the one in the middle. It overlooks the trading floor. But you know, I'll have to escort you up there. If anyone even sees you they'll kick you out, no questions asked."

Jack had never been to the top floor of the building. With the exception of Strong's office on the second floor, every interview Jack had was in a small conference room on the first floor. He did not know that most of the partners and a few senior associates had numerous offices throughout the building.

As Jack and Samantha exited the elevator both could hear the commotion coming from the opposite side of the building—the trading floor. As they came to the end of the hall Jack slowly approached the handrail and looked down. Only half of the first and second floors of the building had offices on it. The back half of the building was open all the way to the top floor and had a walkway that looked out over the entire trading floor. Jack stood there a moment, perched over the rail like a buzzard looking at some road kill, trying to take it all in.

The trading floor resembled stadium seating. There were about seventy executive-style desks, all facing in the same direction, and all of the brokers made phone calls from these desks.

Towards the front of the trading floor, a few steps lower than the front row of broker's desks, were two rows of desks, which were so large they were more like tables, and faced the brokers. The partners, along with the traders and their assistants, sat at these desks.

Chalkboards covered the wall behind the traders. The chalkboards were connected to a pulley system and were constantly moving up and down. The traders sat below these boards, facing the brokers and giving them signals.

The trading floor was designed so every broker could see all of the traders and the chalkboards behind them. The traders had listed all available bonds and other similar investment instruments for the brokers to sell.

As brokers sold bonds, they ran down and erased the bonds from the board. A broker shouted which bonds he had sold the instant he hung up the phone. This helped prevent anyone else from selling the same bonds before the information could be erased from the board. The shouting was also encouraged because the other brokers would then shout accolades that created extra excitement within the room. Whenever this activity occurred, it generated energy on the trading floor that could last all day. It was also a constant motivator for other brokers on the floor who were not selling to keep calling and pitching bonds.

It was much like a sporting event. Brokers were everywhere—yelling, joking, and running up and down the aisles. Customers on the phone could hear and feel the energy as well. As the yelling heightened, brokers would tell their clients, "You need to take these bonds down before you lose them to someone else." The force created on the trading floor was a constant sales pitch that lured customers into buying the product.

The rookies sat at the very back of the trading floor. A combination of seniority and income production ordered the seating towards the front of the floor. The highest producers had the privilege of sitting in the front row. While the partners could work from their offices, they often sat up front with the traders.

Jack looked down in awe at the impressiveness of the trading floor. The décor of the trading floor was just as opulent as everywhere else Jack had seen. Each trader's desk had the most advanced terminals, called "telerates." Teletypes clicked away on each wall with all the stock prices. The brokers were dressed in custom-made suits, monogrammed shirts, power ties, and fancy shoes. Gold Rolex watches adorned the wrist of nearly every broker. Most of the brokers smoked, so cigarette smoke gathered near the ceiling.

Suddenly, one of the men yelled, "The PIMAs are gone." There was shouting, cussing, and accolades by the others as the man who had shouted out walked to one of the chalkboards and crossed out "100 PIMAs." One hundred meant one hundred thousand.

Not ten seconds later, another broker ran up and crossed out "100 GNMA 6.24%" from a different board. He yelled out, "Those Ginnie May's are gone! That's five points for me in case you ladies are interested." The group went wild. A couple of other brokers who were working the same bonds called him dirty names and threw their cigarettes at him. Most everyone was on the phone. Some were pacing while pitching bonds. Others were seated at their desks. But everyone was either on the phone talking or dialing a number or dashing up to erase something from the boards.

"Jack! Jack! Pay attention. Get over here fast!" Samantha called out to him. "Dean's office is right there. And don't tell him, or anyone else, that I brought you up here, okay."

"Don't worry." Jack was still focused on the trading floor. "Did that guy down there just make five-thousand dollars? Does five points mean five percent?"

"I have no idea, but that's not your concern right now. Just act like you busted up here all by yourself." She turned Jack around and pushed him in the right direction towards Dean's office.

Jack did not hear her wish him good luck as he focused on calming his nerves and approaching his final interview. It was now make it or break it time.

Dean Davidson's office had a perfect view of the trading floor. There was a small spiral staircase from the balcony outside of his office door that went straight down to the trading floor. As Jack peered inside the open door he noticed that this was the first office he had seen that was more functional than ostentatious. It was relatively small and with a small desk, and on top of the desk was a bullhorn.

Through the front glass wall, Mean Dean could see his "wards" as they scurried below. Though Dean was a junior partner, he was also the sales manager. He was the one who made sure every broker was on the phone all of the time. And he wasn't sweet about it either. He was a former high school football coach, and was known to be a tough coach at that. To him the brokers on the floor were just older versions of his past athletes; lazy bums all. He could spot someone slacking off in an instant and yelled, booming at the top of his lungs, or used his bullhorn; hence, the name Mean Dean. Now, instead of yelling at high school athletes, he yelled at grown men. It was all the same to him.

When he was not watching his charges from above, he was on the trading floor, weaving up and down the aisles and behind all of the brokers. If a broker was afraid or the least bit hesitant to make cold calls, Mean Dean changed that attitude, quickly and efficiently. Every rookie, and even the seasoned brokers, would rather be on the phone getting rejected by some bank president than feel the wrath of Mean Dean.

If Mean Dean spotted a broker who was not on the phone, he would sneak up behind his chair quickly and quietly. He would then hit the back of the chair as hard as he could and yell at the top of his lungs, "Hook 'em up baby shit!" It always startled even the most seasoned brokers.

As Jack turned to enter Dean's office, he saw the man coming straight for him like a freight train and at first thought that Dean was going to throw him over the handrails. Instead, Dean, with his size forty-five waist, knocked Jack out of the way as he stormed up to the edge of the walkway.

Leaning over the rails, Mean Dean went to work on someone. "God damn it Kyle. Get your sorry ass back on that phone! If I have to come down there I'm going to knock the shit out of you! Get your damn ass back on that phone and now! Don't you dare look at me! Pick it up! This is the second time today I've had to tell you this. Next time I have to come out here your ass is fired! Now get on the phone you homo or you're fired! Hook 'em up baby shit!"

Jack couldn't help but notice how Mean Dean's enormous belly hung over his belt to the point that his belt buckle disappeared, but not enough that Jack couldn't see that the buckle was made of solid gold and was adorned with precious gems. Even more interesting to Jack was the fact that Mean Dean's toupee did not match the color of his hair, what little remained.

Dean quickly turned around to head back into his office. "Who are you and what the hell do you want? In fact, don't bother. I know who you are and you're too late. Get the hell out of here."

Jack was totally pissed off at Dean because of the time wasted scheduling interviews that Dean never bothered to show up to. Now he saw, and heard, firsthand how loud and obnoxious Dean really was. Jack knew that if he cowered then, he had lost. As it turned out, Jack also had an ability to read personalities. He had just never needed to do it before.

With the time invested in trying to get hired, Jack figured there was not much to lose anymore. By now he was too hungry and too angry to worry about it. Enough was enough and he took the offensive. "Davidson, I have called you countless times and arranged to have an interview with you and you've had the audacity to stand me up each and every time. And sometimes when I have called, you never even had the balls to call me back. This is not a game for me. Do you think this is some sort of game? I'm...."

But Dean interrupted Jack.

"Our salesmen here are professionals. They have good sales experience with street skills and a sales background. You don't even qualify for an interview here, much less a job. Take your prissy college degrees somewhere else and stop wasting my time."

This only fueled Jack's rage and frustration, and his conviction to succeed. "I'm not finished." Jack moved closer to Dean, inches from his face, then took a deep breath. "I'm twenty-four years old, and in my lifetime I have sold more than most of your salesmen here will sell in their entire lives. When I was nine I began selling newspapers. I built a route so big I hired other kids to work for me. I worked my way through college without a penny from my parents. I have been a salesman at a clothing store and a waiter for some damn fine restaurants. I have more drive now than I ever had and twice as much as any of those assholes downstairs. If you don't want to hire me then that's fine by me, but it will be your loss."

Jack moved in even closer to Dean. "I did not come here so you could ignore me or pass me around like some cheap whore. I want this job. I will succeed at this job. Do not think I walked into your office to be humiliated and told to go home just like that. This is not the only firm in town that does this kind of business. I am going to work in this industry no matter what. Now, are you going to give me an interview or am I going to interview with one of your competitors?"

Dean slowly turned around and walked back to his desk. He pulled out a cigar and stuck it in his mouth. The cigar had never been lit but you could tell it was often in his mouth. After a couple of minutes of silence, Dean spoke with a slight grin on his face.

"Jack, when I looked at your file I figured you were too much of a pansy to succeed in this business. I guess maybe I could've been wrong. We rarely hire anyone under the age of thirty, and we are especially not that fond of college graduates either. They think too much. College boys want to 'analyze' and 'conquer' the market. So this will be new territory for both of us." Dean sat and leaned back in his chair. "All right, let's see what you can do here. See you bright and early Monday morning. Training starts at 7:30 a.m. sharp. Don't bother showing up at 7:31."

CHAPTER THREE

▼

All Jack could think about from the moment he was hired was starting the training class Monday morning. The weekend was long and the wait excruciating. He was so anxious the night before he couldn't fall asleep. As he lay in bed that night, Jack wanted to prepare for his new job. However, he did not know where to start. Unfortunately for Jack, The Wall Street Journal did not run on the weekends. He wanted to learn more about the business. He wanted to walk in so prepared the next morning that they would praise him. Jack wanted to make Strong, and all the other partners, proud.

Aaron was almost as excited as Jack, but his excitement was more contained since he was not as high-strung as Jack. Aaron had a kind of cool attitude. Like he knew something others did not. Aaron also knew that if all he had to do was to sell then he would be just fine.

Aaron had learned early on that not everyone buys what you are selling. Deals fall apart. People felt guilty, and many had "buyer's remorse." Sometimes they were not really interested in the first place, but felt bad when they turned down the sale, so would often let a salesman carry on with his pitch just to be nice. Maybe they would buy something else, or something cheaper.

Aaron had no illusions that he would make a sale on every phone call he made. He had an "easy come, easy go" attitude and it had worked for him all of his life. Unfortunately for Jack, he had yet to learn this fact of life in the sales world, even though he had spent some time in sales.

So Jack worked himself into a frenzy for no real reason other than that was how he functioned. He wanted to succeed so badly he could taste it. It was not a fear of failure that subconsciously affected Jack. It was his fear of accomplishment that always kept him from truly succeeding. He hesitated at the wrong times. He was nervous when he should have been calm. He faltered when he should have moved ahead. Jack, however, had assets that made him stronger than anything else—his drive and attitude made him thrive when he should have failed. Jack was always good, but never great.

Aaron's carefree, fly-by-the-seat-of-his-pants and summer-breeze attitude was perfect for sales. He would crash and burn, but could then turn around and start all over again. If someone bought what he was selling, great. If they didn't, this was no big deal to Aaron. He would just move on. Aaron never took the loss of a sale personally. After all, it was just business.

Almost anyone on the other side of a sales pitch can recognize weaknesses in the salesman. This is true whether the customer consciously realizes it or not. The customer may not necessarily know if the salesman dislikes the product or not. They may not be aware that he doesn't know much about the product, either. However, a buyer can always tell when a salesman is trying too hard. They can sense his desperation and the begging to make a sale.

It's his hesitations, the tone of his voice, and the lack of confidence that comes across. Of course, the nail in the coffin for any salesman is the failure to close a deal. If the salesman starts showing signs of weakness, or worse, is begging, he might as well just shoot himself in the foot. It doesn't matter what the product is. No sale, no way, not ever.

Aaron's attitude eliminated this problem. Jack's persona just made it worse. It was true—Jack may have been a businessman and a manager, but he was not a natural salesman. Jack was a numbers guy who could learn anything and master it easily and quickly. Basic sales skills can be acquired. Aaron had an innateness for the work, but Jack did not. Aaron had been selling for years. Jack had not.

The only thing that could momentarily calm Jack was talking to Aaron about what was really bothering him. Aaron knew how Jack's mind worked and he knew how to distract Jack's way of thinking. He also knew that he needed to keep Jack motivated and not allow Jack to make it worse for himself. Jack was usually his own worst enemy.

Over the weekend Aaron had begun to prod Jack. "Can you imagine writing a check for almost two-hundred-thousand dollars just for a pool and some stupid shrubs and palm trees?"

"No", Jack said then paused. "By the way, how much did you make off that deal anyway?"

"Standard one percent. They should have paid me more. I wanted more, but they said no. So I didn't need to think twice about quitting."

"Think we'll succeed at the firm?" Jack asked Aaron, but it was a question more for himself.

"And then some. Man, we're a team and a great team at that. With your intelligence and my sales skills we'll make a fortune. I can teach you to sell and you can teach me what it is that I'm selling."

Jack still felt intimidated and anxious. "They told me that if I'm not making more than the U.S. President by the end of the year they were going to fire me. That is a butt-load of money."

"I know. They told me the same thing."

"Hey Aaron, what did Strong say about you being single by the way?"

"He said it was a great business to be single in."

Jack was a little confused by Aaron's answer. "That's not what he told me. He said they needed more family men around."

Aaron had the right response, as always. "Don't worry about it, you'll be fine. He was just selling you. You are way too stressed out about all of this. You need to do something to calm down. Like start smoking. Or something."

"I don't think so. If I start, I'll get hooked. Plus it makes your clothes smell." Jack sighed. "And my wife would kill me, too."

Aaron just looked at Jack with a straight face. He knew that Jack and his wife were having problems, but the way Jack had stated that his wife would kill him if he even just smoked one cigarette made Aaron wonder just how bad the marriage had become. He could also see that Jack was becoming more and more tense.

"Dude, just smoke one cigarette. It'll give you something to do at least. Most everyone who's in sales does it anyway."

Jack tentatively reached for a cigarette. "Fine, just one, but only if it will get you to shut your damn piehole. And don't tell my wife either."

"You don't need to tell me. I know already." Aaron rolled his eyes.

"I know you know. I just feel like I have to say it."

"It doesn't matter anyway. She's going to chew you out for something regardless. Might as well walk in the house smelling like booze and cigarettes and get some enjoyment out of life." Aaron leaned over to light Jack's cigarette. "What's her problem lately anyway? She's been getting really bitchy lately."

"Sometimes…." Jack coughed out, but then could not say anything else as he was coughing too much to respond.

"Did you tell her this job is all commission with no salary?"

Jack looked down. "Yes. And she's not too happy about that at all."

"She'll get over it when she sees how much money you'll be making."

Jack coughed up some smoke before replying. "God, I hope so."

✳   ✳   ✳   ✳

Monday morning, at exactly 7:00 a.m., Jack and Aaron walked into HAYNES, OLIVE, GAGE & STRONG. Training class began at 7:30 a.m. Anyone who knew anything knew better than to show up right at 7:30 a.m. The lobby held a little more than two dozen other trainees, all sizing each other up.

At 7:30 on the dot, as everyone stood around, some talking, others sitting quietly, one man exited the elevator into the lobby. He was tall, thin, and had a coarse-looking face. He appeared to be in his mid-forties. His deep voice resounded throughout the lobby as he said, "Gentlemen, follow me." It was obvious that nobody had any idea who this guy was. Some of the crowd hesitated to follow him, thinking that maybe he was just someone sent there to try and fool them as some had heard rumors of pranks played at this firm. That was, though, until he spoke up again, but not as politely as before. "Let's go ladies. What the hell are you waiting for?"

Everyone corralled into a rather plain and simple classroom. The room had one long table and was placed near the back. There were no windows in the room. Chalkboards lined the front and filled up the entire wall. The only items that hinted of the affluence of the firm were the large high-backed leather chairs.

The man went straight to the point without wavering. Not everyone had settled into their chairs before he starting speaking. No one knew who he was, nor did anyone dare ask. But everyone knew he meant business when he spoke. As he locked the doors to the room behind him he introduced himself.

"Gentlemen, my name is Dan Manikan. Until you pass the Series 7 exam I am going to be your father, mother, wife, girlfriend, mistress, best friend, and your worst enemy. I don't interview anyone because I don't want to know who you are when I fire your ass. The 7 is the hardest test you will ever take, and I don't have the time or the patience to hold your hand."

Someone next to Aaron leaned over to him and whispered, "This guy thinks he's General Patton." Aaron did not move a muscle or react in any way. But Manikan did and his reaction was intense. "I heard that, you little piece of shit. Get out of here, and now! We don't need you here. Anyone else here have something to say?"

The room was totally silent. No one even dared to watch as the young man excused himself from the room as Manikan followed closely behind to slam the door shut. As he was closing the door someone else was trying to get in. Without hesitation he continued to close the door in the young man's face. "You're late. You're fired. So fuck off."

Dan continued as if nothing had happened. "As I was saying, I will teach you everything you need to know to pass the exam and make more money than you have ever dreamed you could. And you're here only because the partners who interviewed you felt that you could make them a lot of money."

He paused and looked round the room. After quickly sizing everyone up he continued his monologue. "That's the last time you will hear me speak to you about money. If you didn't want it, you wouldn't be here. I'm not here to entice you with tales of grandeur and a wallet stuffed with Ben Franklins. I'm not here to motivate you to work by talking about it. I am here for one thing only, and that is to teach you how to pass the exam. As we speak, my secretary is calling the NASD to schedule the Series 7 exam for each of you. The test is in exactly twenty-three days. If you don't pass, then you are fired. This means in twenty-four days, ten of you will be gone. Over one-third of you will fail."

Manikan paused again before continuing. "I can already tell you who will fail. If the person to the right of you and the left of you looks halfway smart, then it looks like it's your sorry ass that will be failing. No pass, no play. Don't expect flowers and don't expect a second chance. We will move pretty fast every day. If you are a dumb ass don't waste my time with your stupid questions. If you're intelligent don't waste my time with your smart questions. And if you can't keep up, well, too bad. I will teach you everything that you will need to know."

He poured himself a glass of water before he continued. "And I don't care who you are. Everyone is on the same playing field starting now. There are three rules in this building and there are no exceptions to these rules. Number one, every single one of you will start work 7:30 a.m. Not 7:35. Not even 7:31. Each of you will work until 4:30 p.m. Not 4:25 and not 4:35. Your job will be non-stop from the time you walk in until the second you leave. For those of you who like to crap while reading in the stall, this is not the place for you. You will not take reading material with you to the restroom. And don't think for a moment that Mr. Davidson has any problem in ferreting you out of there."

A small chuckle came from everyone in the room, but it didn't stop Manikan. "Rule two, you will be out of here at 4:30 sharp. No one is allowed in this building after 4:30. Not even if you forgot your car keys. That goes for every single associate. No exceptions. Early to bed, early to rise, and there are no excuses for being tired."

He then let out a deep breath before he started on the third rule. "Lastly, I don't care if any of you are married or how long you have been married. Your wives are absolutely forbidden from ever entering this building. Not for lunch, not to see the office, not for any reason. No fiancées or girlfriends, either. If any of us sees your wife or your whatever in here, you can kiss your ass goodbye. This is a place of business. You will have plenty of time to spend with them after the market closes. It closes early, and often. You'll be surprised. The market is closed on any day that is even considered to be a holiday. If the market is closed then so are we."

Manikan then made everyone in the room introduce himself. Each listened intently to learn the other's background. There were some experienced salesmen, an attorney, a vice-president for a Fortune 500 company, and plenty of just average guys. There were some with college education, but only six out of the entire group of thirty had college degrees.

Manikan took control again. "Now that everyone knows each other's background, know this. Only about five of you will make any real money here, and only one or two of you will make any serious money. The rest of you will be gone by the end of the year. That's the nature of this beast. Good luck to all of you gentlemen." He then grabbed some legal pads and threw them on the table. He immediately turned to the chalkboards and began the class.

Truth was that Dan Manikan hated training the newbies. Unfortunately for him, the partners had knighted him as the firm's professor. History had taught the partners that Dan was best at conveying what everyone needed to know in order to pass the Series 7 exam. Unfortunately for the trainees, Manikan took frequent breaks and long lunches, and every so often he would just walk out of the room without a word. Sometimes he would head off to make or answer a phone call.

During those brief departures he would grab one of the more successful brokers from the trading floor and throw that guy into the room to fill in. These brokers would brag about how great they were and all the toys they owned. And it was one of these brokers who eventually informed the class that Manikan was also known as "Cadillac Dan."

Most of the tales though were about the money they were making or how they were spending it. They told "war" stories that were often exaggerated. To the broker, though, each trainee was a future competitor, so they went out of their way to scare, intimidate, and embarrass them. There were always constant attempts to establish a pecking order on the trading floor.

The first day was exhausting. The recruits listened intently while taking notes and hanging on to every word that came out of Manikan's mouth. And Dan did not crack a smile or make a joke the entire day. He was a serious man forced into doing a job he did not want to do. Everyone thought they had a feel for Dan's no-nonsense attitude until a phone call came into the room the morning of the third day.

His secretary knocked on the door and when "Cadillac Dan" opened the door she quietly said, "Excuse me Mr. Manikan. The president of First National is on the phone and he said it's urgent. He needs to speak to you immediately. I told him you were in a meeting, but he didn't seem to care."

Manikan looked towards the ceiling and rolled his head around. "Relax Mandy. Put him through in exactly thirty seconds."

With a deep voice and a stone-cold look on his face, he turned to address all of the trainees. "This is a very important phone call. No one had better make a sound. While I'm on the phone I want to you take notes and listen carefully. Listen to the way I address this client. Listen to how I answer his question. Listen to and watch the way I behave while talking to this man and the tone of my voice. This is the real deal. And this is how you make money."

The room went silent. Every trainee made sure that he would not make a single sound. They were silent because of fear. Silent out of respect. More importantly, they were silent because everyone wanted to listen and to learn. It was so quiet in the room that when the phone rang it sounded like a fire alarm. All eyes and ears were on Manikan. Everyone was on the edge of his seat, taking it in. What was he going to say to the president of the First National Bank?

Dan looked at his trainees as he picked up the phone and smiled into the receiver as he began to speak. "Well, well, if it isn't my shit-faced drunken, titty-dancer-loving best friend from last night. I have never seen anyone so tanked. Don't even blame that shit on me. 'Let's go to the Gentlemen's Club. Let's go to the Gentlemen's Club.' That's all I heard out of you all night long. How obnoxious. 'I wonder if Destiny is working tonight? I think she likes me. She's trying to get into med school'. How embarrassing for you. Unbelievable. No, I'm not going to tell anyone. Secrets stay secrets with me and you know it. I do have something special just for you though. I have some California GO bonds you need to take down. The bonds are at a discount, with a six-and-a-half percent yield. And I don't want to hear any shit that you don't have any money either. Yes I think Sheri likes you, but she didn't dance for free last night. I'll call you later or I can have Mandy call you back with the settlement figures. Instead, hold tight for a second and I'll have Mandy finish this up right now. Yea, you, too. See you around, and thanks."

Manikan could not help but laugh every now and then while he was on the phone. He was mainly laughing as he recounted the previous night, and he was laughing because he enjoyed toying with trainees. It was the first time any of the trainees saw Dan crack a smile, much less laugh.

During class Dan painstakingly covered all aspects of the business, including securities laws, types of securities, the products marketed at the firm, and what was expected of everyone working there. Despite Dan's threats in the beginning, trainees had slowly begun to ask questions. Some were good, others not so good. Dan answered directly and succinctly.

Then there was poor Billy. No matter what Billy did, Manikan was on his case. Dan had Billy's number from the start and never had liked him.

It stressed Jack because often he had the same questions, but Jack was afraid to speak up and ask anything. He would rather have Cadillac Dan wondering if he were an imbecile than to open his mouth and prove it. Aaron, on the other hand, was so lost he couldn't ask a question even if he wanted to.

The other recruits felt sorry for Billy because he was a little slower than everyone else in learning the material. He was a nice guy, but he couldn't keep up and made it known by asking so many questions. Dan made it a point to never let him forget it either.

Towards the end of the fourth day of training Billy's hand went up in the air again. He had not yet asked his question when Manikan jumped on him like a starving dog on a bone.

"What Billy? What the fuck is it this time?"

After hearing the question, Manikan went berserk. "You stupid son of a bitch. I have had it with you. Get your crap, pick up your fat butt, and get the hell out of here! You are so fired! You have exactly sixty seconds to get out or I am calling security! Go work for the damn government you stupid piece of shit."

The entire class was in shock. They watched in total silence as Billy, completely humiliated, picked up his things and headed towards the door. He was never seen or heard from again.

If they had not already been intimidated by the man, they were now. No one else wanted to be embarrassed in the same way. Moreover, no one else wanted to lose the opportunity to make the kind of money they believed could be made by working at the firm, which meant not getting fired, which meant not making Manikan upset. Not an easy feat.

What the class did not know was that it was a practice at HAYNES, OLIVE, GAGE & STRONG to hire at least one "whipping boy" with each class. This person was someone who was hired only for the sole purpose to be fired. The point of this was to get the hearts and minds of the rest of the class in the right mode for complete discipline, obedience, and mostly submission. Questions that were asked after Billy's departure were very respectful, measured, and to the point. They were also very limited.

CHAPTER FOUR

▼

The firm that would eventually become HAYNES, OLIVE, GAGE & STRONG had originated in Memphis, Tennessee in the mid-1960s. The founder of the firm was Jordan S. Strong and his company was originally named J.S. STRONG. He had wanted his firm's name to resemble other strong financial firms, with similar powerful names such as J.P. MORGAN and E.F. HUTTON.

Strong started his company with the intention of only trading in bonds and other fixed-income securities. At the time, the market began changing because new banking and tax laws were taking effect. Banks especially were affected by these changes and were soon growing into higher tax brackets, so it became essential that banks placed and sheltered some of their investments into tax-free bonds. Thus, banks needed to buy these tax-free bonds. The only question was where to buy and who to buy from.

Soon after J.S. STRONG formed, about forty similar, but smaller, firms opened their doors in Memphis, Tennessee. Many of these "would-be brokers" had worked for Strong and learned the business under his guidance. These young brokers realized the potential in this new market, left Strong's company, then started many of the competitor firms. Hence, the reason for Strong's speech to all rookies about loyalty. He did not enjoy training his competition.

Problems eventually arose, what with having so many firms with young, and inexperienced management. Fierce competition encouraged unethical practices. Unfortunately, the owners and employees of these new firms often did not understand the bonds they were selling or the true needs of the investors who were buying them.

In the early 1970s, the Memphis firms began acquiring a bad reputation. A reputation that was well deserved in many instances. New, and very aggressive, firms sold every type of bond they could find. Many brokers never researched the projects that the bonds financed, or the management and the cash-flow projections of the entities that were to repay the lenders of the money.

Commission-driven sales slowly bankrupted the investors who bought the bonds. As soon as a bond had a small profit, the broker convinced the banker to sell it for the profit, even if the profit was small. With each sale, of course, came a commission. The broker would then turn around and put the same bank into a different bond. With that purchase came another commission. This practice was known as "churning."

Although a little too late for many institutional investors, The Wall Street Journal began publishing articles criticizing the Memphis brokers. The Journal published one article after another informing the public of the "Shady Memphis Firms" churning accounts. And the articles never distinguished the good firms from the bad firms. For better or worse, they were all identified as "Memphis Bond Firms."

Banks and other institutional investors quickly started protecting themselves from these firms that were based out of Memphis, Tennessee. The first question was always, "Where are you located, Memphis?" If the answer was yes, then the broker lost any chance of a sale.

The crooked brokers soon became astute and started denying the location of their business. Because at this time all transactions occurred over the phone, it was difficult for an investor to determine the true location of a broker.

Institutional investors soon recognized the deceit and began heavier screening of calls. It was unfortunate for new and ethical brokers trying to break into the industry because cold calling became that much more difficult.

As good firms and bad firms alike were struggling to make money, many of the firms slowly moved out of Memphis. In order to stay in business, the firms either disbanded or changed their names and relocated to various cities, including Little Rock, Arkansas; Boca Raton and Ft. Lauderdale, Florida; and Houston, Texas.

Afterward, any of these same companies, honest or disreputable, could get on the phone with an institutional investor and bad-mouth the Memphis firms together. "Heck no, I'm not with one of those crackpot Memphis firms. Here in Houston we have integrity, respect, and knowledge of our investments and of our investors."

And so, J.S. STRONG moved from Memphis, Tennessee, and became HAYNES, OLIVE, GAGE & STRONG, based in Houston, Texas.

This newborn Texas firm was stronger, smarter, leaner, and definitely meaner. The core group had worked together for years. After being together in the game for a long time, the partners had learned through trial and error how to make the firm as efficient and profitable as possible. It did not take long for the partners to become enormously successful.

They were there for each other during the first cold calls when they could barely afford fast-food. They saw each other through marriages, divorces, children, and million-dollar homes. They formed a tight group that had been through thick and thin, good times and bad. Coming from different backgrounds, they had learned from each other and respected each other. The four were as thick as thieves.

The foundation of the firm consisted of Travis Haynes, Tony Olive, Richard Gage, and Jordan Strong. The four partners surrounded themselves with junior partners and senior associates, all who were key players vital to the firm's success. The company had four levels: the partners, the junior partners, the senior associates, and the junior associates. Rookies ranked at the bottom of the latter category and were always called rookies until they made a sale.

The junior partners and some of the senior associates had most of the same privileges as the partners. The real difference was that the partners were owners of the firm. The partners and the junior partners, plus some of the highest-selling senior associates, received seventy-percent of all commissions earned. The other thirty-percent went to the firm, or in other words, the four partners. A few senior associates, and all of the junior associates kept forty-percent of their commissions. None of the brokers had a salary and if a broker did not make a sale, then no one made any money.

Each of the partners had a private office. Top-producing senior associates vied for any available offices. Although it was fairly consistent, occasionally someone moved out and someone else moved in. This would occur if a particular senior associate had a bad month and another senior associate had a good month. Admittance to the third floor executive boardroom was limited to the partners, junior partners, and senior associates. All could invite clients, but only the partners could invite a junior associate into the executive boardroom. It was strictly by invitation only, and the invitations were few and far between.

Despite having private offices, at least one partner was always on the trading floor. The partners, though, chose to work on the trading floor most of the day. It was ideal for any broker to be on the floor in order to keep an eye on the market and quickly and easily locate bonds to push.

All rookies sat at their desks on the trading floor. They were never allowed to leave the desk during working hours other than to use the restroom. A cook came in every day and made their lunch. Rookies, at least until they made a sale and became a junior associate, were required to eat at their desks.

The firm was s
call anyone—girlf
just to appear as i
But it was uncan
on the phone co
desk with rope.
handset just to k

The firm w
push the broker
buy expensive
theory being t
afford, he wou

New brok
tasted a piece
and this cycl
seasoned bro
month.

John P. Bott & Jason L. Fowell

a NASCAR team. As the son of an expert
everything there was to know about Am
American automobiles were the best
believed the same. Gage loved to w
was that they were superior to E
He also believed that Americ
power and speed.
Though the other
Porsches, and other f
would not even c
Cobra any day
Gage wa
He ha
He lear
He r
He h

Every day after class con...
treated the trainees to a few drinks at the firm's local ...
To everyone it was known as HOGS, and was the only bar rookies could go
to after work. Coincidentally, it was also an acronym of the firm's name. The
bar was located on a side street right around the corner from the office, so
heading there was no big deal for most new brokers. It was convenient.

HOGS had a small parking lot in the front, but most of its parking
spaces were on the street. There was a small driveway that led to the back of
the building to another small parking area with a large sign that discouraged
customers from parking there. The sign was for the benefit of a select few who
were given permission to park there. Everyone at the firm who had access to
the "private" parking loved it. They could leave their expensive cars behind
the building and know that their cars were safe. Because HOGS had a side
entrance, those who came to HOGS would always be able to see the fancy
cars that were parked in back.

Richard Gage was usually the first to invite the trainees and young junior
associates out. Gage's personality and cool demeanor relaxed and relieved
each new broker from the stress they constantly felt while on the floor. Gage
was very easy-going and had lots of stories. After a couple of hours in a bar
with Gage, everyone's face hurt from laughing so much. While the senior or
junior associates could stay as long as they wanted, the rookies were required
to leave by a decent hour.

Richard Gage was from the south. Although some called him Ricky, he
was generally known just as Gage. His father was a member of a pit crew for

mechanic, Gage grew up learning
rican-made cars. His father believed
n the world, and like his father, Gage
ork on any American car. His conviction
uropean motors and the easiest to work on.
an cars had the most potential for adding on

partners and associates at the firm had Ferraris,
reign exotics, Gage never drove these types of cars. He
nsider it. He would take a Corvette, Mustang, or Shelby
f the week over a Ferrari.

often heard saying, "The day I drive a Ferrari is the day I die."
d learned how to rebuild an entire engine because of his father.
ned how to drive fast and furious from men who raced stock cars.
astered his training and always drove as if he were in a NASCAR race.
e loved to enhance engine performance any way possible. He even added
nitrous injections and put a turbo charger on anything he could get his hands
on.

Although the other partners teased Gage, they never allowed themselves
to be challenged on the road by him. He was a maniac on the road. And as
much as he coaxed, Gage could never get any of the other partners to accept
his challenges.

They would not race because no one really wanted to know if the car
they spent more than a hundred grand on was not the fastest on the road.
Nor would they race Gage because they knew he had increased his car's
engine's power to some ungodly amount. Regardless, the bottom line was
that no one would challenge Gage, but this was mostly out of respect for his
driving abilities. They knew he was capable of driving a hundred-and-fifty-
miles-per-hour. He would do so only six inches from another car's bumper,
and without any hesitation.

By the time Jack and Aaron started working at the firm, Gage was in his
late forties. His hair had thinned and he was almost bald on the top of his
head. Nevertheless, Gage was a good-looking man and a confirmed bachelor.
He always said that he wore women out before they wore him out, so like his
cars, it was wise to always keep getting a new one.

But there was one very special person in his life. The young son of a
neighbor, and a kid who enjoyed "helping" Gage work on all his cars. Gage
was very fond of the kid and would talk about him frequently, making it a
point that this kid reminded Gage of himself when he was that age. The kid's
name happened to also be Richard, but Gage called him Ricky Too, or just

RT. By the time RT was ten, he could change the brakes on any car in the garage, and with his eyes closed. Gage had taught him well.

Gage kept himself in shape and loved chasing women as much as he loved racing cars. Unless he was in the office, he wore jeans and a T-shirt. When he was younger Gage played guitar in a rock-'n-roll band, and occasionally still jumped up on a stage to entertain the crowd. He loved the attention, especially from the women.

Unlike the other partners, Gage lived outside of town in a moderately priced area but with lots of land. Like the others though, Gage had everything he could ever want on his property. In addition to a few horses and some cattle, Gage had built two garages. The smaller garage was next to his house and had space for five cars. Generally, these were the five cars he drove on a regular basis.

The second garage was much larger. It was a mechanic's dream, filled with professional equipment and tools to work on cars, including drills, lifts, jacks, and air compressors. In addition to a large working area, the garage had enough room for ten cars. Behind the large garage was an assortment of older American automobiles that were in dire need of some tender loving care. Gage enjoyed finding old, used, beat-up, and junked-out cars that he could resurrect into horse-powered monsters. Completed with rebuilt engines, new interiors, paint jobs, and wheels, he showed them off at various car events. Gage would then sell these "reincarnated beasts" to the highest bidder. He never had a problem selling any of them since his reputation for rebuilding cars was common knowledge. He even had had an article about his talents written up in a well-known automotive magazine.

Gage regularly invited the rookies for cocktails, entertaining and educating them with his stories, experiences, and knowledge. There was something special about Gage as well. He never yelled at them or embarrassed them when in front of others. There was not a single person at the firm who did not like Gage. He was extremely intuitive, but he also had a reputation for being wild. Many of the brokers fed off of this energy.

CHAPTER FIVE

▼

After twenty-one grueling eight-hour days sitting in class, each trainee was supposedly ready to pass the Series 7 exam. The six-hour exam was administered at the regional National Association of Securities Dealer's branch office. The test would take three hours in the morning, then they'd get a lunch break, and then they would return for another three hours of testing in the afternoon. A score of at least seventy was required to pass. Upon completion of the test, each examinee received their score before they left the building, so within minutes of finishing the test each knew whether or not they had passed or failed.

The exam consisted of questions ranging from the definition of a basis point, to provisions of the Securities Act of 1933, to situations involving complicated hedge trades. A correct answer could hinge on knowing the difference between "secretary" and "Secretary." Two-hundred questions were chosen randomly from a bank of twenty-five-hundred questions. No one test was exactly the same or any easier than the next test.

Naturally, Jack was very stressed and nervous. He had a fairly good understanding of the material, however, as usual, he put more pressure on himself than was necessary.

Aaron, on the other hand, since he took life one day at a time, was as calm as ever. He assumed he knew enough to pass the exam. He also wanted to bet Jack that whoever had the highest grade had to treat the other to dinner. Jack knew better than to take him up on that bet though.

No notes were allowed in the room where the test was administered. No was one allowed to speak, either. Representatives from the NASD were present throughout the entire exam, including one who stayed in the restroom—just to make sure no one tried to cheat at any time.

Aaron drove, since Jack was too nervous to. While on the drive there Jack sat quietly, reviewing his notes. As soon as they arrived, and Jack had sat down at his station, he began writing notes on the scratch paper provided. He wrote down little catch phrases and formulas he had memorized to more easily recall during the test.

However, no one was allowed to write anything until the test started, but Jack had forgotten that Manikan had told them this in class. Much to his dismay, and immediately before the test began, a proctor walked by and removed everything he had written down.

"You know the rules. You can't do or write anything until the exam starts."

"But they're just my notes," Jack pleaded with her.

"Do you want to take the test today or reschedule for next month? You can re-write them after the test starts you know."

"Today," Jack responded in a quiet voice.

Almost seven hours later, Jack submitted his test for grading, left the room, and stood waiting in a small area they were all told to head to as they waited for their test results. Minutes felt like an eternity. Not a moment too soon, the proctor appeared around the corner with a smile on her face as she showed him his passing grade. Now he just needed to wait to see what Aaron scored.

There were twenty-five people taking the exam that day and quite a few of them were trainees from the firm. The rest were from numerous other brokerage firms from around Houston.

Jack was one of the first to finish the exam. He waited outside impatiently for Aaron. As others walked out of the building, Jack could see on their faces those who had passed and those who had failed.

He looked down at his watch knowing that Aaron should be walking out any second. When he looked up a few minutes later, he saw Aaron walking through the doors. Jack noticed that Aaron's face showed no emotion, which for some reason made him feel even more nervous than he did before he began taking the test. "What's up dude? Did you pass?"

Aaron was unresponsive as he walked towards Jack, then he began talking in a monotone voice. "As I sat there waiting for my results, I could visualize myself picking the proctor up over my head and slamming her into the ground if she told me I had failed. Fortunately that didn't happen. I passed with a damn score of 71. Can you believe it?" Aaron finally yelped out in excitement.

Jack was relieved and had a big grin on his face. "Not really. I would have pegged you for a loser," he joked.

"Yea, that's real funny, you prick. Just what did you get?

"88. And I busted my ass for each and every one of those points, too."

Secretly, Jack let out a sigh of relief for himself and for Aaron. "Come on, let's go to HOGS and throw down a few. Rumor has it some of the partners will be there."

As they pulled into the parking lot and started to head into the bar, Jack and Aaron couldn't help but notice all the fancy cars parked in the back. There were three Rolls Royces, two Ferraris, one black Porsche, and one "pretty" yellow Cadillac. The only thing that distracted them was Gage fishtailing into the front parking lot in his Stingray Corvette. Gage put the "pedal to the metal" to go another few feet, then stopped inches from Aaron's ass. "I see you ladies must have passed the 7. Congratulations. You're not fired."

"Thanks, Gage," replied Aaron.

"You guys are going to have a fantastic time tonight. That I promise you."

The door to HOGS swung open and Tony Olive yelled to Aaron and Jack. "Boys, don't let Gage pull that crap where he stops an inch from running you over. He loves scaring everyone with that trick. Come on in. We've been waiting to see who the winners and losers are."

Tony Olive had grown up in Chicago and moved to Memphis, Tennessee when he was almost eighteen. It was not by choice, so he managed to keep in touch with his old friends back in Chicago. His mother had learned he was running the streets with a very rough crowd, and it was rumored that his father was "connected." Tony never really got a chance to know his father. When Tony was just five, his father was found dead in the back of his trunk with three gunshot wounds to the head.

Although Tony had never lived a day of his life in Italy, one could occasionally hear a hint of an Italian accent, and this was more distinct when he had been drinking. What he said was full of Chicago street slang as well.

Tony Olive was an avid gambler who flew to Las Vegas almost every weekend without exception. Many casinos showered him with everything he wanted, from lavish rooms, a running bar tab, unlimited credit, and of course beautiful young ladies. Strong was a big gambler who also had connections in Vegas. Strong's connections, however, did not compare to the inside connections that Tony had.

It was said that some of Tony's old Chicago friends were running one or two of the casinos he often frequented. These were rumors only because no one was brave enough to ask, and if so, Tony would never tell. Nevertheless, Tony had a rule that no broker from the firm could go to Vegas for the first time without him. Nor would anyone not want to, since anyone who was with Tony was treated like a king when in Vegas.

*   *   *   *

While Jack and Aaron were taking their Series 7 exam Dan had purchased his newest Cadillac. It was a beautiful yellow Fleetwood. Tony and a couple of partners and senior associates felt that the yellow was too "sweet" for Dan. They made sure Dan knew how they felt and teased him all night long.

"Look at the dandy in his dainty little yellow Cadillac."

"What are you doing tonight, honey?"

"You sure do look cute."

That's all Cadillac Dan heard all night. His first retort was less than stellar and it didn't help his cause at all. "Shut up, it's a pretty color." This just sent the entire room into an uproar. After that little comment they laid into him even more. The only other words that night out of Dan's mouth were nothing but profanity. It was all taken in good fun though. The next morning, Dan returned the yellow Cadillac and purchased a black one. The trade cost him a few thousand dollars but he didn't think twice about it. He never did.

The twenty-one-day class did more than just get the trainees ready to pass the Series 7. The class also brainwashed every rookie with the notion that even with their small amount of knowledge, they knew more about bonds than the "dumb bankers" they would be cold calling.

The cold calling was made to seem easier than it was by the precept that the banker *had* to buy the bonds they were selling. The only choice was from *whom* they would purchase the bonds. Like everyone, bankers preferred to buy from friends or well-known and established companies.

Also ingrained into the rookies' minds was that every banker always had money. Bankers often lied and said they did not have any money to invest just to get off the phone. If the rookie believed the lie, then someone else would get the sale, and if the rookie couldn't make a sale they would soon fail in the business.

Most bankers knew how to squeeze every last penny from a mortgage, car loan, or repossessed property. However, there were some who knew very little about their own investment portfolios. Unfortunately for many independent banks, this fact would later affect their businesses in a way neither the FDIC nor the United States Congress could ever fathom or anticipate.

The day finally arrived when the rookies were assigned to their desks to hit the phones. Naturally, they were all nervous. They really didn't know what to say when they were cold calling.

The rookies were given a special block of bonds to sell while cold calling. These bonds were usually bought from another customer or dealer from what was called a "throw away." The bonds were cheap and offered such a high-yield that only a fool would turn them down. The rookies were practically giving away bonds just to make their first sale and open a new account.

One of the pitches would go something like this: "Hello Mr. Banks. My name is John Smith. I'm with the firm of HAYNES, OLIVE, GAGE & STRONG, which is the leading regional investment banking firm in the southwest. We specialize in municipal, government, and mortgage securities. Today, I have some bonds that I have just brought in from one of my insurance company accounts. Maybe you heard about the tornadoes that recently hit Centerville, Texas. Well, my client needed cash to settle all of those claims, so he called me up and said, 'John, I need money. Dump these at any price you can get.' Problem was that our inventory was chock full of these bonds and my trader refused to bid them. But, he owed me a favor and I called it in. Since this insurance company is a great client and a good friend, he gave me a bid. It was low, but he gave me the bid anyway. I was of course completely embarrassed to give my client the bid, so I told him to take the bonds somewhere else where he could get more money. But since I was 'his broker' he didn't have the inclination or the time to go elsewhere. I have the ticket right here in my hand, and I will have to turn it in to my trader before the market closes today. Now I can do that or I can sell them to another client. Or, of course, I could use them to start a relationship with a new client. I manage portfolios for banks of your size. I would like to get this relationship off on the right foot with you and open a new account. I know if you don't take them, one of my other clients will. Although I don't need your business, I certainly want it. I have a cool million ready to go, and if you tell me your routing number I'll go ahead and drop these bonds to your caretaker."

So smooth. So slick. So much bullshit. All of this of course, if you could just get past the secretary and then survive the "I don't have any money" excuse.

The first fifty cold calls Jack made never had a chance to get past the secretary. The next fifty calls only made him more determined to get past the secretary.

Five hours later, and over a hundred unsuccessful attempts to get past the secretaries, he was now ready for blood. He had his pitch all together and ready to go. He was psyched up and determined that no secretary was going to stop him this time. He dialed the number and the phone rang. After the second ring it was answered by a man.

"I need to speak to Mr. Reynolds please."

"That's me."

Jack started to feel a little anxious as he was only prepared to deal with the secretary.

"Mr. Reynolds." Jack repeated.

"Yes."

"Mr. Josh Reynolds?"

"That's right."

Since Jack was not prepared to get the person he needed to speak with he began to panic, and for some reason his mind went totally blank.

"Mr. Joshua Reynolds, the president of the Bank Josh Reynolds?"

"The one and only."

"Ah, crap. I mean sorry. I mean, never, uh, uh, mind. My name is Jack. I got some bonds, you want them?"

"No thank you," was heard as Mr. Reynolds hung up on Jack.

Jack was beside himself. He was embarrassed and completely traumatized as he hung up the phone. He sat there absolutely crushed. It was the first time it ever occurred to him that maybe this was not the job for him.

It certainly did not help when two seconds later, out of nowhere, Mean Dean kicked the back of Jack's chair yelling, "Get your sorry ass back on that phone now! Hook 'em up baby shit."

The phones were set up so that anyone training the rookies could listen in on a cold call conversation with a potential client. The first week of cold calling for each rookie class was also tape-recorded. During that first week, and every day right after everyone left, the partners and senior associates had "comment sessions" about the rookies. Attendance was optional, but they all attended to drink and hobnob with the top producers. Plus no one wanted to miss the fun of listening to what was termed the "boners."

All the comment sessions were held in the first-floor boardroom. When the sessions started, each "boner" was fully edited and ready to go. A cart stocked with the best whisky, scotch, and vodka rolled in. Everyone partook of course. By 5:00 everyone was cracking up at the "best of the boners." At the end the session, once they had stopped laughing, the top producers for that day voted on the best boner of the day. The winner would receive a hundred dollars and be presented the "award" that evening.

The session started off with a short call from Bart. He had cold called the Omaha City comptroller in Nebraska. The only thing Bart managed to say before he was cut off from his pitch was, "This is Bart...."

"Bart the Fart?" interrupted the comptroller.

"Kiss my ass," Bart mustered as the comptroller hung up.

So, of course, from that day on he was always known as "Bart the Fart." None of his fellow rookies ever called him that, but the partners and senior associates did. Bart was complimented for "not taking any shit, even from clients."

And of course, the more drinks consumed, the funnier each boner became.

Unfortunately for Jack, his worst fear came true that day. His call to Joshua Reynolds was a contender for the boner of the day. Although everyone got a good laugh out of it, he was commended for saying, "I got some bonds, you want them?"

When they had left the office that day the rookies had headed over to HOGS to have a few drinks. They were stressed out and panicky after their first day on the job. It was also one more in a long list of rules in order to work for the firm. All rookies could only go to HOGS after work. They never knew who would be there, and no one wanted to take any chances of missing out on a good time, or being yelled at for doing so poorly that day.

Aaron and Jack were the only two rookies who knew each other prior to working at the firm. Initially, they huddled up and talked about their day. The tension was high. Jack was particularly upset about his call to Josh Reynolds. "I can't believe I said that. They're going to fire me before the end of the week."

It was not long before some of the senior associates had come in and yelled out who were contenders and who was the winner of the boner award for the day. Jack could not believe he had won. He grabbed his hundred dollars while everyone in the room congratulated him. They may have been laughing, but he got pats on the back just the same. Even so, Jack was determined to never be a contender, and to especially make sure that he never won this contest again.

Aaron was worried about his performance his first day also. "Whatever. I didn't even get past a single secretary today. I swear my ear is numb. And I don't even know what to say!"

"Yea, me, too. And you know what? I haven't memorized any kind of script whatsoever."

"Script? You've got a script? They're going to fire me, not you," Aaron replied as he finished his drink and signaled for another round. "And did you notice almost everyone had a boner today except for me?"

Jack chomped his ice as he responded. "I just thought that was because you were doing so well. At least no one gave you a new nickname like Bart."

"Poor guy. They wouldn't let up on him would they?" Aaron saw Bart and signaled for him to join them at their table.

Bart pulled up a chair and sat down. "My ears hurt. Do yours?"

Jack responded for both of them. "Yea. It feels like my ear's been smacked by a phone all day." He turned his head. "Does it look bruised?"

Aaron lied. "Yup, it's big and ugly. Maybe you'll grow calluses on your ears. Then you can walk around and be a freak for some sideshow at the fair."

After the third round of drinks had been served, all of the rookies became more relaxed and the group huddled together. They began to talk about their very first day. It turned out everyone thought they were about to be fired. It was a huge relief to all. Apparently no one stood a chance that day of selling any bonds. And everyone failed miserably on their first day, with the exception of the attorney, Floyd, who was supposed to be a rookie.

The partners had hired Floyd knowing that he was an expert in banking laws and in assisting banks in financing projects. His client base as an attorney already consisted of banks and credit unions. He simply called his own clients and sold them bonds instead of legal advice. From that evening on everyone at the firm would occasionally call him "That Fucking Floyd." It was a name that spread like wildfire throughout the entire office. Even future rookies knew him as That Fucking Floyd. And after only his very first day he became a junior partner at the firm.

When everyone realized they were all in this together the enthusiasm for their jobs returned. Initial conversations were full of doubt and questions about how they could possibly succeed at such a difficult job. After realizing they were in the same boat, they spoke of the riches the phone calls would eventually provide. Dreams of fast cars, fine women, and the fancy life a lot of money would bring these young men swirled about them like a tornado. By the end of the evening the bruised confidences had healed.

Although it was only 8:30 p.m. when Jack, Aaron, and a couple of other guys returned to the office parking lot, they were surprised to see so many cars still sitting under the building. Willie was there though guarding the lot full of cars. He also made sure everyone who returned from HOGS was sober enough to drive. If they were not, he called them a cab.

When anyone had asked what was going on inside his response was always the same. "I don't know and it's none of your business either. Now go home. You have to be here early. Go get some sleep."

But as Jack exited Aaron's car he realized he didn't have his keys. "Shit, I left my keys inside. Give me just a second to get my keys before you leave, will you?"

"Sure. Just tell Willie you need to go in real quick," Aaron replied.

Jack yelled across the parking lot to Willie. "Hey, I left my keys inside. I need to go get them."

"That's too bad young man. You can't go in there and you know that. You'll have to get them tomorrow."

"Uh, okay then." Jack turned and looked back at Aaron, shrugging his shoulders in the process.

"Screw that Jack," Aaron whispered. "I'll just distract him, and you go get your keys."

"And just what are you going to do?"

"I don't know. I'll ask him if he needs another cigarette or something. I'll go get Bart and we'll think of something."

"Sounds good to me," Jack responded. In his half-drunken state he mumbled the James Bond theme as he scurried off.

Jack decided to run up the exit stairs since the elevator call button would have lit up by Willie's station. He slowly opened the door to the first floor of the building and stood still, quietly listening for any noise. The only thing he heard was Dan Manikan's voice in his own head. "You are not allowed in the building after hours for any reason, even if you forgot your car keys."

Jack silently crept through the hallway trying to make it to his desk on the trading floor. When he finally arrived at his desk he slowly opened the top drawer. As he grabbed his keys he had never before realized how much noise they made when they jingled together.

He didn't bother closing the drawer after he grabbed them. He turned around to quietly, and as quickly as he could, sneak back towards the exit. The silence in the building was eerie and making him nervous.

As he reached the front hallway Jack heard a faint noise. He panicked and immediately pressed himself flat against the wall and into the shadows.

He could barely hear some giggling. As he listened closer, he recognized the laughter of a woman. As the laughter disappeared he heard men yelling on the second or third floor somewhere. Although he tried, he couldn't determine what they were yelling about. Then he heard a girl laughing not too far from him, but the laughter was gone before he could make out where it exactly had come from.

He cautiously turned into the hallway to make his great escape when an office door across the hallway opened. Jack again quickly hid in the shadows against the wall. When the door closed he cautiously turned and looked down the hallway just in time to see a retreating girl, from behind, wearing absolutely nothing. She turned around, laughing, as she looked back to the room she had just exited. She obviously did not see Jack. He could tell she was a real blonde, and though he was frightened out of his wits that he would be discovered, he did take a moment to observe and appreciate the bouncing boobs as the girl kept dashing back and forth from one door to another. She finally ran into another office and slammed the door shut. She was giggling the entire time. He had no idea who she was, but he thought that she looked good. Damn good.

Jack paused a bit longer before making his next move. The total silence encouraged him to make a break for the exit door. He ran out to the parking lot so fast not even Willie noticed him exiting the building.

CHAPTER SIX

▼

Jack's first day on the phones was not what he had thought it would be. He had read about the market and learned to read the indices and the bond yields. None of that mattered. If a broker couldn't talk to the man in charge of the money it didn't matter what he knew.

Knowledge of the market though was not totally worthless. But it was the salesmanship and marketing that were the keys to breaking into the business. Jack's real education and training started that day on the phone.

As the days rolled by, Jack realized that the secretarial screening was not such a bad deal. It spared him the rejection by some banker or CFO, the humiliation of being hung up on in mid-sentence, and the frustration of another unsuccessful call. The only benefit of a rejected call was that it gave a broker experience and taught him how to accept rejection. Sometimes a secretary would relate some small but significant information about the bank or the person the broker was trying to contact that could help in the future.

Worse than being told to get lost by a prospect was being strung along by one. Some bankers and treasurers were nice. Too nice in fact. They wanted to talk nonstop as they had time to kill. A broker did not.

Over a period of a few weeks, most rookies started to believe that they had locked in a future client. They thought it was only a matter of time before the first sale. This was especially true when they talked about things other than bonds; personal things—fishing, hunting, kid's school, vacations, etc., only to discover that the banker was never going to do business with them. Not with any rookie, ever. When a rookie got the nerve to press a sale the response was something like, "I've had the same broker for twenty years; not going to change now," or "I just wanted to make sure my broker was showing me the best prices." Those were the heartbreakers.

During the next few weeks, the phone did, indeed, turn into the "elephant with diarrhea." Every rookie began detesting the phone. They hated touching it. They despised the phone so much most would not even answer the phone at home anymore.

Both Jack and Aaron watched and understood as their fellow classmates became thoroughly disenchanted. For some it was too much to handle. Some of the brokers couldn't cope with the disrespect of being on the receiving end of so much profanity aimed right at them. The disappointments and repeated failures were grueling, especially if the broker took the denials personally. Some didn't last two weeks.

One day Jack spoke with one of the nicest bankers he could have ever hoped to find. He had called Liberty Hill National Bank and reached the secretary to the president. She had informed him that the president did not handle the bond portfolio and that the portfolio was handled by Mr. Clayton Daniel. She even provided his phone number to Jack.

Jack called and it was Mr. Daniel who actually answered. Jack could tell from Mr. Daniel's voice that he was an elderly gentleman. Mr. Daniel knew everything about bonds and the current market. He could also talk for hours, nonstop.

Mr. Daniel was always eager to converse and was delighted whenever Jack phoned. Jack and Mr. Daniel became friends quickly. And Mr. Daniel had asked Jack to call him by his first name. "My father was Mr. Daniel, so please just call me Clayton."

Jack could, and would, talk with him for a couple of hours a few times a week. Jack listened intently to Clayton and was thoroughly entertained by Clayton's stories about his experiences during World War I. Jack was certain it was only a matter of time before Clayton would buy some bonds.

A few weeks later, when Jack called, Clayton did not answer the phone. It rang several times, but was never picked up. Jack called again the next day. The phone rang and a woman answered. "Is Clayton around? This is Jack."

The woman hesitated before she responded. "I'm sorry, but he's not here."

"Oh, that's no problem. I'll just call him tomorrow."

"I'm sorry, but he won't be here tomorrow either."

Jack was getting ready to ask if maybe Clayton was sick or on vacation when she told him, "I'm sorry, but Clayton Daniel passed away."

Jack was speechless. He was deeply saddened because Clayton had become such a good friend all the times they had spoken over the phone. "I am so sorry. Is this is wife?"

"Oh no, I was his nurse. This is Liberty Hill Nursing Home. Mr. Daniel had been living here for the past twelve years or so."

As it turned out, Mr. Daniel had retired from the bank almost twenty years earlier. He had built the bank from the ground up and was knowledgeable about every aspect of his bank. After retiring, he was given permission to "help out" the bank by talking to brokers about bonds. He was a lonely old man who loved talking to people. A widower with kids in other states who rarely called him, cold callers were often the only calls he ever received.

Clayton could talk to brokers all day long and say whatever he wanted. He just did not have the power to make the decision and say to the broker, "I'll buy." No doubt his passing had shocked many rookies since Mr. Daniel had become friends with so many. Especially once they learned that the bank's portfolio was handled by the bank's president, and not Mr. Daniel. Jack was traumatized just the same.

Aaron, on the other hand, took everything in stride. He was always having fun as well. He too had been cussed out, chewed out, and hung up on. He also had been "stroked" by potential clients who would never buy. But he never seemed to care. After a week or so of calling he started playing a game.

He wanted to see how many bankers he could hang up on first. Most of the financial executives being contacted got a kick out of their own sadistic responses to cold callers. Aaron got a kick out of knowing he was taking that pleasure away from them. As soon as any conversation turned sour, Aaron would hang up. He knew the banker would be furious when he realized he'd lost control of the call. Being pillars in their community, this was not something bankers were accustomed to, or experienced often.

Aaron's game evolved into mimicking the attitudes of the men he called. After a month of cold calling, and being rejected each and every time, Aaron did not care anymore. As Jack sat next to him he could often hear Aaron cussing at the people on the other end of the phone. To Aaron, it became funnier and funnier each time he did it.

He was the only one in the group who couldn't wait to make another call. He was also the only one in the group who never got caught by Mean Dean for not being on the phone. Nor was he ever chastised about his little game either. Mean Dean knew what was going on, but he also knew that this was a learning process, and once a broker got mad enough to be just as rude to some of the people he called, then success would eventually happen.

Jack couldn't take it anymore as he listened to Aaron and his latest call. "No, not fuck me, fuck you. I bet you like that too, right in the.... Damn, he hung up first," Aaron complained as he put the phone down.

"They're going to fire you if you don't cut that out."

"So. Who cares? Neither of us has made a penny in almost two months. How much worse can it be to get fired?"

"That doesn't matter. You're talking to important people. They're all running big companies, with millions of dollars at their disposal. You shouldn't speak to them like that. Have some respect."

"Screw that. Why should I respect them if they don't respect me?"

"You have to earn respect."

"Exactly my point. They don't respect us, so I don't respect them. Besides, it's fun. You should try it. It's liberating, in a weird sort of way."

At this point in their conversation Mean Dean added his two cents. "If you two little sissies don't get back on the phones I'm going to tie your hand to the phone with your necktie. Quit making out and get back on the phones. Neither of you have made a sale yet, now get to it! Hook 'em up baby shit!"

While Dean's comments bounced off Aaron, they frightened Jack. "Don't worry about it Jack, the sales will come. Watch this. I called this guy last week and he's an asshole with a capital A. Let's see how much fun we can have."

Jack called to check the weather and pretended to be on the phone while he listened to a recorded voice tell him the temperature and chance of rain. Aaron spoke with a smile and was courteous to whoever answered the phone. This time he also spoke like he knew the person he was calling.

Some secretary answered. "Good morning, Mr. Peele's office. This is Rebecca, how may I help you?"

Jack sat there, listening only to Aaron's side of the conversation, watching Aaron speak with a big smile on his face. "Hey Becky, it's Aaron. Is that no-good banker in his office today or is he off playing golf again? Now don't lie to me, I know he's playing golf since it's such a gorgeous day."

"Oh no, he wishes he were on the course today. He's in his office, I'll put you right through."

"All right, but he should be hitting golf balls or something, because his handicap is embarrassing."

Aaron applied some of his sales knowledge in his cold calls. He already knew something Jack had not yet learned. The more a broker could act like he truly knew the person he was trying to call, the more likely the broker was to get through. There wasn't a single receptionist or secretary that dared blow off a friend or business associate of their boss.

Unlike Jack, Aaron had also learned that it was not the secretary's fault for being mean. It was what they were instructed to do. They were trained to blow off strangers. It was part of their job. While Jack had snapped at them, Aaron had acted like he had just talked to them yesterday at lunch. It was all bullshit.

Jack listened to the first minute or so of Aaron's call. At first, his conversation with Mr. Peele appeared to be going nowhere. Jack had started dialing his own phone when his interest was suddenly focused back on Aaron.

It was not the words Jack heard that caught his attention. It was the shift in Aaron's attitude.

"I have a better idea, how about you quit pretending you know what you're talking about so we can get down to business." Aaron stopped smiling, but Jack could tell he was still having fun.

Jack could only hear one side of the conversation, but could imagine the responses from the banker. He was trying to concentrate on what Aaron was saying, but he could hear Mean Dean from up above. "Get your ass back on that phone Jack. Don't make me come down there!"

Jack called his home number. Knowing no one would answer, he listened intently to Aaron's side of the conversation.

"Whatever. All you do is manage a bank. I bet you don't even know what a basis point is, do you?" There was a short pause. "Oh please, spare me." He paused again. "Oh, *now* you don't have any money. I call bullshit on that. I bet your customers would be interested in learning that. I don't care how many cold calls you get a day. Do I sound like I'm new to this? You may not like my call, but any one of my bonds are better than the shitty-ass loans you make every day. My bonds are going to save your sorry ass at the end of the year." Aaron listened to the banker for a bit before resuming. "I'll tell you what. I will *allow* you to buy some bonds from me, but it has to be at least a million. Anything less is a waste of my time. I want your business, but I sure as hell don't need it. My bonds will make your portfolio look good. Hell, I should make you buy two million."

Neither Aaron nor Jack could have predicted the events that unfolded next. Jack quietly picked up on the line and listened to the full conversation. When Jack did this Aaron was momentarily distracted, but it never showed. And Aaron tried hard to prevent his enthusiasm from overcoming the attitude he had begun with. "I have two million St. Paul Port Authorities giving you 10% until maturity."

"Are they below par?" Peele inquired.

"They sure are."

"Can I get five-hundred thousand?"

"Nope, sorry. It has to be a million."

"But I don't have that much money."

Jack thought Aaron was about to blow the whole deal. He couldn't believe his ears. By now his own adrenaline was pumping as much as Aaron's.

Aaron could feel Jack's staring at him but wanted Jack to know that he was not losing the momentum. He turned to Jack and mouthed to him silently, "I know what I'm doing." He resumed his conversation without missing a beat.

"My apologies, Mr. Peele. I thought your bank had more assets. I don't deal in anything less than a million. I can recommend you to another broker or one of my rookie associates if you want me to."

After a brief silence, "No, no, I have the money. I'll do the million."

"Excellent. It's a pleasure dealing with someone who's in control of their own bank. I'm going to transfer you over to our trader to close the deal. If there are any problems please don't hesitate to let me know. It's been a pleasure, and thank you for doing business with us."

Aaron's heart felt like it was beating a hundred miles a minute. He screamed up to the trader, "Alex! This bank is ready to buy a million of those Port Authorities on the board. I don't know what the hell I'm doing! Please close the deal!"

After Alex finished the call he yelled to Aaron, "How does it feel to make twenty-thousand dollars off of a single phone call?"

The trading floor went crazy. Everyone cheered as Alex walked towards Aaron with a pair of scissors. It was a tradition in the industry that after each broker made his first sale his necktie was cut off below the knot. It did not matter if it was their favorite tie or not, it was cut. It was an honor and a rite of passage.

For the rest of the day, Aaron walked around with an amputated necktie. He went to lunch like that with Gage and Strong.

Rookies who had not yet had the pleasure of wearing a severed necktie were jealous. That was, everyone except Jack. No one was happier for Aaron than his best friend.

$$\ast \quad \ast \quad \ast \quad \ast$$

As the weeks turned into months some of the other rookies eventually made their first sale. The rest had either quit or been fired. Out of the original class, they were down to just a few, and of these Jack was the only one who had not yet closed a deal. He was relentless as ever though.

Jack felt this job was a life-and-death struggle. He believed his success, or failure, depended on what he did with this job. While he had some sales experience, and he was gifted with the ability to understand the world of finance, for some reason making a sale seemed out of his reach. He was totally fascinated by how different instruments yielded different returns, and also how the same bond could be great for one company, bad for a local government, and disastrous for a bank.

His enthusiasm for his job was the only thing that kept him from being fired. Every afternoon, as they all left the building, he would walk with one of the experienced salesmen from the office, asking question after question.

After a while these men began to avoid Jack as best they could, so he offered to buy them drinks at HOGS so he could learn as much as possible. Fortunately for Jack, all the partners recognized his determination, intelligence, positive attitude, and his perseverance. Otherwise, he would have been fired a long time ago.

Not everyone appreciated Jack's enthusiasm for his job though, in particular, his wife. Getting up at 5:30 in the morning and getting home anywhere between 5:30 and 10:00 at night didn't leave much of a home life for a married couple.

Jack had known his wife, Millie, since they were kids, and while in high school they had gone steady. Not long after Jack had begun college they were married. He knew that she had also wanted to go to college, but Millie had agreed to delay college and go to work so he could go to school. At the time it was a sacrifice she was more than willing to make. She knew that it would not be long before it would be her turn. But there were times when she had to work two jobs, and sometimes the fights that resulted from two people who had too much to do and were very tired became too much for her.

Lately, she had been bringing this up, especially since he had joined the firm and had not brought home a single paycheck. Millie was again forced to work two jobs in order for them to pay their bills, and she was beginning to resent it. She voiced her opinion loudly and often.

Even before Jack left the insurance company there were problems in the marriage. Though his job at the insurance company was secure, the pay was low, and sometimes Millie would bring up the topic of him returning to school to get an MBA. She was tired of working and wanted a family, but not if she had to work outside the home.

Jack knew this, too. He had tried networking with the top executives at the insurance company, but the only person who actually listened to Jack was his boss, Mr. Lange, who had interviewed and then hired Jack because he recognized Jack's skills and intelligence. However, the other executives had little time to spend with someone just out of college. Nor did they make any time to socialize with him.

Once Strong removed the blindfold from Jack's eyes, it was not a difficult decision for him to leave his job to go work for the firm. It was, however, difficult telling Millie that he was quitting a steady job with a decent paycheck for one with no paycheck, no health coverage, no pension, no corporate ladder, and almost no security.

Once again Jack arrived home smelling of booze after a late night of networking with one of the partners and other brokers from the firm. Millie had just arrived home from her second shift job when he walked in the door. His less that sober condition set Millie off. "This is not a life, Jack. This is not the life I signed up for nor the life I want," she yelled. "I'm not working my fingers to the bone so you can go out every night and get drunk with your boss."

Before Jack could respond, Millie cut him off.

"I can't believe you left a decent job for one with no pay or benefits! You're going backward." Millie started to cry.

When Jack reached for her hand, she jerked it back and ranted some more. "You said this job would be big money. Big money fast. I told you it was too good to be true." She blew her nose on a tissue. "I can't remember the last time you brought home a paycheck. We can't afford insurance, much less children."

"You're right, Millie. This job is more difficult than I thought it would be, but I'll get there." He paused. "Even Aaron has made only a few sales," he tried justifying.

"I don't care about Aaron. He's not my husband, you are. We've gone through all our savings and every day you promise the money will start to come in. When, Jack?"

Millie pulled away again when Jack reached for her. She wiped her tears away, picked up her purse, and turned toward the door. "I'm going to stay at my parent's tonight. I'll call you sometime tomorrow."

As Jack watched her leave, he knew their marriage was on the brink of divorce.

CHAPTER SEVEN

▼

Travis Haynes would sometimes make a surprise visit to the training sessions and silently watch the students. Unlike Strong, he never interrupted the sessions, nor would he ever interject any stories or comments during the class. As quietly as he entered the room, he exited.

The interviews with him were different than with the other partners. He often would ask questions some found peculiar. What was asked had nothing to do with education or experience, but would be about something totally unrelated to the firm's business. Haynes would force them to sit in his office in uncomfortable silence for long periods of time. He watched them squirm, leaving the poor applicant wondering if he needed to add more to an answer or just leave it as it was. Often wondering if they had answered the question completely wrong, the interviews were unnerving. If life was a poker game, Haynes was the reigning champion. He was a mystery to every new rookie in every new training class. What they did not know was that he was also a mystery to those who had known him for years.

Haynes was in his mid-forties, was a few inches over six feet in height and had a deep voice that carried far. His voice also had a certain tonal quality, so that when he spoke everyone listened. He rarely said much to the rookies, but when he did they all listened as if it were the gospel.

Haynes constantly watched people, even when they did not know he was doing so. He particularly watched the rookies, sizing them up and constantly learning everything he could about each one. He picked up on their mannerisms, gestures, and personalities. He was an expert in reading body language. He learned things about people just from looking at the kind of clothes they wore. After only a short time he knew the fears, insecurities, strengths, dreams, and desires of every broker. To some, his presence on the floor was almost spooky.

His ability to read others helped make the firm that much more successful. For brokerage firms of this type to make any money they needed to put as many bodies on the phones as possible. Jordan Strong was a natural leader and great at recruiting. Olive and Gage were great at entertaining and motivating. Haynes' greatest skill was telling the other partners which brokers would make it and which ones would not. And he was correct every single time.

The other partners could easily motivate the rookies and associates by talking about money. Haynes, however, got into their psyche. He pushed every button that needed to be pushed. He would place the keys to his Ferrari on a rookie's desk. Sometimes he would call a rookie into his office to look at vacation homes off the coast of Florida. He placed magazines about guns or women, or whatever he thought would get that rookie's blood pumping, on their desks.

Haynes' job was to pick out the whipping boys. He also picked out the first rookie who could and would make the very first sale. He could tell which rookie would make the most money and he knew who would be the first to quit.

Haynes knew who to fire, when to fire them, and most importantly, why to fire them. He was great at thinking outside of the box. He used the firings as tools to motivate the others. In fact, almost all firings were pre-approved by Haynes. He even developed the method and pretense of firing a broker. While he rarely objected to another partner's wishes to fire someone, he usually had the last say so. Haynes was a great puppet master when it came to the rookies and associates, but he never played games with the other partners.

Haynes was also the only reason why Jack had not yet been fired.

*   *   *   *

It had been months since Jack and Aaron began cold calling. The summer was coming to a close on what turned out to be one of the firm's most successful rookie classes ever.

Floyd started everyone off running. By the end of his first month he had grossed nearly forty-thousand dollars. He was immediately segregated from the rest of the class. The partners decided to move Floyd up to be closer to the traders and near some of the senior associates. He also had the prestigious distinction of being the first rookie invited upstairs to the Zeros, and after being on the job for only two months.

Aaron was also coming alive. He was making a sale almost every week and his numbers were adding up. He too started getting a lot of attention from the senior associates and the partners. His best month had grossed a little over thirty-thousand dollars. It was not long before he moved up as well.

Of course, he never saved a penny. The partners encouraged him to spend it before he even received his paycheck. New suits. New shoes. A gold Rolex. And a stereo system with speakers that belonged in a football stadium. And just like that, he was as broke as when he had started.

The other brokers began urging Aaron to buy a new car. Gage let him drive one of his Corvettes during lunch. After work, Olive let him drive his Porsche. Haynes just shook the keys to his Ferrari in front of Aaron's face.

Haynes was always more subtle than anyone else and this was more effective. Strong had a different tactic. He started in on Aaron one evening at HOGS. "Your car is a piece of shit. You're making money now. You need a new car. What are you waiting for? How embarrassing for you. Even worse, you're starting to embarrass us. We can't have that piece of shit sitting in our parking lot."

Bart was also showing signs of life. He didn't make a single sale until he actually learned and became fully informed on one of the bonds the firm was pitching. It was Haynes who sat down with him one day and taught him everything he needed to know about GNMAs, better known as "Ginnie Mays." Once Bart knew what he was selling, he had the attitude and confidence to close almost every deal, and it was not long before he too was moved up towards the front of the room.

Bart was very smart and with a fairly rigid personal code that was probably genetic. And he was the first one in his family, for generations, who chose not to work in law enforcement.

His father had been a Houston police officer for years before becoming a special agent for the FBI in Washington, D.C. Bart's grandfather had been a Texas State Trooper before retiring to Houston. Both of his brothers worked for the Secret Service. His uncle was a DEA agent and his other grandfather was a retired Texas Ranger.

Bart's obsession with law enforcement was apparent. He talked about how he was going to be a cop or an undercover detective but then changed his mind, just to be different from everyone else in his family--but only after being sold by Strong on the firm at a random encounter. There was a little rebel streak in Bart that no one else in his family had. And he was crazy for any police or detective show and movie. One of his favorite movies was Shaft. Bart especially loved the car Shaft drove and talked about it incessantly.

Of course, as soon as he was making money, he also was encouraged to buy new things. Haynes knew what Bart wanted. Haynes could be heard in the hallway, talking to Bart. "What kind of car was that again that's in that movie you keep talking about?"

"It's a souped-up Plymouth Roadrunner. Hot car!"

"Is that what you want?"

"I sure do. I can just see me driving a cherry-red, souped-up Roadrunner muscle car with all the works."

Haynes just smiled and said nothing.

Meanwhile, Jack had yet to sell one bond. No matter how many calls he made, he just could not get the sale. Jack felt his life starting to spiral out of control. He put too much pressure on himself to succeed, and this only caused him to come across as needy for every call he made. He was too hopeful, and his hope was turning into desperation.

It was not long before his desperation turned to begging. "Let's just do this first sale." "Can I get you to buy something, anything?" "I can call you back if you like." "Please trust me." It was pathetic.

The friction was affecting his work and the stress at work spilled into his home life. It was a place from which Jack felt he could not escape. Millie was now spending more of her time at her parent's home. On the off occasion she was at home Jack slept on the couch.

Jack heard his own heartbeat pounding wildly in his chest when he saw the next training class begin. He knew it was only a matter of time before he would be fired. He began to believe that maybe he should be fired. Almost every desk near him was empty and ready for the next group of rookies.

He soon found ways to avoid the phone. He took excessive water breaks. He kept going to the restroom. He would walk up to the boards where all the bonds were listed, pretending to look for a product to pitch.

It took two days of this before Dean decided to act. Mean Dean removed his tie and walked towards Jack's desk and used it to tie Jack's hand to his phone. Neither of them said anything, but Jack felt embarrassed. As Mean Dean walked off he yelled out at the top of his lungs, "Hook 'em up baby shit!"

Haynes had been paying special attention to Jack for some weeks now and had realized a while back that motivating Jack was not the issue. Jack already worked his butt off and Haynes knew this. Leaving the keys to his Ferrari on Jack's desk only made things worse for Jack. The only thing holding Jack back was Jack.

Haynes called Jack into his office to speak with him. "Don't worry, the sales will come. Stop stressing yourself out. You need to act like you don't have a care in the world. Don't let these bankers intimidate you. They put their pants on one leg at a time just like you do."

Haynes did his best to encourage Jack. Much like Aaron had done.

"But I'm not like Aaron," he told Haynes one night at HOGS.

"You don't need to be like him. There's no one right way to do this job. You just need to have a little self-confidence in your approach. Stop acting like every phone call is a life or death situation. It comes across in your voice and your attitude. They may not always hear it, but they can sense it. You know more about the products we sell than anyone else in your class. Hell, you know more about it than most of those who have worked here for years. The problem's not with your knowledge of the product, it's the delivery of your sales pitch. Right now, you couldn't sell beer to a college fraternity. These people need the bonds we sell. And these bonds are everywhere. There are hundreds of dealers like us. What they want and what they are looking for is someone they can believe in. I can tell you this: Gage doesn't know shit about bonds and he never will either. But he sounds like he knows what he's talking about. He projects confidence. He makes the buyer feel secure. The buyers are attracted to that."

"But, I thought I was doing that. I tell them everything they need to know about the bond I'm pitching. It just never seems to be the right bond for them," Jack replied as he looked at the bottom of his glass.

"Once you get past the interest rate and the yield to maturity on a bond, you've lost most of the people you are selling to. They don't know and they don't care about any of that crap. They just want to know that they're not screwing up by buying the bond. They just want to keep their jobs and look good while doing so. And it's your job to make them feel this way."

"I don't know if I can work here much longer. My home life is going down in flames. My wife doesn't understand this job. And quite frankly, I don't blame her. I haven't made a penny in months. Not one goddamn penny. Now you have another training class starting up. I have no illusions about you guys keeping me here much longer." Jack followed his sorrows with a shot of whiskey.

"Let's try a different approach, Jack. I'll tell you a little story about my wife. My wife was a flight attendant. She didn't make much money, but one of the benefits was that we could fly anywhere and pretty cheap. We both loved to fly down to the Florida Keys, or to the Bahamas, or anywhere in the Caribbean. Problem was that we never had any money to even do that. However, when I first started in this business it was easier opening new accounts. The money then began to roll in pretty fast. I never had a problem spending it. My wife, Isabel, however, was always in my face about my spending habits. So one day I decided to cash my paycheck. I put all of the money inside two grocery sacks and walked out of the bank."

"How much was it?" Jack interrupted.

"That's not the point."

"Sorry."

"Don't be. Isabel had just finished making the bed when I got home. I sat her down and placed a sack next to me on the floor. I told her my paycheck for the entire month was in that bag. I told her it was as big as the paychecks from the previous two months. I told her another one would be coming the following month. Then I told her that I thought it was time for her to just know how much money I made."

"What'd she say?"

"Nothing, she just sat there. So I asked her, 'how much is our house payment?' She responded, 'eighteen-hundred every month.' So I pulled out two-thousand dollars and placed it on the bed. I then went through every single bill we had. If the bill was less than a hundred dollars, I just put down a hundred bucks to cover it. Isabel even itemized two college trust funds for our kids, and the money we needed to save each month for retirement."

Jack had a crooked smile on his face as he sat there listening. "Then what?"

"I took all of the money on the bed and put it on the floor. I then grabbed the grocery sack and dumped the rest of the money on top of the bed. I then got up, walked into the hallway, and grabbed the other sack of cash I was carrying home from the bank. I took that and dumped it on the bed also."

"What did she do then?"

"She starting throwing the money up into the air like a little kid. Looking back, it was the smartest, and dumbest, thing I have ever done. She never had a problem spending after that." Haynes smiled. "I definitely created a monster."

"Wow!" was all Jack could say.

"I'm telling you this because you need to change your way of thinking. Stop worrying about everyone else's sales. Stop worrying about getting your first sale. Stop worrying about getting fired. Stop worrying about what your wife thinks about this job. And it's not her fault that she can't comprehend how much money you can make here. But think of all the things you can provide her. I know you're tired of hearing 'no' from everyone you call. I know you're hungry. And you should be angry that you haven't sold anything yet. Maybe you should project some of that anger while you're on the phone. Give yourself some attitude. There are thousands of banks in this country. There are thousands of insurance companies and other businesses that need these investments. There are hundreds of local governments that also need to buy. Twenty good clients will make you a million dollars a year. Imagine if you had fifty clients. That's all you need in this business. You have confidence in the product, and you really know the product, too. You just don't have confidence in yourself. Don't feel sorry for yourself. Feel sorry for the ones who don't buy from you. Screw them. You don't need them all. Just a few."

Jack sat there. Listening. Thinking. Taking it all in. Not saying a word, just slightly nodding his head. It made sense to him. He felt that his slate had been wiped clean. Tomorrow would be a new day. He just needed to execute. "Thanks for the drinks," Jack nodded his head as he got up to leave.

"Anytime. And Jack, one more thing."

"What?"

Haynes smiled. "Relax about the new training class. You just take care of your business."

There were not too many rookies left from Jack's class by fall. Ten became nine. Nine became eight. If they had not quit, they were fired. Each firing was done in the same manner, very public, and very obvious. The entire office could hear when they announced someone's name over the loud speaker, "Charlie, call me on extension 355." Extension 355 was Strong's office.

Everyone knew what that meant. Anyone who received that page was never seen again. They would leave their desk and never come back. Samantha or one of the other girls would come by a few minutes later with a box and pack up any personal effects.

Mean Dean followed shortly to pick up the "Book." The Book was a large three-inch binder that contained phone numbers of every type of business that could and would buy bonds, and that the newly departed broker had been working on. It also contained a description of each entity. The Book listed the address, the total assets and net worth of each institution, or the population of the county. More importantly, it identified the person to call.

The Book also contained gems that could only be mined after numerous failed phone calls. It included hand-written notes from previous brokers in an effort to assist them in trying to make a sale the next time they called.

Typical scribbled notes read: "Doesn't go by his first name, only his middle." "His secretary Angela is a total bitch—and don't call her Angie." "Only buys bonds at a discount." "Non-callable bonds only." Each broker recorded anything and everything that would give him an edge the next time he called.

Mean Dean always held the Book for a couple of days after he had collected it. The brokers knew exactly what to do with this information so they all hovered around Mean Dean. And Mean Dean especially enjoyed the attention and the lavish gifts he received when he had the Book.

In an office with fifty to sixty sales people at any given time, a carrot was always dangling. The Book was often the best carrot. Any number of things could happen with it. Sometimes Mean Dean piecemealed the Book for the other brokers to add to their own books. Sometimes it was a gift, in return for a very nice dinner; one with no expenses spared. Other times it was just reassigned to another broker who called the same territory.

Motivation at the firm was not always positive and several forms were not as pretty as others. Some sort of public humiliation was constantly on display. With so many people making big money egos had to be controlled. A few brokers occasionally needed to be reminded that they were replaceable.

Sometimes, pieces of the Book were distributed to every associate, except for one or two. Those exceptions could be as a punishment, as an indication of a soon to be empty desk, or simply to reinstall the fear of being called on extension 355.

Every desk on the trading floor was lined up next to the other. The brokers could hear each other's phone calls. Sometimes they could even hear the person on the other end of someone else's phone. When the market was hot, it was like a sporting event. Everyone shouting and screaming charged the air with excitement.

When the market turned south it was more intense. Poor estimations in the market produced incredible negative energy. On rare occasions the trading floor could be almost silent. Shouting matches between brokers and their clients sometimes interrupted the eerie silence.

One of the first sales techniques taught to each class was for the broker to visualize himself standing on the desk of the banker. "Long and Strong" was the saying. Keep the prospect on the phone and talk strong through the phone.

The "Long and Strong" attitude, combined with the pressure and intensity of the business, every now and then caused the guys to turn on each other. Fights between brokers had to be busted up as quickly as possible. On more than one occasion someone was sent home with a bloody nose.

Good times or bad, they all worked hard. The tension was often broken by laughter over practical jokes and various pranks. It was the best way to relieve the stress and anxiety everyone experienced daily.

Each day was a new start for the brokers. They knew the possibility of making a lot of money existed with each phone call. The huge chalkboards in front not only showed the available bonds, it also showed who sold what each day. In the mornings this show-and-tell board was wiped clean. This prevented anyone from becoming too complacent or too discouraged. The partners had it down to a science.

CHAPTER EIGHT

Jack walked into work Thursday morning pumped up from his talk with Haynes the night before. He and Aaron, as usual, arrived at the same time.

Jack was motivated and it came through in his attitude. "Today is the day, I tell you!"

"You're darn right it is," Aaron responded.

"You are damn right," Haynes chimed in from behind.

Olive was also walking in. "What the crap are you pansies so cheery about this morning?" Olive looked a little beat up from last night's drinking party. He was wearing a great suit though.

Strong held the elevator door open for everyone. "It is a great day to make money! The sun is shining and the birds are singing."

The five of them walked into the elevator together. Aaron and Jack moved off to the side. Haynes and Strong stood in the back but towards the middle, behind Olive. Olive stood at the front of the elevator doors. Haynes and Strong were both staring at Olive's suit.

As the elevator doors closed Haynes asked, "Olive, is that a new suit?"

"Yes it is. First time I've worn it, too. Fits like a glove, doesn't it?"

"Who makes that suit?" Strong asked.

Olive sensed something was amiss by the tone of Strong's voice, but replied nonetheless. "Not that you two know anything about style, but it's a Pitti Uomo."

Haynes moved a little closer to him. "Sounds expensive."

"You bet your ass it was."

Then Strong moved in a little closer, and as he smirked at Haynes said, "Looks like it has a small rip in the back."

Olive didn't have a chance to even ask "Where?" before Haynes and Strong each grabbed a tail at the back of the jacket. They pulled so hard it split the back of the coat all the way up the middle to Olive's shoulders.

Jack and Aaron stood there, speechless. They didn't know what to do or make of this. They especially didn't know if they should laugh along with Haynes and Strong because they had too much respect, and fear, for Olive.

Both Haynes and Strong stood there laughing their heads off, both gasping for breath. Olive never moved. It happened so quickly there was nothing he could have done anyway. He stood silently, just nodding his head. He acted as though nothing had happened.

"It's ripped right there in the middle." Strong retorted, still laughing, but finally answering Olive's question.

This made Haynes laugh so hard he bent over, totally out of breath.

The elevator doors opened to the lobby while Olive straightened his tie. As he entered the lobby, like nothing had happened, the others faintly heard him say under his breath, "Assholes."

Olive normally commanded a lot of respect. No one in the office, other than Gage, Strong, or Haynes could have gotten away with such a prank to a full partner of the firm. Pranks, like most everything else, were only allowed within the ranks of each group. Likewise, only Olive could have gotten away with his small act of revenge against Haynes and Strong. Later that morning, when everyone else was busy on the floor, Olive filled the arms of both of their suit coats with ketchup. Neither knew until it was time to head out to lunch and went to put on their coats. Both Haynes and Strong began to curse, and with a perfect poker face Olive just said, "Problem gentlemen?"

That morning started out like every other morning for Jack, once he got on the phones. He got past the secretaries, but nothing else. No sales. He was just hoping to find a buyer. It was the same old thing and the positive feeling he had felt when he arrived at work soon vanished.

Jack's now deflated motivation was further burdened by his lack of sales. He thought that he needed a huge trade to keep his job. So at times he only called incredibly large companies with a lot of assets and plenty of capital to spend.

These were the hardest accounts to open, if not usually impossible, especially for someone new to the business and without any connections. Not a single new broker ever opened an account with one of these giants. And unknown to Jack, Haynes and Gage had been listening in on his calls.

They walked up to Jack after his last failed attempt.

Haynes started first. "Are you kidding me with the people you're calling?"

"What do you mean?" Jack asked.

"You've called the Mellon Bank, Chase Bank, Lloyd's of London, Continental Illinois, and Exxon's pension fund. You don't have a chance in hell with any of those guys. You can't get in with those guys off of a damn cold call."

Haynes paused a moment then took a deep breath. "Listen. A bank with only thirty-million in assets can make you about five-thousand a month. If you get ten clients like that you've made fifty-thousand dollars in one month. But you're going at this like you're trying to eat an entire elephant in one bite. You can't do that. You'll choke on it. Until I say otherwise, you are no longer allowed to call anyone who has more than fifty-million in total assets. The smaller guys are easier to deal with. Less red tape."

Gage then continued where Haynes had left off. "Let me show you. Pick anyone in your book with less than fifty-million."

"Okay." Jack randomly chose a bank that was near central Texas.

"Now, I know you can get past the secretary. Once you do, hand me the phone."

Jack no longer had any problems with the secretaries. Though he still had problems once he got past them. He handed the phone to Gage. "She's putting you through."

"What's this guy's name?"

"Mike Tritico."

Haynes pointed to the phone at the empty desk near Jack's. "Get on that phone and listen to Gage. Who cares if he makes a sale? Just listen to how he speaks to him."

"Good morning Mike, this is Richard Gage, down here in Houston. I'm one of the partners with HAYNES, OLIVE, GAGE & STRONG. I'm going to be up in your area next week on business and thought it would be a great time to meet some new clients."

The banker tried to brush Gage off. "If you're trying to sell me something I really don't have any money right now."

Gage kept the same cool attitude in his tone of voice. "Bullshit Mike. I'm not some 20-year-old rookie. At this time of year all of those cotton farmers around you are depositing money in your bank like there's no tomorrow. Now don't tell me you don't have any money."

"Well, it's not that easy. The board of directors has really been on my back lately."

"Aren't you the president of your bank?"

"Well, yes."

"Aren't you on the board of directors?"

Jack could sense that Gage was not only in control of the conversation; he was setting this banker up for the kill.

"Yes. I'm actually the head of the board."

"Didn't you start this bank yourself? It says here you did so about thirty years ago."

"That's true. I built it from the ground up."

"And you're telling me that *you* can't run your own bank?"

"That's not what I'm saying."

"Are you then telling me there is someone else who tells you how to run your own business?"

"No one tells me what to do. I'm the one in charge."

"Well it's good to know I'm talking to the right person. But I don't want you to get in trouble. Let's not do any business today. When I'm in town next week you can see if the board will approve what I have to offer and then maybe we can do business."

Gage was pulling the sale off the table before he even had it.

Jack could sense that Mr. Tritico was getting irritated. He was not irritated necessarily at Gage, but at the idea that someone he did not know was telling him what to do and how to run his own bank. "It's my bank and I can do business with whomever I please. Nobody tells me what to do in my own bank. And I actually have about five million I need a home for, so I can buy right now. What do you have?"

"I have some Rainy ISD Puffs, AAA rated at 7.60%. But I only have one point two million, as it's the last of a new issue and with a 1995 maturity."

"Sounds good to me, and that's a pretty nice rate. Ready for my delivery instructions?"

"Mike, you are the president there; I'm a partner here. Neither one of us has time for delivery instructions. Before we hang up I'll put my trader on the phone with your secretary, and they'll get it done."

After Gage made the transaction he let Mike have some control back. "What day is good for you next week for dinner?"

"Wednesday or Thursday."

"Thursday it is. Want me to bring the wife and make it a foursome, or do you just want to run around like we're bachelors?"

"Why don't we just leave the little ladies at home for this one."

"Sounds good. See you then."

Jack sat there in amazement. Gage was so smooth, so slick. He never hesitated and he never let the banker take control of the conversation until Gage determined it was time to do so. Most importantly, he made this banker want to buy, and buy from Gage.

It also scared Jack. "I never would have known about the cotton farmers."

"I only know that because I have another client in that area. Anyway, that's not the point. Did I ever sound desperate? Like I needed that sale? No. It's all attitude. I wouldn't recommend you cussing on the phone just yet though. I only did it because I knew I could get away with it. You do this long enough and you'll learn what you can get away and what you cannot. You're trying to hunt whales and you've never even been fishing."

*   *   *   *

It was not only the rookies who got fired at HAYNES, OLIVE GAGE & STRONG. Earlier in the week, one of the junior associates, Charlie, had been let go. He had worked at the firm for just under a year. He was producing, but just not enough to keep the partners happy, so they fired him.

The following Thursday, right before lunch, Charlie's Book was passed out to all the rookies. Everyone except Jack got a piece. Aaron was on the phone holding for Mr. Peele, but he could see the look on Jack's face. He knew that Jack thought he was next in line to be fired. Aaron covered the receiver of his phone and mouthed to Jack, "Don't worry about it."

Jack rolled his eyes, "That's easy for you to say. You're making sales. You got moved up. I'm still stuck in the back with the new rookies. You're not about to get fired."

As they walked to the restroom they talked about the incident some more.

"They probably did it on purpose Jack."

"I have been busting my ass up here for months. And for what? To be treated like a little kid by Mean Dean? To learn I don't have what it takes? To lose everything I own? What the hell am I doing here? Who am I kidding? I don't belong here."

Aaron could see the dejection in Jack's face. He heard it in his voice. For the first time, Aaron didn't know how to respond or know what to say to help his friend. He stood there, trying to come up with anything to make Jack feel better. "This isn't an easy job. You know that guy I was talking to earlier? I've called him three times since I made my first sale with him. And each time he acts like he doesn't even know me."

After Jack heard that, his sorrow and self-pity turned to anger. "Are you kidding me? He doesn't remember you? You mean you make sales with people and they don't even remember you?"

"It appears so."

"Have you made any other sales with him?"

"No."

"Try again."

"What?"

"I said, call him back. I want to hear what you say."

"Okay." Aaron walked back to his desk, got the number, and sat down at the empty desk next to Jack. "Okay, I'm calling."

Jack picked up the phone, not only to listen in on Aaron's call, but also because Mean Dean was beginning to notice that Jack was not on the phone.

"Hello, Mr. Peele. This is Aaron Graham. I have some bonds you might be interested in. They're issued by…." but he was interrupted.

"Who is this? What firm are you with?"

Aaron looked over at Jack and whispered, "See?"

Jack was so furious that his competitive spirit began to emerge. "This is unbelievable. This guy has so many brokers he doesn't even remember you? Is he that big of a whore?" He was livid as he got up and approached Aaron. "Give me the damn phone!"

Jack grabbed the phone before Aaron could respond and began speaking. His anger was apparent in his tone. "Is this Mr. Peele?"

"Yes, who's this?"

"That doesn't matter. It's not like you would remember anyway."

"Excuse me?" Peele responded in an agitated voice.

"Do you realize this fine young associate you have been talking to has sold you bonds in the past? Are you telling me you buy from so many different brokers that you don't even remember him?"

"I just buy from whoever has the best deal."

"I can't believe we've done any business with you in the first place."

Aaron was beginning to freak out, waving at Jack and mouthing, "What are you doing?"

Jack turned his back to Aaron and continued berating the banker. "I'm going to close this account. We can't do business with someone like you. You're too much of a liability for us, not to mention a liability to yourself."

Nothing but silence was on the other end of the phone for a few seconds. That was until it was replaced with a meager, confused voice from the other end of the line.

"What do you mean? What liability? You don't want my business?"

"What do you mean what liability? If the market goes up you don't even know whom to call when the "cheap" bonds aren't delivered to you. These other brokers will take the bonds, mark them up some more, and then sell them to someone else. And when the market goes down you can bet your ass they'll deliver some piece of shit bond to you that will have cost your bank a ton of money."

For the first time Jack envisioned himself "Long and Strong." "We want your business, just not that kind of business. We're not here to show you the "bond of the day." But if that's what you want, you can use one of the other hundred places that call you. I'm here to manage portfolios and to make sure you make money. If you want to send me your entire portfolio, then we can talk. I'll look at it and tell you what you need and don't need. I promise you, if we manage your portfolio the only thing you will ever have to do is look at the bottom line and then smile. Those are the terms, take it or leave it."

"So who should I deal with? You or that other guy, what's-his-face?"

Jack looked at Aaron. "You can deal with what's-his-face, whose name happens to be Mr. Aaron Graham by the way, mostly about the bonds, but I can talk to you if you have questions about something else. I'll do the portfolio analysis."

Peele was thinking out loud as much as he was talking. "Hmmm. Interesting. Sounds good." There was a short pause before he began to speak again. "I'll tell you what. I'll mail you my entire bond portfolio. Look at it and tell me what you think. It probably would be easier for me to deal with just one firm. And you're right. There's too much liability dealing with so many firms. You guys can manage the portfolio for the next quarter. Let's see how your returns do and we can go from there. Agreed?"

"Sounds good. I'll give you back to Aaron and he can give you our info."

Gage had been watching and listening the entire time. Later, he told the other partners about Jack's conversation with this particular banker; and it was someone they knew and had done business with off and on for years. Gage finally concluded, "You start to make money whenever you are too hungry or too angry."

"He's both," Strong responded. "He had nothing to lose on that call. That's probably why he was so aggressive."

"But he basically just made money for someone else. He's not going to make any money just doing that," Strong replied.

"Aaron will though," Olive pointed out.

Haynes suggested that they invite Aaron to attend that evening's escapades upstairs.

"No way," was the consensus from the others.

"He's not making quite enough money yet and he hasn't even grossed ten- thousand dollars in one week," Olive blurted out.

Haynes interrupted them. "That's not the point, ladies. The point is to get Jack fired up some more. His frustration gave him the attitude to get a banker to agree to deal exclusively with us. That's pretty damn good. Besides, I guarantee Aaron won't accept until Jack is invited also."

"All right, let's go find out then." Strong walked off toward Aaron's desk to deliver the invitation.

As Strong started to walk away Haynes whispered, "Make sure Jack can hear you."

Jack watched Strong approach Aaron's desk a few rows up from his.

"Aaron, you did well last month. You're doing even better this month, especially with today's sale and what Jack managed to get for you, and for the firm. We think it's time for you to join us upstairs after the office closes for the day."

Strong was mostly facing Jack, but talking to Aaron. Aaron happened to look at Jack for a moment, and when he did so Jack mouthed, "You'd better go."

Aaron thought for a second. "There's no way I could have maintained that account that Jack saved. I have to give him credit for that one. Plus, Jack made us the only firm that this guy's going to deal with from now on."

"Doesn't matter. It's your account, not Jack's. It's your money, not Jack's. And it's our firm, not Jack's."

Aaron was confused and a little frightened. He did not know just how to respond to the invitation by Strong. He felt excited to finally be asked to join the coveted Zeros, but also conflicted since his best friend had not been asked.

"I can't do that. And Jack will be the one analyzing the portfolio anyway. I don't even know how to do that. So it's also kind of Jack's sale, too. It's an honor to be invited to hang out after hours tonight, but I can't go unless Jack goes."

"Sorry. No can do. Jack is not producing. As I said, it's your account, not his. Maybe one day he'll be invited, but that day is not today. So suit yourself."

Strong quickly turned around and walked away, and as he did he ever so slightly nodded his head at Haynes. Haynes ever so slightly, and with a slight smile on his face, nodded back.

It was the last Friday of the month. The closest Jack had come to making a sale was the one he had made for Aaron the day before. The morning started out like all the others. The trader, Alex, informed everyone on the trading floor the best bonds of the day. The only thing unusual was that Strong was standing behind Alex erasing one of the boards.

Strong then wrote everyone's name up on the board. He addressed the room when Alex finished. "For this office to thrive, every desk has to produce at least two-hundred-thousand dollars a year. Some of you are averaging enough each month to gross the two hundred we want. And some of you aren't." Jack felt Strong was talking directly to him. Strong continued. "We're now going to increase the amount of rookie training classes and will no longer start a training class every quarter. We will have a new group of trainees start every six weeks. The training classes will also be a little smaller." Strong then looked around the room, and it seemed to Jack that Strong was focusing just on him. Strong slowly began to stroll back and forth. "We obviously don't have enough desks for everyone. And some of you have slacked off of, too. However, if any junior associate consistently produces more than one of the senior associates, that senior associate is gone. Regardless. At the close of business on the last day of every month we are going to scratch a name off the board. I think you know what that means. One bad month and you're gone. Now get on the phones and get to work."

Snapshots of the trading floor on this day were like any other. It was always loud and very busy. Brokers ran up and down the aisles yelling and screaming about bonds bought and sold. Brokers cussed up a storm as they hung a phone up when rejected. There was pointing and shouting, and tension was felt everywhere.

Occasionally two different brokers would sell the same set of bonds. The commissions were large, so it was a situation that had to be solved quickly before a fight erupted. Alex, Strong, or one of the other partners might find some additional bonds from the market. Sometimes they found a bond nearly identical to the one sold—the maturity of the bond might have been slightly different or it was callable. For the most part though, the purchaser never knew the difference, and no one made an effort to inform the buyer of the switch.

Despite the firm's new approach on terminating brokers, Jack was surprisingly relaxed after Strong's speech. The fact that he had finally accomplished a sale, even if it was not his own, gave him a sense of confidence he had not felt since he had begun working for the firm. Although he had "danced" with someone else's client, nevertheless, he had finally danced. His conversation with Peele was the first time Jack had been in control of a sales call from start to finish. And it was the first time in months that Jack did not believe that this job was impossible.

He sat there cold calling that morning and closing his first sale never crossed his mind. It felt like he was starting anew. Jack spoke to everyone he called as if he really did not care if they were interested or not. He also ignored the net worth or the assets of the company. He didn't even pay attention to what the secretaries said when he called. The only thing he really noticed that morning was how beautiful all the secretaries in the office seemed to be.

Haynes' secretary, Terri, was walking past Jack while he was dialing the phone. As she passed him she happened to glance right at Jack, smiling, and he gave her a big smile in return. While Jack was put on hold, he looked up and saw Bart looking at him. Jack then mouthed, "Terri is so damn fine I can't stand it." Bart gave him a thumb's up sign then went back to his call. Floyd had also seen the look the two had given each other, and he made a kissy face at Jack. Jack kissed the air back at Floyd. Aaron was walking back to his desk and stopped to see what all the kissing was about.

"What, you and Floyd have a thing going on now?"

"Kiss my ass, Aaron. He's just messing with me because I was checking Terri out. She's smoking hot."

"You're telling me. I'd give anything to see her naked," Aaron whispered back.

"Shut up. Can you imagine what—,"Jack was forced to stop in mid-sentence as his latest prospect was put through.

It had been fairly slow that morning. Market prices had gone up making the bond yields go down. The only sales made that day were brokers telling their clients their bonds had gone up in price and they should sell them while they had a profit. Of course, the brokers also had a new bond to put their client back into immediately. The brokers made a little bit of money coming out of the sale of the newly sold bonds but the real money was putting their clients back into a new bond.

Jack had learned how to spot some of the "buy signs" in customers. This latest prospect was practically flagging Jack down with all of the buy signs. Jack's voice was deeper than normal. He was likely mimicking the customer. Jack would get a little bit loud, and then calm down. He would get excited, and then compose himself again. He could feel this sale coming.

He started "romancing" this customer. Jack backed off and started to pull the bonds off the table. He felt as if he was catching a marlin. He let the customer run the drag for a while. When he got tired, Jack slowly reeled him back in. It was masterful and Jack felt powerful.

Jack was on the phone almost forty-five minutes with this guy. He answered questions with questions. He quizzed this prospect each time, learning more and more about the guy's business and some personal information as well. Jack even changed the bond he was pitching, telling the prospect why a bond with a seven-year maturity was better for him than one that matured in twenty years.

Finally, Jack heard those magic words. "I'll take the bonds." Jack was ecstatic. Months and months of hard work for this one phone call. It was true elation like he had never felt in his entire life. He hung up the phone, closed his Book, and jumped on top of his desk and screamed down to Alex, "Those million Baton Rouges are sold!"

The whole office started clapping and cheering. Jack was excited as he jumped off his desk, landing hard on the floor, not that he would have cared, much less noticed if he had hurt himself. Aaron had dashed back from his desk and was "high-fiving" him. Bart and Floyd were cheering so loudly Jack could barely hear what Aaron was saying.

Jack gleefully walked towards the front of the room. He went up to the board and marked off his bonds. There, Alex waited with scissors in hand, ready to cut Jack's tie. He grabbed Jack's tie, opening and closing the scissors quickly up in the air as he prepared to cut his tie off. "Good sale. So who did you sell them to?"

Jack failed to respond. His face turned white. White as if he had seen a ghost. His mouth dropped. His eyes were open very wide and he was in shock. Jack dropped the eraser that he was holding in his hand. He stood there for a second completely silent. Alex let go of his tie and Jack ran back to his desk to check his Book.

But he had already closed it. It was hundreds of pages thick. He began thumbing through it. Looking for *that* page. Looking for his last call. Jack had been so excited about this call that he had not been paying attention at all. He had no idea who he had sold the bonds to.

He called several prospects that he thought might have been the one. Each bank looked the same to him as the next. He spent hours looking for who it was, all to no avail. Jack's first would-be sale was not to be.

Jack left the office that evening feeling completely devastated. He just wanted to be home. It was such a long drive home that evening, too. Jack wanted to be with his wife. He parked his car in the garage as usual. Millie was not at home, not that he expected her to be anyway.

As he walked in he noticed a manila folder on the kitchen counter with a note on top. The note started, "Dear Jack." He slowly opened the folder after reading the note. Inside were divorce papers with little tabs that stated, "Sign here."

CHAPTER NINE

▼

The next two weeks for Jack were not good. He had yet to complete his first sale and had moved into Aaron's apartment with nothing more than the clothes he owned. The car that he had owned since college was falling apart. Jack had not made a penny in almost six months. Any other person would have broken down by now, but for some reason Jack kept going. He didn't know what else to do. It was only Aaron's success that kept Jack coming into the office everyday, that and the fact that he had no idea what to do with himself all day, and he didn't want to be alone.

Aaron was now grossing at least five-thousand every week in commissions, but he continued to spend every penny he made. He bought more custom-made suits. He upgraded his stereo system. He bought another new color television, but this was for Jack's bedroom. Aaron figured Jack could use the distraction.

Everyone was paid only once at the end of each month. The partners encouraged Aaron to buy more stuff, especially after each paycheck. Aaron would run up enormous amounts of debt, and by the end of the month would pay the bills when he received his paycheck. He then spent the rest of his cash as if it had an expiration date. While he had new clothes, new toys, and a bigger apartment, he was living paycheck to paycheck.

It was frustrating for Jack; not that Aaron had money, but that Jack did not. Aaron often tried to treat Jack to dinner and repeatedly tried to buy him something nice. Anything. Not out of pity, but because he wanted to share his newfound success. After he came home to find the new television in his bedroom, Jack would not allow Aaron to buy him anything else. It was bad enough he was being fed and housed by his friend. The only other thing Jack accepted from Aaron was a brilliant red, Italian-made tie, but only because Aaron insisted on buying Jack a "happy divorce" gift.

"Think about it Jack. You're getting divorced at the perfect time. You have no money, no income, and no fancy car. She can have half of that all day. You don't own crap, you poor broke bastard. How lucky can you be?"

"It doesn't make me feel any better you know. But thanks for trying."

Aaron had never sugarcoated his words when he spoke about Jack's wife either. "She was turning into a bitch anyway. And why would you want to be with someone who won't support you?" All Jack did was sit there and say nothing. "She'll be fat in a year," Aaron continued. "Fucking fried-chicken-eating bitch." Sometimes what Aaron said made Jack feel better; sometimes it did not, and right now he wished that Aaron would just stop talking and leave him alone.

It was a usual Monday morning, except for the ten new rookies on the floor. The class appeared average and a few did stand out. Both Aaron and Jack recognized the only woman from the new class. In fact, she was the only woman broker on the trading floor. Her name was Maye. She was in her mid-thirties, single, fairly attractive, and she kept herself in shape. She was the kind of girl that the more you got to know her, the more attractive she became, but she was also smart and determined to make it in this business.

Both Aaron and Jack recognized her because she had been trying to get interviews and into the training class the same time they had been. Unbeknownst to them, she had been running the gauntlet for a year.

This was the 1970s. Women's liberation was strong on the streets and moving into more businesses, but within the finance industry it was still a man's world. None of the partners at HAYNES, OLIVE, GAGE & STRONG wanted to hire a woman broker. Nor did any of the brokers want to work side-by-side with one. Women, during business hours, were only useful for making copies, typing letters, answering phones, and getting coffee.

Quite obviously, becoming a broker was more difficult for Maye than for everyone else. Mean Dean, Alex, Olive, and Strong wanted nothing to do with her, and they made it perfectly clear each time she contacted any of them.

So Maye tried a different tactic. Every Friday she sent a little gift to each partner. At first they were small gifts. With each passing week each gift became more elaborate, and more expensive. And each present was perfectly tailored for each recipient. It was uncanny how she knew just what to give each one.

Every time she sent a gift she followed up with a phone call. "Did you get my gift? How is the new training class coming along? Ready to work with a woman broker yet?" Maye's tactics soon were becoming quite the talk around the office.

One Friday no one received a gift. The partners began calling each other with the same question. "Did you get your gift?"

"No," was the common response.

"Wonder what's going on. Think she gave up?"

"Hope not. I've grown to like my little gifts every week."

The following Monday, Dean, Alex, Olive, and Strong each received a beautiful bouquet of flowers. The whole office was buzzing about how a woman had sent flowers to a man. And not just to one man, but to four. A small note was attached to each bouquet and said the same thing. "If I'm not in your next training class you will not like my next surprise. With *all* my love, Maye."

The four of them huddled together that afternoon and discussed the situation. They talked about how much they enjoyed getting gifts from Maye. They also discussed her perseverance and aggressiveness in pursuing them, and how her approach to being hired by the firm was becoming effective.

Haynes and Gage soon joined in on the discussion about hiring a woman, making the argument that they needed a woman broker to keep up with the times. "And it's not like we're hiring some ugly bitch, Olive said. "And she seems pretty cool, and puts up with all of our shit, too. How bad could it be?" They didn't know whether they made the right decision or not. As the future would tell, though, Maye was great at opening accounts on the road, and was the only broker to make cold calls on the road. This suited everyone, since she was then never at the office to make anyone feel uncomfortable. But she was just not so good at making a second trade with the same client. After a while, but behind her back, she soon became known only as "One-Trade Maye."

Another broker who stood out from the latest class was a guy whom everyone only knew as Swamp-Ass. He was from so far down in the sticks of southern Louisiana it was unbelievable. There were rumors that he and his family actually lived in the swamps. His real name was never quite known on the trading floor because no one could understand a word he said, what with his thick Cajun accent. So no one ever figured out what he was talking about. How he ever got hired eluded them all.

Fortunately for Swamp-Ass, various members of his family were officials in charge of counties, cities, and banks all over Louisiana, as well as in a few other southern states. He was practically guaranteed to succeed in this business by his connections alone. Swamp-Ass did fairly well in whatever language he was speaking. However, he never called a single person who was not a family member. Not that he needed to. The guy had a lot of connections.

The rest of that class was standard white male. That was, except for Eddie McClendon, or as he was soon to be called, Fast Eddie because he could talk faster than anyone else. He was a black man in a white man's world and was the only black broker who ever succeeded at the firm. Fast Eddie also was one of the few who had a college degree. He was wild and liked to have a good time, and he always dressed impeccably, even to the point of being obsessed that his shoes were always shined and spotless.

Anyone who spoke to him on the phone would swear that he was white. In the 1970s, banks, insurance companies, and other businesses that bought bonds where almost exclusively dominated by white men. Never once did any of Fast Eddie's clients suspect he was black.

And Fast Eddie never let them know. He constantly told racial jokes whenever he was on the phone, and he would laugh harder than anyone else at the joke's punch line. The irony was that he had more "redneck" clients than anyone on the floor. Many of them were highly prejudiced against African Americans. If they only knew how much money they were making Fast Eddie they would probably have had a stroke.

It was a different story though if he called an institution run by another black man. His voice would change and he and the other guy would talk trash about "the man" and how the man was trying to keep "us brothers down."

And anyone within earshot of Fast Eddie, while he was not on the phone, was sure to hear his favorite word. Every other word out of his mouth was some form of the "F-bomb." He'd hang up the phone and scream across the floor, "I just sold 100 motherfucking GNMA's to this sorry-ass-honky fuck in Mississippi."

At first, he was hired so the firm would not get sued for discrimination, same as they had done with Maye. But as it turned out he made money—lots of money. So the partners were happy.

$$*\quad*\quad*\quad*$$

Jack was sitting at his desk, quietly eating his lunch, when his phone rang. It was the banker Jack had spoken with two weeks before. It was the banker who had wanted to buy bonds from Jack but who Jack never got the information in order to do so. It was the same banker that Jack had searched for hours in his Book and had caused him so much grief.

"Hey Jack. I don't mean to bother you, but I've been sitting here waiting to take delivery of those bonds I bought from you two weeks ago. Then this morning I suddenly realized I never gave you my wiring instructions. Do you still have those bonds?"

There was silence at Jack's end of the phone. He began to get anxious, something he had not felt for a while. This time, though, he was not going to blow it. "I am so embarrassed that I neglected to obtain all the necessary information last time we talked. Truth be told, I couldn't find your phone number to call you back, and for some reason I also forgot to write down your name."

"My name's Chris Kanter. You do remember selling me some bonds a few weeks ago?" Jack noticed the humor in Mr. Kantor's voice, as well as his sincerity and how courteous he was towards Jack. At once he remembered his name.

"You're going to have to forgive me Mr. Kanter."

"Call me Chris, please."

"How did you find me?"

"I had your name written right here on my pad, but I didn't write down the name of the firm you worked for and I forgot what you had told me." They both got a laugh out of the fact that they both had messed up. "Thank goodness my secretary overheard me ask you what firm you were with, and I really thank God I had said it out loud. And I'm sure we're both grateful that she has an excellent memory. So since I had not heard back from you I thought I'd give you a call."

Jack was astonished at this turn of events. "You have no idea how much I appreciate your calling me."

"Well, I thought to myself during our talk that I've never had anyone interrogate me about my bank the way you did. And no one has ever shown me one bond and then told me later it wasn't good for me, much less tell me why. I think I then realized that you were the first broker to ever call me and sound more interested in my business than your own."

"Well, thank you. I certainly don't want to harm your business or hurt this firm's reputation."

"Do you still have those bonds by the way?"

It was music to Jack's ears. "Hold on, let me check." Jack looked up on the board and noticed the bonds had been recently marked through, sold by Aaron of all people, and only that morning, too. Jack was suddenly in a total frenzy and yelled out, "Where's Alex? Where the hell is Alex?"

Alex was off the trading desk and using the restroom when Jack rushed in, and in a complete panic. Alex was standing in front of the urinal but Jack just grabbed Alex and pulled him away from the urinal all the while talking a hundred miles an minute. "I need bonds. I need those bonds I sold but did not sell two weeks ago, or whenever, or something. I need them now. Find more. He's on the phone now. He's waiting!" Jack was talking so loud and so fast Alex couldn't understand a single word coming out of Jack's mouth. Plus Alex was cussing up a storm since he had peed all over his pants when Jack had grabbed him away from the urinal. They were out in the hallway when Alex finally yanked his arm out of Jack's grasp. "Can I please at least zip up my damn pants?"

Jack began to run back to his desk to pick up the phone. Aaron grabbed him as he was rushing by. "Look at me Jack. Breathe. Take a deep breath. He wants to buy from you. You will not lose this sale. Just relax. Let it happen." Only Aaron could see Jack's eyes beginning to well up.

Alex yelled down to Jack, "Good news and bad news. Good news is that I found the same bonds. Bad news is that the trader who owns them will only sell if you take delivery of his entire block. Two million. I can try and find something else if you want me to."

Jack started to feel a sense of dread, not sure what to do. He finally composed himself and got back on the phone. Jack spoke candidly to the banker. "Chris, sorry for the delay. I have your bonds. But you have to take delivery of the entire block. I can find something else for you though."

After a moment of silence, Chris inquired. "Well how many bonds are we talking about?"

"Two million."

"Oh, that's fine. I thought you were going to say twenty million or something. I'll take them all."

Even though Jack tried to stay calm and in control, Chris could hear the relief in Jack's voice. "Excellent. Now if I can please have your wiring instructions we can get this deal done." Jack looked up at Alex and gave him a thumb's up.

Chris was laughing on the other end. "Certainly. Though would you do me a favor? I have another million bonds coming due next week. I'm going to have to put that money somewhere. Can you call me back next Friday with something good for my bank?"

"It would be my pleasure," Jack replied happily.

They talked a little bit longer before Jack finally hung up the phone. He just sat there in his chair. Finally leaning his head back, past his shoulders, and almost over the very top of the chair. Aaron looked back at Jack with a smile on his face. He was as relieved as Jack.

A few minutes later all of the partners walked in from lunch. Alex was busy on the phones, but managed to tell them about Jack's sale. "Really?" was their response.

Jack's first sale was almost as orgasmic as it was anti-climatic. And it was not just Jack who let out a huge sigh of relief. Everyone in the room had done so as well.

Strong strolled to the front of the room, grabbed the scissors off the desk, and then all four partners walked towards Jack.

"That sure is a nice tie you're wearing," said Gage.

Jack solidly responded, "First time I've ever worn it, too. It was a gift."

Olive walked up and grabbed his red tie and looked at the brand. "My, aren't we fancy!"

Haynes admired it also. "Well, here's to your lucky tie then."

Strong then grabbed Jack's tie and without hesitation cut it off and threw it across the room at Alex. "Nail this baby to the wall. This one will stay here forever. When people whine that they can't do this job we'll tell them Jack's story." Strong looked back at Jack. "How much did you make by the way?"

Jack's eyes blinked wide open. "I don't know."

Everyone looked at Alex for the answer. "Those bonds had two points on them."

Jack immediately knew the answer to his own question. "That's two percent of two million. Forty-thousand dollars!"

Gage looked Jack straight in his eyes. "You got it buddy. Nothing like making forty-thousand dollars off of a single phone call now, is there?"

"No there certainly isn't," Jack responded with a smile.

Jack's new account turned out to be just what he needed. Over the next two weeks Jack sold a total of three-million bonds. The transactions closed before the end of the month, meaning Jack got paid his commissions for that month. Payday turned out to be a Friday.

On his very first paycheck from HAYNES, OLIVE, GAGE & STRONG, Jack grossed fifty-thousand dollars. For the first time, he felt a whole new world open up for him. As Jack stared at his paycheck he realized that it was all worth it. The monkey was finally off his back. He could now look forward to each day knowing sooner or later he would make more money. And what was even better, he was finally moved up to the desks with the other junior associates. He was no longer a rookie. He could go out to lunch rather than have to eat at his desk. And he was back with his best friend.

After lunch that day, Strong and Haynes took Jack to the bank. Knowing that Jack would want to save his money, they made Jack withdraw most of the cash after depositing his paycheck. Jack had never seen that much money, much less walk around with it stuffed in every pocket he had.

The three of them then headed to Haynes' favorite tailor, Mr. Martin, who was waiting with a forty-year-old bottle of single-malt scotch and a dozen Italian, hand-made ties. Mr. Martin was always on call to customize new suits and shirts in honor of a broker's first payday, and Haynes had called ahead to make the arrangements.

Next the three headed to Neiman Marcus, one of the best department stores in the area, so Jack could buy a few more essentials, which included a lot more suits. Jack had always wanted to shop at Neiman Marcus but never had the money to do so. Everything was hand-picked by Haynes and Strong, but Jack paid for it.

Each new designer suit was ten times more expensive than Jack had ever paid for one before. At first, their way of thinking was backward to Jack. He had always purchased suits first and then found a tie to match. Not these boys. They picked out a "power tie" and then found a suit to match. Naturally, a power tie required a power suit. And power suits were never on sale or on the clearance rack. By the end of the day the wool was pulled back from Jack's eyes and he could see that buying the tie first made perfect sense.

Strong and Haynes made sure that the next time Jack walked into the office he would look like a million bucks. Jack's custom shirts were embroidered with his initials on the French cuffs. His silk suits fit him perfectly. Jack's wrist sported a gold Rolex that shined brilliantly. His feet were clad in fabulous Italian shoes that were so comfortable Jack felt like he was wearing slippers.

The next task was to have Jack buy a new car, but they were running late and wanted to get to HOGS right after everyone else was already there. The plan was to have Jack make a grand entrance in his new clothes, all the more to impress the rookies, and to throw down a couple of drinks before the gang headed to dinner. The timing worked well for Jack as his wallet was getting thin.

They went straight to HOGS. When they arrived, Aaron and Olive were standing at the bar joking around. Haynes shouted out to the bartender, Jeremy, and pointed at Jack. "Open this gentleman a tab and put all our drinks on it."

Jack was too caught up in the moment to even think about disputing the suggestion. For the next thirty minutes Olive entertained them with stories of Las Vegas. Olive spent a good portion of his time trying to convince them that they should immediately drive to the airport. The more they drank, the more they were tempted to go, but they were all getting pretty hungry. A juicy steak was all they could think about.

Haynes had Jeremy call for a new limousine and then close out the tab. Jeremy brought the bill over and handed it to Jack, who then began to slowly go over it to make sure everything was correct. In a long and drawn-out process, Jack pulled out his money and started to pay. Haynes, Olive, and Jeremy all stood there shaking their heads impatiently, not that Jack noticed, as he was too busy trying to figure out what to tip Jeremy.

Finally Haynes had had it and spoke up in an agitated tone of voice. "What the hell are you doing?"

Jack looked up in bewilderment. "Well, I'm paying the tab."

Haynes did not say a word as he shook his head. He looked up at Jeremy. "Should you tell him or should I?"

Jeremy responded as if it was a chore. "I'll tell him, damn it."

Jack was totally confused, as he had no idea what was going on.

Jeremy spoke very matter-of-factly as he leaned across the bar and placed his face just inches from Jack's. "Here's the deal. If you're with these guys then you are a high roller. And if you are a high roller then you need to act like one. Even when you're not with them you need to act like it, especially if you want to get the girls. You need to at least pretend like money doesn't mean a thing to you."

"Okay. I think I get what you mean, but continue."

"I'm standing here watching you pay this bill. First, you looked down at the tab with your fingers all over it like you were going to open it up and perform heart surgery on it. The only thing you need to know when you look at a tab is to see how many Ben Franklins it will take to make it go away. Second, you never keep that much money in your wallet."

"Okay, but why not?"

Jeremy rolled his eyes as he continued. "Because I know guys like you. Tightwads. After staring at the bill you reach back for your wallet. You unbutton your back pocket. You pull it out and keep it hidden underneath the bar so no one can see it. You pick out a few bills and hand them to me. You close your wallet and watch me go back to the register to get your change. When I bring it back you take the change and count it out, calculate my tip to the exact percentage you've always given, and then you carefully put the rest of your money back into your wallet. Next, you quickly fold your wallet, put it safely back in your pocket, and finally button up. You act as if your wallet was a vault."

"So what?"

"So what? Are you kidding me? If I was a young lady standing over there checking you out, I just lost all interest. Women don't want to hang out with someone like you. Whether she realizes it or not, she just saw you guard your money like Fort Knox. Interpretation—you don't have any money, or if you do, then you are a cheap-ass prick. So now she's totally turned off and there will be nothing you can do or say that will ever change her mind. You lost her before you even knew you had her." Jeremy raised his eyebrows and bobbed his head towards a table of young women who were looking over at them.

"Yea?"

"Yea, that's right. From now on you carry your money in your front pocket. It's easy to grab. Wham, bam, your money is out and ready to party. It gives off that subtle hint that you don't make a big deal about a tab."

Olive took over from there. "You may not be a wise guy, Jack, but at least look like one. You just grab the money and throw it on the bar. You then turn your back and walk away like it don't mean shit, especially if some sweet thing is near you and checking you out. It's all attitude. And no one is going to steal it either, at least not here. You then reach for your smokes and look for a light."

"I really don't smoke."

"You do now. Here, take my pack. And buy yourself a gold lighter from the jewelry store, too." He and Jeremy exchanged glances then Olive continued. "As I said, it's all about attitude and making an impression. It's a certain overall look. And it's a sweet icebreaker with the ladies."

Jack sat there, taking it all in. "Okay. I think I can do that."

Strong then broke in. "While you're at it, buy yourself a gold money clip, too. Solid gold, not some gold-plated sissy crap." Olive nodded at Strong then looked back to Jack. The lesson was winding down. "From now on you keep all your Ben Franklins in the money clip. Capiche?"

At this point Olive pulled out his money clip, stuffed with cash. He took a quick sniff and the look on his face was almost angelic. "Forget about anything else. There is nothing that smells like money." He took another sniff then put the clip back into his front pocket.

Jack and Aaron just sat there, wanting to know more. Learning how to spend money like a high roller was cool and they knew they could get used to it, fast. Even sweeter was that for both of them it was no longer an act.

As the group turned to leave, Jeremy and Olive nodded to one another. And the untrained eye missed the exchange of a little baggie for some money.

Everyone jumped into the limousine and they left HOGS. As usual, the limo was fully stocked with booze and smokes. The party never missed a beat. There were just the four junior associates, Aaron, Jack, Floyd, and Bart, all excited to be having their first real dinner with the partners. Also with the group were two senior associates. It was a rowdy gang by the time they reached the restaurant.

Gage had called the restaurant from HOGS so their table would be waiting for them whenever they arrived. They all had drink after drink, cigarette after cigarette. The party continued as the limousine stopped at a liquor store so Gage could buy more cigars and ultra-premium Scotch.

When the limousine finally pulled up to the steak house everyone stumbled out, heading straight to the bar where Gage bought everyone a fifty-dollar glass of single-malt Scotch. He made a toast, slammed the drink down in one gulp, then ordered another round as they made their way to the dining table.

Just as with everything else when it came to the firm, dinner was an experience like nothing the junior associates could ever have dreamed. One bottle of vintage wine after another made its way to their table. The partners were regulars at the restaurant and were treated like royalty. Their favorite waiter, Scott, had learned a long time ago not to ask if they needed another bottle. He would just bring a bottle or two of the very best the restaurant had to offer, even before a bottle on the table was completely empty.

A few thousand dollars later, they paid the check, gladly over-tipped Scott, and headed out the door. From there they drove to a topless bar. Again, Gage had called ahead and a table was ready for them, and in the back. There was very little light at the rear of the club, and this was just how the partners liked it.

Jack, Aaron, Floyd, and Bart looked at each other in amazement when they had finally sat down. This was no "every man's" strip club, but something a lot nicer, and a lot more expensive. The partners called it a "gentlemen's club." Jack was learning something new by the minute, and he loved it all.

The women at the club recognized the partners, since the men came to the club on a regular basis, and even had their own table. And, as any stripper knew, clients who sat in the back, away from the stage and lights, were the ones with the real money. They were more than willing to spend it on a beautiful girl, especially one who would do a little extra something. Practically every girl in the place ran over to them, jostling for the best place, which caused a few stares from the other patrons of the club. Not that anyone from the firm who noticed would have cared.

A short time later a handful of Marines walked into the bar. Gage called the cocktail waitress over and told her that all the drinks for the Marines were on him, and that they could have anything they wanted. He also placed a Ben Franklin on her tray for each Marine. She conveyed his message to the group then gave them the money. This was met with a round of hoorays from the Marines. They were grateful, and repeatedly came over to thank Gage and to ask if he, or his friends, needed anything.

After a bit, Gage walked over to the Marine's table and sincerely said, "I'd appreciate if you boys wouldn't waste one more second of your time talking to me, but to take pleasure in the young ladies at this club and to just enjoy yourselves. I cannot begin to tell you how much I appreciate what you do. One day, a long time ago, someone did this for me. Maybe one day you'll have the chance to do the same."

Again, they profusely thanked Gage. In response he handed each of them another Ben Franklin. As Gage began to walk away they told him they would always have his back, then thanked him yet again.

Gage had been a Marine and he paid tribute to the soldiers out of pure loyalty and compassion. It was something his father did, and it was something he knew he would do for the rest of his life.

Six-thousand-dollars later, and all with grins on their faces, they staggered back into the limousine and headed to another gentlemen's club.

CHAPTER TEN

▼

The next few months turned out to be good for everyone at the firm. Jack made a few more good trades. Aaron opened a few more accounts. Fast Eddie was starting to bring in the big bucks, too. And Floyd and Swamp-Ass were able to keep up the pace they had started with. But it was Bart who remained a couple of steps ahead of them all. His family's contacts and jobs with the government were good and solid.

Bart was doing so well that he pulled into the office one morning with another brand new car. He kept his souped-up Roadrunner, but had upgraded to a Lotus. Bright cherry red with black trim. He screeched into the parking lot each morning and peeled out every afternoon.

One afternoon, at quitting time, Bart was nowhere to be seen. Both Jack and Aaron were waiting in the parking lot next to his Lotus, wanting to go to HOGS. They stood around for quite some time until Willie made them leave.

As it turned out, Bart had been invited to the Zeros. Those who had never been invited had no clue what happened at these parties, but from the way Bart looked the next morning it must have been fun.

Jack and Aaron arrived at work earlier than usual the next morning and waited for Bart to pull in. There were no screeching tires when Bart arrived this time. And Bart looked like he had been praying to the porcelain throne all night long. He slowly, and painfully, got out of his car and looked at them. "All I can tell you is that they told me if I was late I was fired."

That was not good enough for them. Aaron took charge. "What do you mean that's all you can say? I don't think so! At least throw us a bone."

Jack wanted to know just a little of what went on at one of the parties. "So, what goes on at the Zero?"

"Sorry. I already told you, no can say. And that's all I'm going to tell you." Bart paused a second as if to clear his head. "And it's not Zero. It's Zeros. As in all the zeros in my paycheck."

Aaron was not pleased. "How the hell would we know that? Oh, this is some bullshit."

Jack then noticed that Bart was wearing a short-sleeved shirt. "Uh, Bart, your shirt. Are you allowed to wear whatever you want to now?"

The look on Bart's face when he realized he was not wearing the proper attire said it all. "Oh, damn, I didn't even notice. I'm not dressed right. Crap!" He looked up and sighed. "And it's hotter than hell today. Now I'm going to have to wear my coat all day long." Bart put on his coat and asked, "Can you tell I'm wearing short sleeves?"

"Not really. But you're going to burn up inside with that coat on, especially since your desk sits in the sun."

It was almost lunchtime and Bart couldn't take it anymore. He was sweating bullets. He started to take off his coat when Aaron reminded him not to. "If they see your shirt it's your ass."

"Hey. I made a lot of money this month. I don't think they'll do anything." Bart began to take off his coat.

While they had been talking they had not noticed Mean Dean patrolling through the aisles and heading their way. "Wrong answer!" came booming from behind them. "Get your coat and get out of here!"

"Come on, man. I didn't make it to the cleaners last night or this morning. It's all I had to wear."

Mean Dean had a malicious grin on his face. "I'll make a deal with you Bart the Fart. I'm going to lunch now. You have until I get back to be at your desk, and wearing the appropriate shirt."

Bart submissively inquired, "What time will you be back?"

Mean Dean hated when he had to repeat himself. "You have until I get back from lunch to be at your desk, and wearing the proper attire. And I'd hustle if I were you."

Bart took off out the exit stairwell and screeched out of the parking lot. He returned from the store so fast his chair had barely stopped spinning.

As soon as Bart had dashed out, Mean Dean then directed his attention to Jack and Aaron. "I actually came over here for you two ladies. Strong wants to see the both of you in his office. Now."

They silently stood up from their desks and headed to Strong's office. Neither said a word. Both wondered what was wrong now.

When they entered Strong's office, Kate told them to take a seat. "Do you boys want one last cigarette before you go in?" she joked.

Jack was none too thrilled. "What does that mean?"

"It means you need to just relax. It means you two have pissed him off somehow. It means you better have a cigarette in your hand so when you walk in you look calm. He's on the phone now, but he'll be off soon."

They both had just sat down and started to light up a cigarette when Strong yelled for them to get their asses in, and quick.

Aaron looked at Kate as they passed her desk. "If I get fired can I ask you out on a date?"

Kate was still quietly laughing as the door closed behind them.

Strong began speaking quickly and intensely. "We have an image at this firm. It's an image that we have worked very hard to achieve and one that we take seriously. We are not about to lose it because of you two dickheads."

Jack and Aaron had no idea what Strong was talking about. They both dressed as they were told, even down to their underwear. The made sure they were clean and shaved each day and kept their hair cut as was dictated by the partners. And they both had been making a lot of money lately.

"I don't think we quite understand," Jack said.

"I'll get there if you shut the fuck up. I pull into our parking lot every morning. We have clients who pull into our parking lot every other day. They see the same thing I see. You two are an embarrassment to this firm. You are an embarrassment to me. Jack, that car of yours is the biggest piece of shit I have ever seen."

Aaron chuckled since he had been saying the same thing to Jack for years.

"And you have no room to laugh Chuckles. A truck? Are you kidding me with that good ol' Texas boy crap? I don't even know where to start with you. You are not a cowboy. And even if you were you will not drive a truck to this office anymore."

"Sorry sir," Aaron responded.

"You two are making some serious money now. Today is payday. Tomorrow is Friday. If I pull into this parking lot Monday morning and I see that piece of shit you're driving Jack, or that farmer truck you're driving," as he glared at Aaron, "you're fired." Strong had a little "what am I going to do with you" smile on his face as he quieted down, then spoke in a softer tone. "I can't believe I let you two get away with this for so long."

Jack let out a sigh of relief. "Not a problem sir, we'll leave early today and get it done."

"No you won't. Your ass is on the phone until the market closes."

"Yes, sir!"

"And one more thing. Neither one of you better buy some freakin' family car with four doors. It had better be something that doesn't embarrass this firm or myself. If it does, then you are fired."

On Monday morning Bart's car was not the only one burning rubber as it pulled into the parking lot. Jack had a brand new Corvette and Aaron a new Alfa Romeo Spider. They pulled in right behind Bart. Aaron and Jack had raced to work from home. They each exited their cars laughing while walking towards the elevator. As the doors to the elevator opened, Aaron spoke to Bart. "That sure is a fancy coat you have on."

As the doors closed, Jack smiled at Aaron and said to Bart, "And it looks like there's a little rip on the back your coat, too."

$$\ast \quad \ast \quad \ast \quad \ast$$

Aaron and Jack were eating at a fancy restaurant one evening when Jack ran into his old boss. He had not seen or talked to him since he left the insurance company. Jack saw that Mr. Lange was sitting at the bar with a group of other men, some of whom Jack recognized as his ex-coworkers. When Jack had worked there Mr. Lange had always trusted Jack's judgment. Because of that trust, Jack always had a special fondness for the man.

Jack left the table and approached Mr. Lange at the bar. "Mr. Lange. It's so good to see you again. How are you doing?"

Mr. Lange was as excited to see Jack as Jack was to see him. They talked a bit, catching up on what each had been doing since Jack had left. Jack, though, did not have much of a chance to divulge much information since Mr. Lange was so happy to see Jack that he monopolized the conversation.

The conversation then changed to what each was doing lately. When Jack left the company he had never told Mr. Lange what he was going to do, feeling that he needed to get going before he let too many people know. Mr. Lange began to tell Jack that he had changed jobs within the insurance company. "It's more of a promotion actually. It's what I've wanted and waited to do for years. It was the whole reason I went back to the University of Houston and finally got my MBA."

Jack was silent for a moment, not saying a word. His mind was working a mile a minute, digesting this latest information.

Mr. Lange finally interrupted Jack's silence with a simple, "I know that look. What've you got going on in that head of yours?"

"What did you just say you now do?"

"I've been transferred over to investments and portfolio management."

Jack was still quiet, so Mr. Lange continued. "Well, I don't manage all of the portfolios, just a few of them right now. As time goes by, I may, but I'm still new at this. That's why I'm here tonight. I just went to a seminar about financial instruments. I'm here with some of the other guys I met there."

"What exactly was it about?"

"This one was geared toward fixed-income securities. You know, bonds. What kind of bonds we should look for to put in the portfolios. Stuff like that."

Jack still sat there saying nothing. He just looked at Mr. Lange, and finally spoke up. "No shit."

Jack pulled out his pack of cigarettes and offered Mr. Lange a smoke. Lighting their cigarettes with his gold lighter, he winked at Mr. Lange. "I think God is smiling at me right now."

Jack then told Lange where he was working and what he was doing. They spoke for a while. Lange was amazed at how much Jack knew about bonds and the economics of the market in general. Jack drilled Lange on the assets of the insurance company. It almost felt like a cold call to Jack, except he was not on the phone, and it was not cold. Lange listened for a few minutes then interrupted Jack. "Hold that thought Jack. Let me grab the guys from the class and introduce you to them."

Jack couldn't believe his good luck. It was like a gift from heaven when Lange had said that. However, Jack was not that good in front of strangers so he was getting a little nervous. He noticed his palms getting sweaty, but also knew that he could pull this off if he could just calm down some.

By then Aaron had walked up. "What, you just walk away without a word? Leaving me all alone, too. Were you just going to leave me at that table all night? I looked like an idiot over there! So I ate your steak."

"You are not going to believe what just fell into my, well, our laps. But your salesmanship and my knowledge have to be as one, starting right now."

Jack quickly explained what was going on and all the men they were about to meet. Aaron caught on and saw the group of gentlemen walking towards them. He noticed each of them had a cocktail in one hand and a cigar in the other. He opened a tab at the bar and ordered everyone another round.

Aaron lined them up and Jack knocked them down, and they felt like they were shooting at fish in a barrel, it was that easy. Some of the men had walked into the restaurant barely knowing anything about bonds. Initially, a few felt pressured, but Jack's solid knowledge and Aaron's cool demeanor and sales skills made any feelings of being forced to buy go away. It was not long before everyone was feeling confident in doing business with Aaron and Jack, and the firm. They did not know exactly what they were buying yet, but they knew whom they were buying from, and that's all that mattered.

When Jack and Aaron walked into the office the next morning there was already a little commotion going on. Maria, the office manager for the firm, was chewing out Strong and Haynes. She was on another one of her tirades about the secretaries that the firm hired.

Among other things, Maria was in charge of all the administrative staff at the firm, meaning that she was in charge of the young ladies who worked there. Maria worked hard to make sure all the girls were punctual, hardworking, and looked professional. Those were none of the traits that the partners were really looking for in a secretary though. The partners had their own ideas of what made a good secretary.

And Maria was the only one who ever yelled at the partners. Secretaries had a "shelf life" of no more than a year or two, so Maria had the job of constantly training new girls. It was not something she enjoyed doing. Just as a girl was properly trained she usually quit, though every now and then one would be fired. Not that Maria was ever privy as to the reason why.

Maria was determined as she spoke forcibly to Haynes and Strong. "The girls you make me hire are barely qualified to do the jobs they're supposed to do. Some of them can't even type! It's as ridiculous as it is unbelievable. You have never hired anyone I've suggested or wanted. It seems your only criteria is what they look like, and that is no way to run a business. Then it's me who has to take up the slack, and I can't do it anymore. Things have got to change."

Haynes finally interrupted her with his head down and in a worn-out voice, "All right, all right. Who do you want us to meet? This time we'll consider her. Okay? Just please stop yelling."

Maria addressed both of them. "Her name is Rose. She's very intelligent and I think she can really make a difference in this office. She has a lot of experience. Wait here and I'll go get her."

As Maria was leaving the floor Gage and Olive were just entering the area. Maria passed them by as she was heading to the lobby to get the new girl.

"What's going on?" Gage asked the two of them.

Haynes responded in a tired voice. "Oh Maria wants us to meet a new girl to work here."

Maria soon returned with Rose, who was dressed professionally and had a conservative appearance about her. Maria had a proud look on her face as she and Rose walked towards the partners. That was until they heard Olive's booming voice. Olive had not heard Maria's tirade and he also had not seen them approaching since he had his back to them. He yelled at the top of his voice. "Score! New meat! Is she that quiet redhead waiting up front? You know I'm a sucker for redheads. Do you think she's wearing red panties to match her hair?"

Both women stopped dead in their tracks. Maria turned and looked at Rose, just in time to see Rose turn around and walk out of the building.

Maria did not even try to stop her. She just stood there silently shaking her head. "Why do I put up with this crap?"

Haynes smiled back. "Because we pay you oh so well."

Strong could not help himself. "She was too old anyway. Keep them under twenty-five if you would please."

"She was only thirty!" Maria retorted quickly.

"Too bad. I said under twenty-five. We like them young. And, by the way, thank you for your future cooperation." Strong nodded his head and winked at her.

There wasn't anything else Maria could do but stew and think about finding another job, but the pay at the firm was enough incentive to keep her working there. Though the partners liked their secretaries young and beautiful, they did know that a well-run office required brains and organization, and Maria fit the bill perfectly. Plus she was not bad to look at either. Paying her a high salary was well worth any grief she gave them.

The excitement of the day had just begun. After Maria had left the floor, Aaron boldly walked up to all of the partners and threw down the bar tab from the night before. He told the partners they owed him a thousand dollars from the restaurant's tab, plus another four-thousand dollars from the "gentlemen's club."

"Bullshit," said Olive. "What makes you think we owe you this?"

Aaron turned and yelled over to Jack. "Make the call."

Jack picked up the phone and called Lange. The night before Jack and Lange had discussed a little game they would play on the partners the next day. They spoke on the phone for a few minutes while the partners listened, all with a curious look on their faces. Jack then put Lange on hold. "He has four million to put wherever I tell him to put it. That tab has his drinks, as well as four other portfolio managers, on it. It was a *very* entertaining evening last night. I think this comes under the heading of a company expense. What do you think Aaron?"

Aaron had a sly grin on his face. "I tend to believe so, too." He turned to the partners. "So, what do you think?"

"Done," came out of Gage's mouth first. He had a devilish smile when he looked at them, too. "We'll talk more at lunch." Olive glanced back at Jack, looking pleased, but also, what seemed to Jack, a bit jealous. "The market's open. Now get your ass back on the phone and help pay for that bill."

Jack and Aaron kicked ass and took names as they phoned their new clients. In less than a day, Jack and Aaron both had sold nearly twenty-million dollars in bonds. They were the top producers for the month.

Everyone fed off the energy that was created by Jack and Aaron that morning.

The whole office was wild. The market was roaring. Brokers ran up and down to the trader's desk erasing bonds from the boards. Everyone yelled when someone else screamed out a sale and the amount of the commission. The cheering and hollering was only interrupted by Fast Eddie, who was cussing up a storm, or Swamp-Ass hollering at the top of his "Cajun" lungs when he made a sale. No one had yet to figure out a single thing he said. Alex was going crazy at the trader's desk, looking for product.

Every single broker was buying and selling bonds. Alex was answering calls on one phone while dialing on another, all the while trying to write down available products on the boards. No one wanted to be left behind. As it turned out, that day was the firm's most profitable ever.

CHAPTER ELEVEN

▼

Not only was it an incredible time for the firm, but a great time for Aaron and Jack. The partners invited the two to go to a lot of different places with them. They attended sporting events, charity auctions, galleries, and of course, topless bars.

One day, Gage came down at noon and grabbed Aaron and Jack as he was heading out for lunch. Gage wanted to ride with Jack in his new car. He was talking trash that Jack's Corvette was still a virgin and needed to be shown how a real man drove her.

They all walked to the elevator, but as the elevator doors opened, out rushed Olive, cussing up a storm. He walked out with only the left half of his coat on. The other half was on the floor. Strong and Haynes were standing in the back of the elevator with a look of innocence on their faces.

"I'm not picking that shit up," Olive replied. He obviously was none too pleased.

"Will somebody get a hanger for his coat," Strong calmly stated. It was funny to everyone, except Olive.

Somehow Olive recovered enough to agree to head back out for some lunch, even though at the moment all he could think of was a way to get back at Strong and Haynes for the latest rip-the-new-suit coat prank. This was the firm's favorite prank, and it did not take long for everyone in the office to have had his suit coat ripped at least once. Because of his exquisite taste for fashion, Olive always seemed to be the main target between the partners.

Gage drove Jack's Corvette to the restaurant, and drove the car hard. Jack inwardly cringed every time they turned a corner fast or set off like they were in a race after each stop. All Jack could do was think about what all this hard driving was doing to his new car.

Lunch, though, was all business. Questions were fired back and forth about Jack and Aaron's new accounts. The partners were impressed by how the two had handled the group of investors and how they had worked as a team. The firm had never before considered teaming brokers together, since they always figured if a broker worked alone he would be more aggressive and thus make more calls and then more sales. This was something different, and if it worked they liked it. And they liked it even more when they heard the final tally from all those new accounts. Combined, the portfolios of the new clients were almost eight-hundred-million dollars.

But the best part of the lunch for Jack and Aaron was not the food. It was the invitation. The invitation everyone wanted. The invitation they had been working towards for months. It was an invitation that was elaborately extended to just them. The coveted invitation to join the Zeros.

Best of all, they learned it was a permanent invitation. Once a broker was invited to the Zeros, he was always invited. Any day and every day the Zeros got together. It was like a fraternity. In fact, it was frowned upon if a broker was not a regular at the Zeros once he had been invited. The only way a broker lost his invitation was if he was fired or quit.

The Zeros had very special rules, and while there were only a few rules, they were very strict rules. Rules handed down by the partners. Strong began listing the rules. "Rule One: Only partners can invite someone to Zeros. Rule Two: You cannot tell anyone about the Zeros or what goes on at the Zeros. It has to remain a secret and a mystery to those who have not yet been invited. Rule Three: You can never be late to work and you can never miss work because of a late night at the Zeros. Rule Four: There are no exceptions to these rules."

Lunch was quick and intense. The partners were strict about returning to the office, mainly to get Aaron and Jack back on the phones. No one can make money when they are away from the phones. Well, other than One-Trade Maye. The partners had decided to let her be, and let her do whatever it was she wanted, since she managed to bring in enough money to keep them happy. Plus, they had to have one woman broker working at the firm. It kept the women's libbers off their backs.

On the way back to the office Gage pushed Jack's driving ability. He kept telling Jack to drive faster and harder than he was used to doing. Gage then taught Jack how to take corners faster than he had ever taken them before, and it was not long before Jack was starting to feel good about the way he was driving. He was having fun and previous thoughts of what it was doing to the car soon left his head. Gage also taught Jack how and when to use the clutch as a brake, when to hit the gas, and how to drive using the emergency brake.

It was all fun and games until Jack hit the curb on the driveway heading into the parking lot of the office and fishtailed. He did not damage his car since he hadn't hit the curb that hard, but as the car's engine died, so did Jack's excitement.

Gage all at once turned to Jack, and was suddenly serious. He looked at him with a stone-cold look that told Jack that something important was about to be said. Maybe it was more tips on how to drive, or how to avoid hitting curbs. Jack sat silently and waited for Gage to speak. "Before the Zeros tonight we need to talk. Aaron, also." His voice was level and even, matching the look on his face.

"Are we in trouble or something?"

Gage exited the car. "No, I don't think so. But I want to keep it that way."

Jack sat there wondering what Gage had meant. It was a confusing statement coming from Gage. Jack kept thinking, "Keep what? And what way?" Jack just stared as Gage walked away wondering what had just happened.

Jack quickly grabbed Aaron and pulled him into the men's restroom when they returned to the office. He repeated exactly what Gage had said and how he had said it. They bounced ideas around for a bit trying to decipher what Gage meant. Jack thought it was something related to being in the Zeros, but knew they couldn't ask anyone else, as much as they wanted to.

Jack worried about what Gage had said. "What the hell could he have been talking about? But the fact that he said 'we'll talk about this tonight' is a good thing, right? Tonight means after work at the Zeros. It sounds like we're still invited to the Zeros."

Jack was nervous about what Gage had said, but Aaron's cavalier attitude served him well. Aaron went back on the trading floor as if nothing was wrong. Easy come, easy go was his motto. Aaron figured that in a worse-case scenario he could always find work for a competitor. He knew it. More importantly, the firm knew it, too. And even though Jack now felt this as well, the knowledge still could not keep him from getting more upset as the day wore on. It seemed like the clock did not move an inch all afternoon. A new client finally put Jack's worries to rest.

The morning had passed quickly for Jack and Aaron, but the afternoon felt as if it lasted forever. The anticipation of going to the Zeros and the "talk" from Gage was killing them both. The rules were so strict and this fact only fueled their curiosity and excitement.

Aaron called clients and cold called like a machine. His goal was to make another sale that afternoon. He didn't care if it was to a new client or to an old one. He just wanted to sell something to someone in order to have a sale to throw into the partners' faces, just in case.

Over the past months, Aaron's cold calling attitude never really changed. He was just as quick to chew out someone on the phone as he was to hang up on him. He cussed and called them names whenever he felt they needed it.

He had received many different reactions to his tactics. Although he made a couple of sales when he was overly aggressive, most reactions to his behavior were quite unpleasant. On this afternoon, however, he received a reaction he never expected.

A man who was the president of an insurance company had angered Aaron by not responding to questions, responding meekly, and basically doing not much more than making Aaron do all of the talking. This time, though, he mumbled something that Aaron could not make out at all, and he was tired of repeating himself to this guy. All at once Aaron went into his aggressive and abusive mode. Jack could hear Aaron from his desk, which was now next to Aaron's.

"Why don't you take that dick out of your mouth so you can speak clearly?" That was just the beginning. Aaron ran off a few more homosexual activities before he stopped berating the man and began to hang up the phone.

But then Aaron heard something even he could never have expected. After the first few words from the man there was a brief silence on the other end of the phone. A moment later Aaron heard the man's voice again, but this time with a peculiar tone to it. It was this that held his interest. All Aaron said was, "I'm listening. Go on." It did not take long for Aaron's eyes to pop wide open.

Aaron was stumped. He spun his head around like an owl and looked at Jack. Jack really did not know what was going on, but he could see the puzzled look on Aaron's face. Jack lifted his shoulders and mouthed, "What?" But Jack had to quickly turn back and get on the phone as Mean Dean had begun to yell at him from the stairs.

Aaron looked at Jack to regain his composure and began to pitch a bond before he was interrupted. Whoever was on the phone was not interested in the bond. "That's not what I meant. Talk to me about, about the, about the other thing, you know, the other thing you said."

Aaron was still baffled, trying to remember exactly what he had said to this man. He sat there not knowing what to say. The silence on the line was only broken at the other end of the phone. "Go ahead, I'm listening."

All Aaron could muster was, "So you want me to talk dirty to you?"

The man responded. "Yes, just the way you did, earlier."

"You mean like talk dirty, like gay homo talk dirty?"

"I'll make it worth your while if you can get me excited." The man went silent again. Those were magic words, and the only words Aaron really needed to hear. A new account. Another sale. Which meant money to spend. Aaron began with the dirty talk, and then sold what was selling. A couple of minutes later he wrote out a trade ticket for a million bonds before hanging up the phone.

Unbeknownst to Aaron, while he was giving the man exactly what he wanted, Bart had walked over and tapped Jack on the shoulder. He had noticed, and was curious to what was going on, as Aaron was halfway under his desk and acting weird. He and Jack were soon listening to everything Aaron was saying. After Aaron had finished with the call he turned around to get up, only to be surprised to be met with stupefied looks and mouths wide open.

Jack chimed in first. "I knew you were gay. Known it for years. But Aaron, that's okay. Your secret is safe with me."

Bart tried to say something, but was laughing so hard he fell on top of Jack's desk then on to the floor. Of course, this brought the attention of others in the room; all wondering just what was going on at Jack's desk that was so funny, and wondering why Bart had fallen.

Jack started laughing pretty hard himself, but managed to gather together some semblance of decorum, while trying to keep a straight face. "You're going to have to warn us next time that happens." Bart by this time had gotten off the floor, but was still laughing. Jack continued. "We need to make sure we're not on the phone you know." Jack couldn't hold it in any longer, and wiped tears of laughter from his face. "We can't work like this. Not in this kind of environment. Are you two going steady now? Is he your boyfriend?" By now Jack and Bart were back to laughing so hard that a few others had gotten up to check out what was going on. No one ever wanted to miss out on a prank or a joke.

Aaron could see Floyd and Eddie coming his way and had to think fast. "Fuck off, Jack. You too, Bart. I just made a lot of money. You won't be laughing when I'm buying another car. Plus, he said he had some others who might be interested in buying from me." Aaron tried to sound manly, but was not fooling Jack or Bart. "Can you guys just do me a favor and keep quiet about this for me, please?"

That pathetic plea did not help Aaron's cause. Both Jack and Bart razed him even more. They also could not stop laughing. "Did he invite you to a bathhouse, too?" But both stopped once Floyd and Eddie walked up to Jack's desk. They had wanted to know what was going on, but no one was going to tell. Some secrets were meant to stay that way. Plus, Bart and Jack got a dinner out of it all. And a very good laugh. It was a story that Aaron and Jack would laugh about for years to come.

But it was Aaron who laughed, all the way to the bank, because this account not only became one of Aaron's better accounts, but it brought in a lot of clients who wanted the same "talk." Aaron often received calls, and all looking to get the same sales pitch. All he had to do was talk dirty to them.

From that day on, Aaron tried to make those "special" calls from the privacy of the conference room. All too often, though, he had to make his calls while crammed under his desk. Aaron did not do this because he was ashamed, or because the guys were making fun of him. He did this so he could talk as dirty and as explicitly as possible. And for some reason, Mean Dean never made any comments when Aaron went "hiding" under his desk. He was on the phone. He was making sales. That was all that mattered.

By 4:32, everyone who was not allowed to be in the building had left. It was amazing to Jack and Aaron how no one really ever noticed who stayed and who remained. Like ants with marching orders, all the workers gathered their things and walked out.

It occurred to Jack and Aaron that they had always done the same thing, too. Despite the rumors, no one ever paid any attention to where everyone went until they were either in the parking lot or at HOGS. There was something else they realized at that moment and that caught their attention. They had never seen any of the secretaries leave at 4:30, and yet had never wondered why.

The office manager, Maria, was packing up to leave for the day. They saw her come down the stairs. The two secretaries that had been down on the floor at quitting time headed upstairs right at 4:30. Maria coolly smiled at Jack and Aaron, and as she walked by said, "Enjoy yourselves."

Bart came around the corner as Jack and Aaron followed the girls upstairs. Bart did not know that Jack and Aaron were now on the guest list. He rushed over and smacked each on their backside like they had scored a touchdown. Bart told them to follow him to the upstairs boardroom. The three of them were laughing and cutting up like little kids.

It was all fun and games until they got to the top of the stairs. Strong was standing outside the doors to the Emperor's Lounge. "Bart, go on inside and make yourself a drink. We'll be right there. I just need to talk to these fellows." It was a cordial suggestion to Bart, but it sounded more like a command to Aaron and Jack.

Jack and Aaron's ignorance of the situation caused them both to feel intimidated. One never knew what was going to happen at the firm. They each looked on as Bart walked away. Strong then led them into Olive's office.

Olive was there with Haynes and Gage, both who were sitting on a leather sofa.

Haynes spoke first, and in a very calm voice. "You boys are making a lot of money now and there will be a lot of parties that you will be invited to, and there will be a lot girls that you will meet. With all your cash you might find it hard to always spend it, but we're here to help you find things to buy, and it's important that you know this. But there is one thing we don't want you to buy or do. We do not want you getting mixed up with the wrong crowd, if you know what I mean." He looked at Olive when he said this. "That means no drugs. Nothing. Not even marijuana, and certainly not coke."

Gage continued with the speech. "Did you know that marijuana kills your ambition? If you think it expands your mind, it doesn't. It's a depressant. It brings you down. You probably think it only relaxes you, but it doesn't. It makes you move slower. It makes you think slower. Your total reaction time to everything is slower. Hell, it makes your life slower. That is not what we are about at this firm. We need aggressive individuals. We need men who know what they want and go after it. You two have been raking it in lately. We want you to keep making money. It's good for us and it's good for you. And I know how much fun it is spending it."

Both Jack and Aaron were somewhat surprised by this whole conversation. Jack finally spoke up. "I don't really understand what this is about. We don't use drugs and we never have."

Olive finally spoke, even though the other three partners were giving him a stern look. "Some of the brokers in this office like to party a little harder than others. You might see some of the guys doing things at the Zeros that you have never seen them do in this office before. They may offer you something."

Strong interrupted. "If that's what you need to keep you on the edge, then you better be careful. It'll keep you going full steam ahead, but only for a while. That stuff is expensive but it fits in with your lifestyle. It's something the rich and famous do."

Gage then interrupted Strong. "Man don't tell them that shit."

Olive interrupted Gage. "It's the 70s man. Everyone's doing it. It's what all the high rollers do. It's not even illegal."

Haynes finally spoke up. "No, that's wrong. It is illegal, unlike booze." He looked at Aaron and Jack. "We just don't want to see any of that from you two, okay?" Both swore they'd never use drugs, not that Jack thought he would want to anyway. Alcohol kept him pretty wasted as it was, and the last thing he needed was something else that was illegal.

Strong got up to open the door so Aaron and Jack could leave. As they walked out, they heard Haynes start in on Olive again as he and Gage got up to leave as well. "Don't be telling that crap to anyone else. It's hard enough to keep some of these guys in line already. I'm tired of having some of our top producers turn to nothing because of that shit."

It was the first time either Jack or Aaron noticed any friction between the partners.

CHAPTER TWELVE

▼

Usually the only activity held in the Emperor's Lounge on a regular basis was whenever the Zeros met. The room was twice as big as the largest conference room downstairs. The hardwood floors were covered with Persian rugs. There were two luxurious leather couches towards the back of the room, all in shadows.

An extraordinary and massive bar lined one entire side of the room. In one corner of the room was a complete seating area with glass coffee tables. It resembled the bar area at a posh restaurant.

The liquor was neatly organized. Scotch on one side. Bourbon on the other. Vodka and gin were placed between the two. There were bottles of tequila on ice, ready to go. Nothing less than super premium was ever served at the Zeros. Shot glasses lined the bar, just waiting to be filled. Countless other bottles of wines and liqueurs lined a shelf behind the bar and were stocked in the refrigerator.

On the left side of the room was a blackjack table. A small Las Vegas-style sign read, "$100 minimum bets." This was strictly enforced. And there was not an empty chair at the table. Brokers made their bets as one played dealer for the night, and with his own money. The other side of the room had a large poker table. Again, it was set up like one would see in Las Vegas. Every seat was taken. Men were drinking and placing bets.

On the latest stereo system light jazz was playing in the background. The room was designed to keep the top producers happy, and the rumors and stories that did leak out were intended to keep the rookies, and brokers not yet selling enough, motivated. It worked.

It was one big, continuous party. Everyone was drinking, laughing, and having a good time. When Aaron and Jack walked in, there was a shot contest between the secretaries going on at the bar. Brokers gambled on who could down the most shots in the shortest amount of time. These wagers were also hundred-dollar minimums. As the night wore on the amount of the bets increased, as did the number of girls who participated.

Following Jack and Aaron into the Emperor's Lounge, Gage ran behind the bar and called to Jack and Aaron as if he were a real bartender. "Gentlemen, let me pour you only our best."

Gage set up three shot glasses and a bottle of chilled tequila. As he poured the shots he began to speak. "I want you two to know that I don't approve of the shit Olive was talking about. But it's Olive's thing for some reason. I don't like to see that here. I know some of the guys here do that crap, but they really need to do it somewhere else. I don't like it, but if I don't see it going on, there's not much I can do about it. I just don't want to see you guys pushing grocery carts on the street. You're better than that, and we all know it."

"Yes sir," Aaron replied.

Gage continued. "Some of these guys, especially those around Olive or Strong, are high as a kite even as we speak. Some of us have to put up with it because they produce. But the minute they stop producing, then they're out of here." They picked up their glasses as Gage toasted. "Here's to being single, drinking double, and sleeping triple. Now go and have a good time."

Drinking was the real game at these parties. Everyone's personality changed, especially the girls. These were not the girls Jack and Aaron knew during the day. They all had alter egos for these parties. They even used a different name. Samantha was Sissi, Terri was Tipper, Mandy was Mitzi, and Kate was Kitti. A different name allowed them to create a new personality, one that the girls could easily slip into.

The girls were more than flirtatious. They teased the men. They danced with one another provocatively. They had tequila contests. The girls were no fools though. Everything came with a price. Fortunately for them, price was never an issue.

All at once a man entered the room. His name was Steve and he had shown up with a handful of girls. He only stayed a few minutes before shaking hands with Olive, then left as quickly as he had arrived. To the untrained eye it was a cordial parting. A closer look would have seen the exchange of a little white baggie for some tightly folded bills.

The girls who had arrived with Steve also came with the same "party favors" but knew to keep them out of sight other than for those who wanted to partake. They were all looking for a good time themselves and were regulars to a Zeros party. They picked up where the other girls left off. Some of the secretaries flirted and showed a little skin, some did more. Steve's girls, on the other hand, had looser morals, if any at all. After a few drinks, one by one, they left the Emperor's Room with a broker.

One of them was flirting with Aaron for a bit. Aaron had not caught on to what was transpiring until Olive walked by and whispered in his ear, "You're going to hurt her feelings if you don't screw her." She struck out with Aaron, but quickly found someone else. There was always someone else.

Everyone drank the night away. Plenty of people ran around like fools. Brokers played poker. Steve's girls ran around totally nude and used the Xerox machine to make copies of their breasts and other body parts, which they were more than happy to pass around. An endless supply of liquor kept everyone's glasses full.

Jack, Aaron, and Bart sat at the bar visiting until Mitzi, Kitti, and Sissi grabbed them, and a bottle of tequila, and led them to another room. It was someone's office that the guys had never been to before, but it had three large sofas within, and was very dark. The girls were flirtatious and eager to please, no matter what. Aaron and Jack were nervous, since neither had ever had sex with someone with an audience in tow, let alone an audience also having sex. It made Jack uneasy, and for once Aaron was not feeling as cocky as he usually did. However, the girls knew that a broker would never be invited to the Emperor's Room unless he had been making some serious money, so they had no trouble treating these boys like kings, and it was not long before the three forgot that there were others in the room. Alcohol will do that. So will a beautiful and naked girl on your lap.

The Zeros was one big party that lasted most of the night. There was a strict rule that everyone had to be at work at 7:30 the next morning if it was a workday. Jack and Aaron managed to get out of there around 2 a.m., wondering how they were going to function the next day. It was going to be a very painful morning.

Another perk of being invited to the Zeros was the open invitation to go to Las Vegas with Olive. Olive frequented Vegas often and regularly had free airline tickets sent to him by the casinos. He handed them out like candy at the Zeros. At least once a month Olive would head to Las Vegas, and he often invited a few brokers to tag along. Most usually accepted the offer, but now and then a broker would decline, and then Olive would order them to come along. They were told that they either came along or they would be fired.

The first few times a broker would head to Vegas they were somewhat segregated from the partners. Although the associates had free rooms, and enjoyed themselves to the fullest, they did not have the privilege of hanging out with the partners. Once a broker had gone to Vegas a few times, and kept being one of the top producers, would he be able to tag along wherever the partners went. Brokers new to the trip though managed to tag along, though at a distance far enough not to make the partners angry.

This was not only the natural progression of things, it was part of the firm's constant molding of associates. The associates were treated as first-class citizens by the casinos. But those who were personally invited by Olive, and were allowed to be with Olive, were treated like royalty.

An invitation to accompany Olive to Vegas was one thing. However, to run in Vegas with Olive was another milestone altogether, and something everyone wanted. Otherwise, the associates had to gamble at separate tables, tables frequented by tourists. Olive's gaming table was reserved just for him and his chosen guests, and was always surrounded by women who were at Olive's beck and call. Only the best for Olive.

Young associates were still being taught how to spend their money. They were placed at tables with ten-, twenty-, and fifty-dollar minimum bets. The bets made at Olive's table were much larger. Most of the young associates could not yet comprehend gambling with so much money. It was one thing to buy expensive items that a broker could see, touch, feel, and use. It was another to simply gamble away tens of thousands of dollars in one sitting. The vision of Olive's lifestyle opened their eyes as the firm's constant training worked its magic. It would only take one trip to Vegas for an associate to work harder to spend his way into what Olive called the "Partner's Circle."

The following Thursday, right before lunchtime, Strong had some of the brokers go out and buy new sunglasses before returning to work after lunch. The only other instructions they received were that the new sunglasses had better be cool. It was an odd command, but no one questioned it.   Like robots given an order, they did what they were told.

There was always a reason for everything, not that some of it ever made sense, but if they wanted to keep their jobs, they did what they were told. Once all returned, the sunglasses were closely inspected by Strong and Haynes who then took their time over each pair, whispering comments to one another about the choice each broker had made. The four brokers were then chosen and told to leave with Haynes. The "chosen ones" piled into a new 30-foot custom motor home that was parked in front of the building. It was Gage's newest toy.

This was the first time that any of them had left the office before the market closed. No one knew where they were going, and no one asked.

Haynes spoke up as he opened a bottle of champagne. "New shades require a new car. Something much more expensive than what you have now. We need to find the right car to compliment those sunglasses. Everyone here knows how to spend a lot of money even on the smallest of items. Now we're going to take you to the next level."

Gage's new RV was stocked with liquor and the finest cigars. Everyone drank, anticipating and wondering what dealership they were heading to. A shot of adrenaline hit each and every one of them as Gage pulled into the parking lot of a Ferrari dealer.

Jack, Aaron, Floyd, and Bart were the ones chosen, and then chauffeured by Gage, to buy a Ferrari. Everyone exited the RV except for Gage. "I don't do Ferrari gentlemen." As Gage drove off, Strong shook his head then gave him the finger. "Asshole doesn't know what he's missing."

A salesman greeted Strong and the four brokers virtually floated in on a cloud as the walked into the showroom. Jack joked that he felt ridiculous living in an apartment but shopping for a Ferrari. Strong overheard the comment and blew his stack. He chewed Jack out and told him he better have a home, and a condo downtown, in the next couple of weeks or his ass was going to be fired. "And the same for the rest of you ladies." He turned and glared right at Aaron. Aaron just nodded his head. There was not much else he could do, especially as he could not take his eyes off of the cars.

The showroom floor seemed ablaze as they gaped at every current model on display. The doors to each were open and ready for the excited group to sit in each car. The four behaved like little kids in a toy store right before Christmas. Everyone took turns sitting in each car's driver's seat. They eagerly placed one hand on the steering wheel and the other on the gearshift. They played with all the buttons and honked the horns. The hood of each Ferrari was popped open to take a look at the engines, not that these guys would know what they were looking at, but it was what Strong and Haynes did, so they did it, too.

Over the next few hours each broker chose a Ferrari that Strong and Haynes felt fit each best. All of the cars were given a final detail and were soon parked out front. Electricity filled the air as the keys to four new Ferraris were placed in the hands of these young men.

Then two salesmen drove up in a new Ferrari for Strong and Haynes as well. As he jumped in, Strong yelled at everyone, "Follow me."

"Where to?" Bart asked.

"To San Antonio. And keep up ladies. No excuses allowed." He smiled at everyone as he tore out of the parking lot.

The road to San Antonio was an easy and fast two hour drive in a Ferrari. It was a great highway to drive such a car, and an even better road when racing against five others. All were glad that there were few people out on the freeway that day.

The sound of six Ferraris with the "pedal to the metal" could be heard for quite a distance. The few other cars on the highway quickly got out of the way, seeming to part like the Red Sea, as each car roared by. Each man constantly tried to pass up another. Every now and then the road became clear of cars and the pack of Ferraris would fly by at 150-miles-per-hour.

About a third of the way to San Antonio, Strong led everyone to a gas station to fill up. It was the only building they had seen for miles. To everyone's surprise, Gage was already there. He was leaning on the side of his car, offering a cigarette to some smoking-hot cowgirl. She was wearing tight jeans, a very small, and tight, white see-through top, and a black cowboy hat. As soon as the others arrived she smoothly left, but not before giving Gage a passionate kiss.

All the brokers realized it was a planned meeting when Olive appeared a few minutes later. It must have been one of the firm's many watering holes. Under an old mesquite tree behind the station they sat around and drank a few beers at a picnic table.

A few minutes later a sheriff walked around the corner with one hand on his sidearm as he pointed at the crew with the other. "What the hell is this?"

"Lunch!" Gage yelled as he hurled a beer bottle at him.

The officer caught it and yanked the bottle top off with his teeth. He then drank the beer down in a few gulps. After he let out a big belch, he threw the bottle in the air, drew his pistol, aimed right at it, then hit the bottle in one shot.

The guys held their breaths. "Did you see that shit? My aim's off a bit. Barely got the mother." He then looked at Gage. "Gage, you old son of a bitch, where the hell have you been?" The younger associates let out a sigh of relief.

Gage got up and they hugged as if they were long-lost brothers. As it turned out, they used to race when they both lived in Tennessee. In fact, they went back so far they had played kickball together in the streets. And both had families who had lost their farms to a bank when times got tough.

Both had moved to Texas around the same time and remained close. Where Gage was better suited to a big city, his buddy moved to the country and became a sheriff. They only spoke occasionally these days, but no one could tell. They picked up as if they had just seen each other the day before.

It turned out to be the perfect setup. Everyone was granted immunity in his county because of Gage's friendship with the sheriff. He radioed ahead to the other officers working their speed traps to let them pass without incident. With this call, they were soon on the road again.

Each man jumped into his own Ferrari as Gage stayed back for a few minutes and chatted with his buddy. The thrill of not worrying about a "Smokey" pulling them over was exhilarating as they raced out of the parking lot. Anxiety also crept into their blood, since as they were all leaving they noticed what Gage was driving. His 1967 Shelby Cobra. The kicker was that they all knew that where the Shelby left off, Gage picked up.

A nervous burst of excitement and energy was helped along and sparked by the other partners. It was the kind of energy that only little boys feel when they jump on to their beds so the monster underneath does not grab their leg. No one knew what Gage had done to his Shelby Cobra, and though they were all dying to find out, they all also wanted to get as much of a head start as they could. Not that it would have mattered.

Sure enough they were impressed. Everyone watched their rear-view mirrors as much as they watched the road ahead. They were all cruising at a hundred-miles-per-hour and were a few miles down the road when they first heard him approaching. It was not long before Gage appeared in the mirrors behind them, like the Grim Reaper.

No matter how fast they traveled, Gage kept coming. Bart happened to be the last car in the Ferrari train when Gage caught up. At a hundred-and-twenty- miles-an-hour, Gage was hanging two inches from Bart's bumper.

Bart hurriedly pulled out of the way as Gage tailgated the next car, who happened to be Olive. Olive eventually changed lanes and flipped off Gage as Gage sped on by. One by one, Gage passed each car except for Haynes. Haynes refused to allow Gage to pass. They quickly left everyone behind as Haynes accepted Gage's challenge. They disappeared over the horizon.

The group approached the San Antonio city limits before they knew it, and the traffic outside of the city eventually slowed everyone down. They arrived at one of San Antonio's finest River Walk hotels, the Palacio del Rio, in a roar. Pandemonium hit the entrance as all the valets raced to park eight exotic cars. Each valet was given permission to drive the cars around the block, then the cars were parked in a row, right in front. It was the best marketing tool any hotel could ask for.

Each broker checked into their own suite with no luggage, so no one went up to their room. They grabbed their room keys and headed to the bars on the River Walk.

San Antonio's River Walk was one restaurant and bar after another, all along a slowly winding river. The boys walked from bar to bar, threw back drink after drink, shot after shot. Dinner consisted of nothing more than whatever snacks were offered at the bars. It was a wandering party that always targeted the next bar. A flock of women followed the men as they threw hundred-dollar bills around like there was no tomorrow.

As the devil's hour approached Strong led the group back to the hotel.

Floyd asked, "For what? It's still early." Olive just stared at him, even though most of the others were laughing.

"There's a savings and loan convention starting in the morning. None of us have a clean suit and none of you ladies have any luggage. We need to get up early and have the tailor come fit us for suits and shoes. It'll take them a few hours to get everything finished."

Bart had purchased enough tailored suits to know how long it took. "No way is there enough time for that."

Strong retorted in his usual lecturing tone. "It'll be done. For the right price, it will get done. And don't confuse hand tailored with customized either. Everyone needs to be in my suite a 6:00 a.m. No excuses."

As soon as 6:00 a.m. was uttered they dispersed without saying another word. Plus they each knew what "no excuses" meant.

By the time the four arrived at Strong's room the tailors had already been there for an hour. Strong's suite was large enough to accommodate half a dozen tailors and all their assistants. The brokers came into the room one by one and a flurry of activity began. Each tailor was assigned to an individual broker, and within minutes the tailors were sifting through the various fabrics. They then went to work; chalk in one hand and pins in the other.

There was no breakfast other than coffee and Bloody Marys. Measurements were taken precisely and quickly. Shoe sizes were recorded. The color of everyone's hair and the tone of their skin also noted. The tailors spoke among themselves but never once asked for anyone's preferences. The associates had no say in the matter. All was chosen and decided without any input from them.

As quickly as it all started, it ended. The tailors were gone in a flash. "The suits will be here by four," was heard as the door shut behind them. The tailor's assistants remained to clean up.

Eventually the eight gathered in the lobby, ready for an early lunch. But lunch, at that moment, meant margaritas. Margaritas soon led to tequila shots. Their path to total intoxication only ended because they knew they still needed to buy more clothes. Anything and everything not provided by the tailors. Plus, everyone was hungry by then for some real food, and the River Walk was a gourmet's dreamland.

The last stop of the afternoon was to the bank. Each man needed to have enough cash on hand for any situation that might arise for the coming evening. The look of the bank employees' faces as thousands of dollars in cash was handed out said it all. Then everyone headed back to Strong's suite at the hotel. Sure enough, right before four, there was a knock at Strong's door. With their assistants behind them carrying boxes of shoes, the tailors rushed into the suite, frantic and sweaty.

Surprising to some, but not to the partners, everything fit perfectly. Nothing needed to be altered. These tailors were the best, and each associate immediately realized it. Everyone had his own distinct, custom tailored suit, accompanied by a perfectly matched tie. The associates were awed by how debonair and professional they looked. Every suit had an unknown price tag, undoubtedly marked even higher under the circumstances.

Jack turned to Aaron. "How much do you think this will cost? I don't know if I have enough cash." Aaron did not have a chance to respond when Gage interrupted. "Don't worry about it boys. This is a company expense. It comes under what we call 'marketing and advertising'. "

Strong led the way downstairs to the savings and loan convention. The convention was taking place in a large banquet hall at the hotel. When they arrived, there were dozens of bankers hanging around outside the area leading into the banquet hall. And all were wearing the same banker's outfit: A dark gray or navy suit, with a tie to match. They looked like funeral directors to Aaron.

Gage stayed outside while the others went in. He began courting the bankers as they all stood around, and it was not long before most of the group accompanied Gage to his suite, which was the largest the hotel had to offer. With the men mingling about outside the small area in front of the banquet hall, it had become stuffy and all were ready to get out of there.

The room inside was equally stuffy, if not more so. A dozen or so very large tables were filled with hundreds of men listening to a presenter. To Jack's surprise, as well as all of the other associates, Cadillac Dan was the speaker at the podium. He entertained the crowd with fancy financial talk as the audience nodded their heads in agreement.

Soon, Dan finished his presentation and the brokers were told to spread out and make some "new" friends. They were also told to invite their new friends up to Gage's suite, but to do so in an orderly fashion. Haynes first met each banker arriving at Gage's suite, greeting each new prospective client as if they were the only person around. Haynes then handed them off to Gage who would lead them to where the food and bar was set up, giving a sales pitch the entire way.

Each banker was also asked if they needed anything else, as the room was well stocked not only with the finest food and liquor, but other amenities. As the food and drinks disappeared, staff from the hotel magically appeared with more. There was hotel staff working inside the suite as well. Bartenders, waitresses, servers. Each knew what to do, and did it well. No one even noticed they were there. "We aim to please" was the partner's motto for the evening.

It was not long before most of the bankers from the convention had made it into Gage's suite. Some came up by themselves, others in groups. The room eventually was filled with them, so the partners had devised a plan that allowed a banker to only be in the suite long enough to become a new client. Then back to Haynes they went for a closing speech, a handshake, and a promise to call soon. Plus an open tab in the hotel's downstairs bar. Most of the bankers were willing to become new clients, since once the liquor started flowing they became more relaxed and more willing to do business with the firm. They drank, smoked, cussed, and yelled for more booze and smokes.

At the center of it all were the partners. Their ability to get some the conservative bankers to let their guard down was uncanny. Ties were loosened and sleeves rolled up, though no one at the firm, no matter how hot it got in the room, did so. It was not long before Strong and Olive joined the group upstairs, and it took even less time for the four to weed out who they would let loose, once they were assured of a new client, and who would stay.

Haynes soon escorted those deemed too conventional by the partners out of the suite, all the while keeping up the routine of being their best buddy and selling them on the firm and how much money they all were going to make. Haynes joined the other bankers by the bar downstairs. Those who were identified as being not so conservative were invited to stay as long as they wished.

And at just the right time, just when the associates and the remaining bankers thought it could not get any better, the entertainment arrived. A handful of women walked in looking very professional, that was, until they removed their overcoats. The women mingled throughout the suite making acquaintances. These sophisticated bankers, pillars in their communities, did whatever they could to hand out their room keys.

Banker and savings and loan conventions were prime scoring targets for the firm and they never thought twice about spending thousands of dollars for one night of individual meet-and-greets. Long ago, the partners learned that alcohol brought out the primal thoughts and actions of most men. It relaxed even the most uptight individual. Alcohol made them feel confident. It made them do things they would not normally do. Booze lowered their inhibitions. It also made some regret what they did and said the night before. That's if they could recall the night before. Alcohol also created a false sense of trust and being ready to pick up where the last party left off.

These relationships, bonded by alcohol, simple pleasures, and sinful secrets, were very profitable for the firm. No banker hesitated to buy bonds from any of the partners or associates who provided such entertainment. For some, these special conventions were the highlight of the year. With one weekend only, the firm would make ten times the amount of money it spent in a month's time of entertaining or cold calling. Dozens of new relationships formed with HAYNES, OLIVE, GAGE & STRONG after each convention. These bankers could buy bonds from any other firm, but after one night of partying most would now only deal with the firm. These were business relationships sealed with alcohol, and for some, sealed with secrets.

CHAPTER THIRTEEN

▼

The following Monday morning Alex and Cadillac Dan were in front of the trading boards telling the brokers about a new bond. One of the rookies from the newest class walked in about two minutes late. Cadillac Dan turned and pointed at him. "You're late, so you're fucking fired. Get out of here." He barely missed a beat as he kept talking about the bond as the young man slunk out of the room, not even looking back.

This bond was a different instrument than what they had been selling. It worked another way, but still had a price and a coupon that indicated its return on investment. The bond was selling at par, with a ten-percent coupon. When Alex and Dan were finished, Strong stood up and yelled out, "Let's get to work. Shove them down throats or up their asses! Make it happen."

Jack had been keeping up with what was available in the bond market, so he understood how the bond worked and why. Aaron did not. "I have no idea what they're talking about Jack."

"Don't worry. I'll explain it later," Jack whispered back.

Bart did not get it either, but he felt confident enough to ask, so spoke up and asked Alex to explain more about the new bond.

Strong stood back up. "All you need to know is that it sells at par, ten-percent yield, and you make a commission. Now get on the damn phone and sell the damn bond."

"But I don't understand…" but he was cut off by Strong.

"You don't need to understand shit. Sell the damn bond! I don't care if you convince one of your clients to sell something else to buy this, but you had better sell the damn product." Bart knew not to say anything else by the look on Strong's face.

Everyone got on the phones and started calling. The tension could be felt throughout the room, until a new rookie yelled out something about selling five million of the bonds. He ran up to Alex all excited about his sale.

"We just have to change the coupon to fifteen-percent and he'll buy five million!"

Alex sat there with an impatient look on his face, and glad that Strong was not around to hear that a client had jerked this broker's chain so hard. Had Strong been present, he would have done and said untold things to this client. Alex finally muttered, "What?"

"Just change the coupon to fifteen-percent and he'll buy."

The room started to fill with laughter. Alex finally responded. "You dumb piece of shit. You can't change a coupon on a bond. The coupon on a bond never changes. The price will change and the yield will change, but the coupon never will."

"So should I call him back and tell him?"

"No. He was just messing with you. Call him back another day when you know what the hell you're doing."

A moment later Strong returned to the room still filled with laughter from the rookie's error, and asked Alex what was going on. The look on Strong's face when he was told, and then the stare Strong aimed at the rookie, made the entire room get quiet, fast. Most were thinking, "Another one bites the dust."

Not long after Strong had returned to the floor Aaron had a buyer on the phone. Aaron had put the buyer on hold as he yelled up to Alex. "I haven't even pitched a bond yet, but this guy says he has to have at least an eight-percent yield or he won't buy. What do I sell him?"

Alex was quiet for a second after he told Aaron to hold on. Strong leaned over and conferred with Alex. Haynes joined in their huddle since he was sitting on the other side of Alex at the trader's desk. Alex typed something on the computer before he finally responded. "Sell him our new bond at 103. It'll push the yield down below nine percent, but he'll think he's getting a deal. And you can keep the extra three points on your commission. Man. You need to call this dumb ass every week."

Aaron proceeded to sell the bond at three dollars over par, when it could have been bought at par. The higher price made the yield return lower. The buyer thought he knew what he was talking about, but since he didn't, would regret the buy later on. It did not matter though, because the most important thing was that the buyer was happy, and that he was happy now. Aaron was even happier, since on a million-dollar trade he grossed an extra thirty-thousand dollars over what he should have made.

Returning from lunch that day, the partners were heard yelling at each other as they were coming down the hall. They were yelling, but also laughing. "I told you to lay off all those pitchers of beer," Haynes could be heard saying to Gage. "And that'll teach you to put so much sauce on your ribs too," replied Olive. "No wonder you never know what you're eating!" Gage just glared at them both.

They had been to a barbeque place, but for some reason known only to them, had to leave earlier than they had planned. Gage had been gnawing on a large rib, pulling on the bone with his hands while chewing on the meat, when the bone slipped out of his hands and smacked him on the front of his face, covering his face and head with a lot of sauce. Sauce was also flying through the air, landing on Haynes and Olive, and unfortunately, a woman seated at the table next to theirs.

Haynes had then dared Gage to throw a rib dipped in sauce at Strong since he had somehow managed not to get hit with any of it. It was only fair that everyone be anointed. Gage initially declined, until Haynes bet him a hundred dollars he would not do it.

Strong returned the favor by squirting barbeque sauce on Gage's suit, and adding more to his head and face. "Now you're wearing a matched set. Love the hat," Strong smirked. Olive then offered Gage two-hundred dollars to shove potato salad inside the back of Haynes' shirt. It was not long before a few of the patrons were calling for their waitresses. The guys decided to get their dessert boxed up and left the restaurant. Of course they left a large tip to cover any mess that needed to be cleaned up, and for the unlucky woman to get her clothing cleaned.

But ribs, barbeque sauce, and potato salad were not the only weapons of the day. Olive walked in smelling of coleslaw, with a few pieces still clinging to his suit, all thanks to Haynes. About an hour later, the coleslaw began to emanate a strong odor. Although the stench was getting worse, it was fairly amusing to everyone. Everyone but Olive. Olive noticed Haynes sitting at the other end of the trading desk eating some key lime pie from their lunch.

Haynes was savoring a bite of the pie while on the phone with a client when he noticed Olive was looking at him. He raised his fork with some pie on it, gave Olive a quick wink with a smile, and took a bite. Olive smiled back and began walking towards him. Though Haynes was on the phone with a client, he did put up a small fight, but Olive wrestled the pie away anyway. Olive took one bite of the pie and winked back at Haynes.

Neither of them said anything. Haynes knew what was coming. Olive then took the rest of the pie and smashed it all over Haynes' head and smeared it down his face. Haynes never missed a beat, moved a muscle, or blinked an eye. He sat there still talking on the phone, covered in key lime pie, and closed a sale of two-million bonds to a buyer who never had a clue what was going on at the other end of the line.

As the afternoon wore on, the smell from the coleslaw was becoming unbearable, so in front of everyone on the trading floor Olive decided to strip out of his clothes. He casually walked upstairs in just his boxers and socks to get the spare suit in his office. Gage walked by him cool and collected while coming down the stairs. Olive did not take much notice of him. When Gage reached the bottom of the stairs he ran up to the trader's desk like a little kid and began whispering to Haynes. Both began to laugh quietly. A moment later the entire office could hear the yelling and profanity. Olive eventually emerged at the balcony cussing at Gage. He was now just in his boxers and his legs were covered in ketchup. He knew it was Gage who had put it there.

Everyone on the floor started cracking up. The humor was not lost on Olive though, as he always did appreciate a good practical joke. Wearing only his boxers, he strolled out of the building and to his car. He soon returned wearing a pair of silk pajamas that he usually kept in his car. He returned to where he had been sitting at the trader's desk, sat down, and started making calls like nothing had happened at all.

Olive had a habit of getting home late. In an effort to avoid any trouble with his wife, he would put his pajamas on in the car and sneak into the house. He would turn the TV on softly and lay down on the couch. His wife, Anna, would come down in the morning and he would just tell her that he had fallen asleep on the couch watching television. It worked every time.

Later that night at the Zeros the shenanigans did not stop. Ice cubes were flying across the room, soon followed by celery sticks, fruit, and coffee grounds. And the more alcohol that was consumed, the funnier it seemed to get. Men and women ran around the room totally naked, though a few of the men still had on their underwear. Floyd was running around in just his socks, showing them off, though no one could see what the big deal was about his socks. For some reason he made it a point to show them off to everyone he could, using his penis like a pointer. He was finally told to put that "cocktail weenie" away by Olive.

Olive then decided to make a copy of his "manliness" at the Xerox machine. "It pays to advertise you know," he said as he handed out the copies to all of the girls. It created only one small problem. Earlier, he had been having a little fun with one of the girls, so Olive's marketing scheme left a smear on the copier's glass.

No one who had attended the Zeros that night ever wanted to use that particular copy machine again, and whenever they saw someone do so, they would all burst out laughing. So the firm bought a new copy machine and moved the old one out near the trading floor for the "exclusive" use of the rookies. Of course, once a rookie became a member of Zeros, he too stopped using the machine.

★   ★   ★   ★

It was a Friday, right before quitting time, when Olive invited Aaron, Jack, Floyd, and Bart to go to Las Vegas. While Olive was well known by every casino in Vegas, he had special contacts at one place in particular. All anyone had to do was mention Olive's name and they were automatically upgraded to what the casino considered its best accommodations and first-class treatment.

The casino always sent a private jet for Olive and whoever were his guests for the weekend. Olive's invitation also meant that each broker had to bring a lot of cash, and also wire even more to the casino.

Olive's invite on this day was to celebrate the four chosen to become senior associates. Senior associates were not only selected by how much money they brought in, but it also depended on how well they fit into what the firm's partners deemed worthy. The "image" Strong was always talking about. It was also contingent on who was the most obedient.

By the end of this trip, these future senior associates would really know what it meant to be a "high roller." Aaron, Jack, Floyd, and Bart were the four who had met the requirements so far, and had been invited to Vegas by Olive. Strong, Gage, and Haynes were going, too, since it was a celebration of sorts, but all three were running late.

The casino's private jet landed at a small airport in southwest Houston. The boys walked towards the plane on a red carpet. Floyd could not believe his eyes. He had a huge grin plastered across his face. A small set of stairs led up to the jet. A gentleman suddenly appeared from the plane, quickly walked down the steps, then up to them to take their bags. As they entered the private jet their eyes fell upon plush leather seats and a fully stocked bar. The plane also came with three beautiful "stewardesses" who would attend to their every need.

Olive cranked up the stereo, and a bottle of whisky quickly filled empty glasses. The cabin's interior was charged with energy and excitement. Everyone was ready to party and just waiting for the others to arrive.

Olive was acting a little more hyped than he usually was and as if he had never even been to Vegas. After the first sip of his drink he yelled out, "Viva, Las Vegas!" And he continued to say it about every ten minutes during the entire flight. Before the plane took off, the boys noticed that one of the stewardesses, wearing a very short skirt, brought out a mirror and handed it to Olive. She smiled and pulled out a small vial filled with white powder that she emptied out on to the mirror. Olive pulled out a sterling silver blade from a gold carrying case and cut the powder into equal lines in a matter of seconds.

Despite the many parties they had attended together, Jack, Aaron, Floyd, nor Bart had ever seen any drugs being passed around, or even used. They certainly had never seen any of the partners do drugs, though all assumed that Olive did since he talked about how it was okay to do them.

Olive pulled out a little straw also made out of sterling silver. "I bought this at the jewelry store last time I was in Vegas." He stared at it lovingly. "I just had to get it. You boys will just have to roll up a Ben Franklin."

All four of them were uneasy and did not say a word. Then everything seemed to move in slow motion as they watched Olive snort one of the lines. "Viva, Las Vegas! Who's up next?"

Still no one said anything and it immediately caught Olive's attention. "This is Vegas baby. Sin City. You boys need to relax. You're high rollers now, so start acting like one. Roll up a hundred-dollar bill and do a line. And you'd better have a hundred-dollar bill, otherwise you're out."

Floyd was the first to respond, probably because he was standing closest to Olive. "I'm not doing that shit." There was some hesitation in his voice, but he tried to sound convincing. Olive did not take too well to what Floyd had said. "Either get with the party or get off the damn plane. In fact, I don't even want to look at you right now. I can't have some square asshole running with me in Vegas. Man up or you're fired!"

Floyd still did not move. He could feel Olive's stare. The tension could be cut with a knife. And it was clear to all of them that the drug had changed Olive's attitude, making him more cruel than he usually was. Olive turned extremely aggressive towards Floyd. There was no debate as far as Olive was concerned. One little associate with one partner breathing down his neck, telling him that if he did not snort some coke he would be fired. The pressure was too great. Floyd finally folded.

All the while Bart was looking on wondering what he could say or do to stop this from happening since he and Floyd had become good friends, but he did not want to have Olive choosing him next. His strict moral code would have made for some serious choices, and at the moment he did not want to have to make those decisions.

So Bart did not say a thing, but he had a hundred thoughts running through his head. Some were good; some were bad. What to do? He knew that Olive would force him to go next as it seemed lately that Olive was on his case more and more, and for no reason that Bart could figure out either. He was making more money than he ever dreamed. But what would his father think? Was this living? Or was this dying? One random thought after another, all in a matter of a few of seconds.

Olive had a devious smile on his face. He looked directly into Bart's eyes and said one thing. "Who's next?" Olive then turned his attention to Jack and Aaron. "Its party time, boys." It could have been the same for the rest of them, but before Olive could force Bart to go next Gage walked in. "Man put that shit away. And leave the boys alone. What the fuck is your problem?"

Olive leaned back in his chair and shrugged his shoulders. "It's Vegas man, what's the harm? I'm just trying to show the boys here how to have some fun. Just forget about it."

Gage, though, was not going to forget about it, as he could tell that Olive had gotten to Floyd, and this angered him even more. "What you do is your business. I don't want to see that shit again and I don't want to see you forcing drugs on anyone else again either." Gage stared at Olive in disgust. "What is going on with you lately?"

Haynes and Strong then boarded the plane, unaware of what had just transpired. Then they saw the drug paraphernalia. They each took sides. Haynes sided with Gage. And though Strong did not totally agree with Olive when it came to drugs, he sided with Olive. Taking it now and then was no big deal to him, and he figured if he didn't get hooked doing drugs now and then, no one else would do so either.

Strong was also of the "party" opinion. "It's only for when we go to Vegas anyway, so who cares? You guys are making a big deal out of nothing. Just have a drink or something." He bent down and snorted a line of coke himself.

Haynes turned and looked at Floyd then started in on Olive. "Look at this kid. He's shivering." He looked at Olive. "What the hell were you thinking?"

The tension finally broke as the door to the cabin shut. The other stewardess brought a round of drinks out for everyone. She spoke in a sexy little voice saying, "I'll be in the back if anyone needs me." Olive was the first to jump up and follow her. He felt it wise to leave the area and no one was sad to see him get up and leave.

As the plane readied for take off, Haynes pulled out some cards and started playing poker. And so went the next five hours. Bart was still in a state of shock after witnessing what happened to Floyd and spent as much time with him as possible to make sure he was okay. Jack and Haynes played some poker, and Haynes dealt him few good hands in a row. Haynes then invited Bart to play.

Bart had eventually calmed down once he saw that Floyd was going to be okay, but he was angry with Olive and still kept an eye on Floyd. The plane landed, but Olive and Strong were too high from the drugs and booze to be able to move fast. Everyone rushed to the waiting limousine, impatiently waiting for Olive and Strong to stumble to the car. The party never really missed a beat since the limousine was stocked with whiskey.

When they arrived at the casino the door to their limo was opened immediately by the bellhop crew who took the luggage to each broker's own suite. As soon as Olive exited the car all that was heard from any employee of the casino was, "Good evening Mr. Olive." "Welcome back Mr. Olive." "Glad to see you again Mr. Olive." Olive had the privilege of not having to check in, as he had his own suite.

A hotel clerk quickly moved from behind the front desk and handed Olive a batch of room keys for everyone else. Without needing to sign anything they meandered to their rooms. They were told to gather in Olive's suite after getting settled in. The sun was setting and the city was coming alive.

The partners had bigger suites than the associates, but Olive's suite was the largest and most posh. Bart was reluctant to go at first as he was still upset about what had happened, but Aaron and Jack convinced him to head up to Olive's suite. Plus, Floyd was starting to feel better and said that they all had better go, or they'd get fired.

They walked into Olive's penthouse suite and stood beneath an incredible crystal chandelier. Looking around, they saw a baby grand piano, a large dining table, a TV, and a massive hot tub that they could see through the bathroom's double doors. They made themselves a drink from the fully stocked bar and walked out to the balcony. From the top floor of the casino it was a perfect view of the Las Vegas strip.

After a few more drinks, Bart eventually loosened up after the incident on the plane, and it was not long before the group was ready to hit the casino. The elevator back down to the main floor provided a straight walk to the blackjack tables. None of the open tables had enough seats for the four associates to sit together though.

Before they had a chance to notice much else, a man came up to greet Olive. He was dressed in a dark silk suit with a red tie and with a matching red silk handkerchief. Gold flashed from his fingers. He was as Italian as they came. When Olive saw him, they walked towards each other.

He greeted Olive in a deep, Chicago-Italian accent, "Antonio Olivarto." It was the same accent Olive had when he had had too many drinks. The two men hugged and kissed each other on the cheek. "It's good to see you, Tony."

"It's good to see you too, Joey."

Neither of the associates had ever heard anyone address Olive by his full name. A moment later two others walked up to Olive with the same greeting. Each received a hug and kiss on each cheek. "Hello Mickey. Hello Lou."

The men also greeted Strong, Gage, and Haynes, too. Jack noticed though that none of the other men kissed them on the cheek, but did give all a quick hug and shook everyone's hand.

Olive introduced his guests. "This is Jack, Aaron, Floyd, and Bart. They're with me. Soon to be senior associates too, if they behave this weekend." Olive was looking right at Bart when he said this. Without hesitation, after Olive's introduction, they received the same greetings as did the other three partners. It was a first for the four of them to hug a complete stranger.

Joey looked at the guys and said, "So these are your new guys, eh? Please make yourselves at home in my casino. If there is something we have not provided or if there is anything you need, please just ask. And I hope tonight that the cards are hot and the women even hotter."

Joey turned towards the pit boss and gave a small nod of his head. With this subtle gesture a new table immediately opened up just for them. A moment later a dealer arrived and placed a small "reserved" sign on the table. The group was led to the table by a cocktail waitress who seated them, then quickly took their drink orders.

There was no minimum bet posted on the table. The partners pulled out wads of cash. Each immediately changed in thousands of dollars for chips. In the blink of an eye, a handful of sultry, gorgeous women appeared. After a few cigarettes were lit, everyone became acquainted.

It was Bart's first trip to Vegas, and actually his first time ever betting. He sat at the table and pulled out fifty dollars to wage. He soon felt a malevolent stare from all of the partners. He wondered what was wrong now.

Olive leaned over and spoke in an agitated whisper. "You are fucking embarrassing us. Especially me, so you'd better fix it or you're fired."

Bart did not say a word, as he was totally confused. Aaron knew how this little game worked though and whispered to Bart a few tips.

Gage had a more relaxed approach when showing associates how to spend their money. He had not really noticed Aaron telling Bart the rules of the table since he had been distracted by the blonde on his left arm nuzzling his neck. He casually said to Bart, "Come on man. We chase dollars, not pennies. Pull that money clip back out and pony up."

Olive leaned over again and maliciously whispered something else to Bart. "You have until I fire your ass to put some real money on the table."

There was a sexy brunette wearing a very short skirt and a blouse that did not leave much to the imagination leaning against Bart. She bent over, showing him all her assets, and whispered in his other ear with a soft sensuous voice. "Come on Barty, pull it out and show me whatcha got."

Bart reacted in a calm and cool manner as he unrolled his stack of "Ben Franklins" and placed the pile of money on the table. He half chuckled, turned and smiled to the brunette and said, "You want a quarter inch or a half inch." He grabbed the girl and planted a hard kiss on her lips. "Let's see if you bring me luck sweet ass." "Oh, you are a big boy," the brunette whispered in his ear.

Bart grabbed about a quarter-inch stack of hundreds and placed his first bet ever. "That's my boy," yelled Gage, who was barely heard over the howling from the other men and shrieks from the other girls.

Olive spoke to the others as if he had now somehow bonded with Bart. "That's my boy. I told you he would be fine." Bart could hear the false tone in his voice though. He was not Olive's "boy."

The blackjack gods were watching the table as the dealer hit all of them with high cards and crowned Bart with blackjack. The high cards kept rolling in for all of them. The table was on fire. In no time stacks of hundred-dollar chips left the dealer's pile and into the gamblers'. The hundred-dollar stacks were replaced with thousand-dollar chips. The energy around the table was intoxicating. The women were captivating and ready to have fun. It was the perfect combination that only Vegas could provide.

To Jack, Aaron, Floyd, and Bart it was a dream come true. Drunk, rich, and surrounded by beautiful women, they gambled like there was no tomorrow. But no one realized what was really going on. It was all orchestrated by Joey, to make sure the newbies were given the time of their lives. One single nod of Joey's head brought the sinful pleasures these four had always desired. They were in heaven and would sell their souls to stay there.

One by one the partners left the table for one of the bars inside the casino. Eventually they huddled up at a bar talking about how the night had been going, throwing back one drink after another. The girls of course followed since they knew where the real money was. It didn't take long for the four associates to realize that not only had the partners left the table, but so had the girls. They went to join the partners at the bar, where everybody drank down a few more. They then decided to ride around the strip to see what else they could do.

Waiting for them were two limousines. One for the partners, and their girlfriends, and the other for the associates, and whatever girls wanted to go with them. Aaron had had his eye on one in particular, but was disappointed when he saw her step into the partner's limousine. As it turned out there were plenty of young ladies to go around, and a girl accompanied each man to ensure that no one spent the night alone. This was all arranged by Olive to make sure that the guys had a memorable time. And what a time they had!

A phone call by one of the partners eventually woke the boys just a few hours after they had gone to bed. "Meet you downstairs by the bar in ten." No one had gotten any real sleep and they all woke up tired, and alone. The girls who had partied with them, and returned to their suites, were not the type that spent the entire night.

No one had mentioned to the guys that this trip was not just for pleasure, but it was also a business trip. All the partners were gathered at the bar sipping Bloody Marys when the four associates arrived, bleary-eyed but there. They knew better than to be late. They were so tired and hung over that not one of them even noticed the partners were in golf attire.

Mickey walked up and greeted Olive with a kiss and a hug. After greeting everyone else, he addressed the group. "Everything's set up. You tee off just after 12. Everyone else who's coming is staying at another one of the casinos. We have a limo taking them to the golf course."

Bart was the first one to speak up. "No one told us we were playing golf."

Mickey was the only one to respond. "No shit. Don't worry about it. I'll take care of you gentlemen. The club has everything you'll need." He looked at the partners. Go on ahead. I'll make sure these boys get some clothes and clubs, then I'll send them along." New shirts, pants, gloves, and shoes were purchased without a thought. They even purchased golf clubs that would most likely never leave Las Vegas.

It was a thirty minute drive from the main strip of Vegas to get to the lush greens in the middle of the desert. As they entered the clubhouse they were individually greeted by name from people they had never met before.

Unbeknownst to the boys, a select few of the partner's best clients were playing that day. No formal invitation had been extended by the firm to any of these gentlemen. This "chance" meeting was no coincidence however. As far as anyone knew, it was mere happenstance that these bankers were playing golf at the same course and at the same time. Way outside of Las Vegas, where, surprise, surprise, their brokers happened to be playing.

Each partner paired up with one or two of their clients, and an associate was added to the foursome for good measure. After checking in with the golf marshal, Strong turned and asked the group a question. "Are we playing for five-thousand dollars per hole gentlemen?"

"Yes." But the response from everyone was unnecessary.

Everyone, that was, except the associates. Jack nearly crapped in his pants as he walked back to their cart and looked at Aaron. "What...the...hell? Five-thousand dollars? Per hole!"

Gage had overheard him and said to the group, "It'll just be the "men" today. This time let's just have these boys watch and learn."

The guys were never so glad to hear those words. They were weekend golfers at best. Of the four associates, Aaron was the only one who played golf on a regular basis.

The partners, on the other hand, were pretty good at the game. It was more than obvious from the first drive that they played regularly. Then there were the bankers. They looked as though they were trying out for the PGA Tour.

There was no chance anyone would have a better score than the bankers, and the partners knew this. A five-thousand-dollar-per-hole bet was not a wager. It was not even gambling. It was a kickback. But outside of Las Vegas, no one knew the difference.

It was Saturday night and not long before everyone picked up where they had left off the night before—drinking, smoking, and gambling at a private table. A new set of girls surrounded them. Different girls, but they all had the same attitude and beauty as the previous ones. Ready to party, and party hard. After first running around town for a while then having dinner, they returned to the casino tables. They were drunk and spending cash as if it had an expiration date.

This time, however, the money left their pockets and returned to the casino. And then some. Olive was especially down in his chips. In fact, he owed the casino more than two-hundred grand. In his state of mind, fueled with booze and cocaine, he didn't even notice. Nor did he care. Win, lose, or draw, these men were having the times of their lives.

Olive lost a few more big hands and ran out of chips. He asked Mickey for a fifty-thousand-dollar marker. Mickey looked at Joey for approval, and with a nod of his head Olive had fifty-thousand in chips pushed towards him. Olive played a few more bad hands and decided he wanted to try his luck at the craps table. The associates had no choice but to gather their chips and head over to that part of the casino, trailing after Olive like trained dogs.

Joey was already there waiting. He greeted all of them as they approached the craps table. He then spoke privately to Olive for a bit. No one could really hear what was being said, but the conversation ended with Olive saying he would wire the money to the casino on Monday.

Joey turned his attention to the younger associates. He made sure they were all enjoying themselves. Then pleasure suddenly turned to business. Joey began inquiring about the bond market. He asked Jack if they could make some money together if he jumped in.

Jack and Joey talked for a while as they strolled up to one of the bars. When Joey had walked off, Olive came over. Olive shared stories about his childhood and growing up in Chicago with Joey. He bragged on and on and told Jack what a great guy Joey was and how he took care of his friends. Olive's sales pitch was interrupted by a blonde who had come up to him and swiftly dragged him away. Aaron and Bart came up to the bar to talk with Jack.

As Olive was walking away, Bart asked one question under his breath to Aaron and Jack. "If Joey is such a great guy, then why do I feel like I'm standing next to the devil?" Jack felt the same way and said so. All Aaron could do was nod in agreement.

They stayed up all night partying again. No one had slept when the limousine pulled up Sunday morning to take them back to the airport. Dazed, exhausted, and still drunk, they all piled in.

They were about to pass out on the plane when Haynes walked up to the guys. They could tell he had something important to say by the way he stood over them.

"You four listen, and listen good." Haynes made solid eye contact with each of them before he said anything else. "Never, ever, do business with Joey, or anyone associated with him or his casinos. I don't care how nice you think he is or how much he asks you about bonds. I don't even care how much money he promises to send you. And I don't care if you are broke and starving for a commission. Do you hear me? Never. Do we have an understanding?"

One after the other each responded with a solid, "Yes."

✱   ✱   ✱   ✱

Monday was just another day as far as everyone else was concerned. The boys who went to Vegas did nothing but sleep the rest of their Sunday and walked in that morning feeling just fine. Except for Bart, who was starting to have a burning sensation when he went to the bathroom. It was a little gift from one of the Vegas girls that would require a shot of penicillin later in the week.

None of them said anything about their weekend trip. Nor did anyone else as Strong pulled Jack aside to talk some business without even saying, "Good morning." For some reason, Strong was running around like a chicken without a head. The question as to his frantic behavior was quickly answered when they learned Strong's biggest client was visiting the firm that day.

The president of a large Texas bank soon arrived accompanied by a few of his vice presidents. Strong and his client were in meetings for the remainder of the morning. Jack was brought in to meet with them on a new product idea that could benefit only certain investors. As lunchtime approached, Jack was still working out the kinks. The entire investment's success depended on the future of the market—bear or bull. It gave everyone something to think about before Strong left for lunch with his client, and of course the VPs who were tagging along.

Other than the client visit, it was a fairly normal day at the office. A sale here and there kept the office busy. Lunch had come and gone and Aaron had not opened any new accounts or sold any bonds that day. He had spent nearly every penny he had while they were in Vegas, so he really needed to make some sales.

Aaron did have one client in particular he could call to make a sale. It had been a few weeks since Aaron had last called this banker. And every time he called he made a sale. It was a one-hundred-percent success rate with this guy. All he had to do was talk dirty to another man. Late lunchtime was his prime calling time for this client since the partners and most senior associates were out of the building. Fewer people meant fewer ears to overhear. Fewer listeners also meant less teasing, something Aaron tried to steer clear of.

The last few times he called he was able to sneak away into the conference room and really get down and dirty. That was not an option today because Strong would return any minute with his client and he knew that they would head straight to the room.

Aaron dialed his client's number. He turned his back and crawled under his desk. Not long after, Bart could hear the gay pornographic dialogue coming out from underneath Aaron's desk.

Bart had an idea and he signaled to Jack. Jack's execution of the plan was simple and flawless. Jack grabbed his phone's handset then leaned over towards Aaron's desk and held the phone right behind Aaron's head. He then pushed the button on his phone to "intercom."

Aaron's voice could be heard throughout the entire office. Aaron was distracted for a second then regained his composure. He turned, gave Jack and Bart the finger, and then mouthed some obscenities at Jack. He then turned back around, stuck his finger in his other ear, and focused on the call. He never missed a beat but knew he would later pay the price for this commission.

Aaron's homosexual love talk over the intercom had been going on for a few minutes. Two things that were not heard over the intercom were hesitation or modesty. The whole office was in tears and literally falling to the floor, they all were laughing that hard. Even Mean Dean was coughing up a lung from laughing so hard.

Aaron described one obscene act after another. It was all man-on-man, and very explicit phone sex. Interrupted here and there with some panting from the other end of the line. Feigned satisfaction at Aaron's end. Total satisfaction from the other.

Then Strong came rushing around the corner. His face was red. The vessels on the side of his head looked like they were going to explode. He had just returned from lunch with his clients and they could hear the conversation going on. The hardwood floor shook with every step he took. "Who? What the? Get off the fucking intercom!" His screaming scared the crap out of everyone and the room fell silent, though the few still laughing stopped as fast as they could, or turned their backs so Strong could not see that they were still laughing. Everyone knew better than to be the person Strong was mad at.

Jack quickly hung up his phone and Aaron's call was silenced. Strong stopped in his tracks. He did not know whether to find out who it was or go back to his client. He chose his client as he now had to do some customer confidence rebuilding.

A minute later Aaron came up from under his desk. He received a nice round of applause. He may have been a little embarrassed, and was still a bit mad with Jack and Bart, but he never blushed. He proudly yelled out his commission and screamed "I'll take that shit to the bank any day," which drew an even greater applause.

Eventually Strong walked his client to the door, then walked straight over to Aaron, asking just one question. "Did you close the deal? Tell me you sold something."

With a crooked smile on his face he responded, "As a matter of fact I did."

Strong had a smirk on his face. "Talk about shoving bonds up someone's ass." He turned, walked off and shouted out as he turned the corner. "That's a salesman gentlemen!" He never mentioned it again during market hours. It was, however, a running joke at the Zeros from then on.

CHAPTER FOURTEEN

▼

Haynes had been building a house for over a year and it was finally finished. It was on an acre and half and not too far from downtown Houston. Since the house was on a cul-de-sac, the front yard was small relatively compared to the backyard. There was a circular driveway that surrounded a large fountain. The only thing that was not finished was the backyard. A huge patio had been installed, but nothing else. There were a few patches of grass here and there. The rest of the yard was nothing but dirt and high weeds. The trees had never been pruned either.

Even though Haynes wanted to have everyone over, his wife kept telling him that the house was not ready. "There's no pool." "I haven't finished all the decorating." It was always one reason after another.

Strong did not care what Haynes' wife said, so on his own initiative he had one of the secretaries send out invitations to everyone at the office. But Olive took it upon himself to take over the invitations. He hand delivered each one to every broker's desk. He had chosen a particularly nice invitation, too. It was a copy of Olive's Xeroxed "Little Captain." The invitations were delivered Friday morning, for a party that same night.

While this was nothing new to Catherine Haynes, she nonetheless was upset. But with a phone call here and there it was all taken care of. Food and alcohol was ordered. Maids, waiters, bartenders, and caterers were summoned to make it happen. Money always made it happen.

It was a cool evening with very little humidity that night. A rarity in Houston. Instead of staying inside, the party moved itself to the back patio. As everyone threw their cigarette butts into the dirt they went over ideas for Haynes' backyard.

Haynes was soon reminded that Aaron used to do landscaping for a living, so Aaron was summoned to join the discussion on what to do about the backyard. As he and Haynes walked around the backyard Aaron fed him one idea after another. A pool here, palm trees there. Aaron was thorough about the ideas he was proposing to Haynes. He was meticulous about where he placed plants so they would not drop leaves or flowers into the pool.

Haynes liked what he heard. However he was concerned because he could not figure out what to do with the rest of his yard. "I don't want to deal with mowing and landscaping all the way back to the fence. That's too much of a hassle, and with gardeners everywhere all of the time there will be no privacy."

Aaron jokingly responded, "You could just cement the whole damn thing if you want to."

As it turned out, Haynes loved it. "Whoa. Now that's an idea!" Haynes then decided that he wanted the rest of his backyard laid with concrete, all the way to the property line at the back.

Aaron tried to talk some sense into him. "You are kidding, right? It won't look good. No greenery, no color. It'll look like crap in fact."

"No it won't." Haynes paused for a second to think. "Maybe I just need a bigger pool."

"Then your pool will be too far from the house." Aaron stood there thinking for a moment. "But that gives me an idea. Why don't we move the deep end of the pool towards the back of the property and then have a beach-like entrance to your pool at the front." Aaron could feel that Haynes was warming up to the idea, so he went in for the final sale. "Then the water actually starts up here near the house and then slowly gets deeper for the next thirty feet or so. And you can even add a water volleyball area. It'll be like some resort."

Haynes loved the idea. "Like a beach. A beach pool. Now, that's what I'm talking about. Have you ever seen one before?"

"No. Never even heard of it either. The idea just came to me." Aaron also thought of how much money this was going to cost and who he could recommend to do the work. "You're still going to need some palm trees and colorful plants around. And it won't be cheap."

"I got money to spend. You be the point man on this and I'll buy you a Ferrari when it's all done."

"Thanks, but I already have one."

"Then you'll have two."

Strong had walked up by this time. "Two what?"

"I told Aaron I'd buy him a Ferrari when he finished my pool and he starts bitching and crying that he already has one. Can you believe him?"

"Why does he get a Ferrari? He wouldn't even be here if it wasn't for me. So I should get the Ferrari."

"I'm not buying two Ferraris. Fucking forget it. But let's do this instead. Aaron, you buy Strong a Ferrari when you get yours."

"Why do I have to buy him one?"

Cadillac Dan had approached the three by now. "Buy one what?"

Strong started the explanation. "Haynes is buying Aaron a Ferrari. So Aaron has to buy me a Ferrari. It's pretty simple actually."

Cadillac Dan picked up where they left off. "Well logic only dictates you should buy me a Ferrari then."

"Oh crap," was the first thing that came out of Strong's mouth. "Fine, but then you have to buy a Ferrari for someone."

"For who? There's no one else in on this."

Aaron immediately yelled out to Jack. "Hey dude, get over here, quick!"

Jack walked up to the group, followed closely by Bart and Olive.

Aaron picked up were they left off. "Cadillac Dan here is going to buy you a Ferrari."

"Sweeeeet!" Jack initially reacted.

Strong was quick to inform Jack that meant that he then had to buy Olive a Ferrari.

"Oh that's no good. Why do I have to buy Olive a Ferrari?"

Strong was so matter of fact in his response. "Because Olive has to buy Bart a Ferrari." Olive was not pleased about having to buy Bart a Ferrari though, and was going to say something, but then decided to let it go.

Bart was fairly happy as he looked around and found no one else outside. Bart was bobbing his head and smiling. "This worked out well for me."

Until Haynes spoke up. "Wait, so everyone here is getting a Ferrari except for me? Oh this sucks."

Aaron interrupted. "But the pool was my idea. I shouldn't have to buy a Ferrari."

"You wouldn't even be here if it wasn't for me, remember? And the party was my idea." Strong poked Aaron on his forehead.

Haynes picked up again. "This whole thing was my idea and I'm not getting one. That's not even fair. No way. Bart you're up. You are buying me a Ferrari. That's it. This circle is now complete. No more Ferraris for anyone." The entire thing seemed silly to the associates, but everyone was getting a new Ferrari, and as Bart reminded them, it all evened out in the end.

Almost two months later the pool in Haynes' backyard was complete and a week after that, seven new Ferraris were in the parking lot of HAYNES, OLIVE, GAGE & STRONG. From that night on a new practice began at the firm. Many of the partners had two or three of the same make and model of certain cars. Each time a partner wanted a new car he would choose an associate to buy it. The associates did not have a choice in the matter. They were also required to pay for it in cash. It forced the brokers to work that much harder.

Jack had been diligently reading the market for months. The product he had discussed with Strong's client was a viable way to make some easy money for everyone. For a short period of time, the prices on the bonds would be falling, making them cheaper to purchase. Investors could purchase the bonds at the current price and not take delivery of them for a few months. By then, the bond market would have turned around and the prices would increase on the bonds.

The same investors could now sell the same bonds they had ordered for purchase a couple months prior, but now at a higher price. The client, instantly, would have purchased and sold bonds without any money leaving his hands and would simply receive the profit from the transaction. The broker, of course, always received a commission.

After informing the partners of this opportunity in the market, Strong made the presentation to the trading floor for everyone to begin pushing the sales. After Strong finished, Jack stood up to speak. "We can only do this for a short period of time. This "gift" in the market will not last forever. You cannot sell these bonds for delivery past the next two or three months, max. The market will likely correct, and if it does, your clients will start losing money. A lot of money. So don't push the delivery past the next two or three months."

Strong interrupted Jack. "Shut up Jack. You don't know that."

"You're right, I don't, but—" Jack was interrupted again.

"Just shut the fuck up Jack. Get your ass on the phone. Everyone, get on the phones and sell the bonds. Shove 'em down their throats or up their ass! Make it happen!" He stormed out of the room and everyone got to work. It was, as always, business as usual. No questions asked.

Gage was an American muscle car lover, and as it turned out, Bart was as well. Bart frequently visited Gage's home and garages. Gage, Ricky Too, and Bart were always taking something apart or putting something back together again. It was not unusual for Bart to hang out at Gage's house over the weekend. He enjoyed more than just the cars at Gage's home. Beautiful women were always there, enjoying his pool and hospitality. So, it was common for Bart to call Jack and Aaron to come over to hang out, especially since Gage encouraged a select few to come and visit.

When Bart called them on this particular day it was for something a little different. Jack and Aaron arrived to see a handful of scantily clad, pretty women walking in and out of Gage's thirty-foot RV, followed closely by Bart.

Jack was first to ask. "What's the deal?"

"We're taking this baby to the beach. The bar is stocked and the women ready to party. Y'all in or what?"

Gage was standing next to the vehicle, affectionately stroking the hood to the engine. "Of course they're in. This baby is purring. Wait 'til we get her out on the open road."

Aaron shook his head. "It's an RV Gage."

Gage was excited, bouncing around as he spoke. "Think again my friend. She has an all-improved in-take system, better exhaust flow, and new brakes. Plus I installed a…"

Bart quickly interrupted him. "Whoa, cowboy, don't tell them everything. Gotta save something for the second date. They'll see."

The group piled into the RV and headed towards the Gulf of Mexico for a long Fourth of July weekend. There was no food in sight, but the RV was stocked to the brim with beer and hard liquor. It was before ten in the morning and the occupants had graduated from Bloody Marys to Mexican beer with tequila chasers.

Gage had a beer in one hand and the steering wheel in the other, cruising down the freeway. The speedometer gauge was about ten degrees over the last marker, which read eighty-five-miles-per-hour.

The RV flew on down the fast lane, passing everyone else. Gage was forced to slow down as a red Camaro driving in the fast lane failed to yield to his own faster vehicle. Gage started tailgating the Camaro and laying on the horn. As the Camaro sped up, so did Gage. There was no way for Gage to tell how fast he was going. The speedometer hand had circled all the way around back to zero. When the freeway opened up, Gage moved to the right lane to try and pass the Camaro. Everyone in the RV was laughing and egging Gage to go faster. As they passed the Camaro, Gage opened the triangular window on the driver's side. He smiled at the teenager cruising in the Camaro, stuck out his hand, and gave the driver the finger.

Only Bart knew that Gage had installed a turbo charger on his RV. Gage had also installed nitrous for that extra kick. As Gage was about to use the nitrous he noticed a police car in the shade underneath an overpass.

For the Texas State Trooper using his radar gun, it must have been a sight to see. A thirty-foot RV flying down the freeway, and passing a Camaro.

The officer clocked Gage at 111-miles-per-hour. Gage and the teenager both slowed down and watched for the officer in their mirrors. It was probably disbelief that caused the officer to hesitate before he finally turned on his siren and lights and pulled onto the freeway.

The officer caught up to them where they all had pulled over. He then walked up to the Camaro and calmly looked in. The kid inside did not move an inch, and the officer knew he wouldn't. He then walked towards the motor home.

Gage opened the door to allow the trooper to walk in. Gage was very calm as he said, "What seems to be the problem officer?"

The officer slowly responded as he looked at all the empty beer bottles on the RV's kitchen counter. He responded in a voice only a Texas State Trooper could. "What seems to be the problem? You seem to be the problem. You're speeding, and it appears you've been drinking, too."

"No sir, not me." Gage pointed to the others in the back. "They've been drinking. There's no law against that is there?"

The trooper looked at the girls in their small bikinis before scanning the rest of the RV. He took a few steps inside and picked up one of the empty beer bottles. Bart chimed in at this point, "If you want a cold one, they're in the icebox. Don't be shy." No one expected that from Bart. Even Gage's eyes got big.

The trooper turned and looked. Bart stood there with a pleased look on his face. The trooper lowered his head and shook it. "Son of a bitch." He finally looked back up. "Damn it Bart. What're you doin' here?"

"Just heading to the beach. What are you doing here Trooper Lee?"

"You maniacs are tearing up my freeway at over 111mph, that's what I'm doing here."

"One hundred and eleven? Impossible. Even if we were, are you really going to write us a ticket? Are you really going to go into a courtroom and tell a judge that a thirty-foot RV was going a hundred and eleven miles an hour down a freeway? Racing a Camaro?"

"You were racing the Camaro?"

"No. I'm just saying."

"Damn it Bart, save it." The trooper was agitated but definitely amused. "How's your granddad doing by the way? We sure do miss him."

"Oh he's good. I'm sure he's wondering when you're going to retire and go sit with him on his porch."

Their conversation ended as quickly as it started. Trooper Lee, a good friend of the family, just let it go. All the punishment they would get was a little warning joke from the trooper. "I'm going to tell your granddad on you Bart."

The RV drove off on its way. When Lee saw the frightened look on the kid's face in the Camaro, he couldn't help but laugh. He leaned up to the window and suddenly smelled the odor. He let the kid go, too. He figured the kid urinating on himself, and on cloth seats, was punishment enough.

Although it was technically owned by Haynes, the firm had a beach house near Galveston, Texas. The two-story home stood on stilts to protect it from storm surges. Of course, it had all the toys a grown man could want or need: mini dune buggies, all-terrain vehicles, dirt bikes, and jet skis. Inside, there was a pool table, foosball table, and large TVs in every room. There were several bedrooms, each with its own full bathroom.

Other brokers from the firm came and went as the holiday weekend passed. Olive showed up Friday night, partying hard with a few girls. In the mix of everything Olive convinced Aaron, Jack, and a couple of the girls to take off in Gage's RV. Bart rushed to the motor home when he saw his two best friends getting in.

Gage's RV was still a roaming party. The booze was abundant as they took off into the night, heading south, and before anyone in the RV realized, they had passed over the border into Mexico. The drunken reactions were all the same. "Woo hoo! *Andale! Andale!*"

What happened next was a mystery to everyone except to Olive. A full night of drinking soon caught up to everyone in the back, and they all had passed out after their little orgy. Focused on the road, Olive though kept driving.

Yelling and commotion woke Bart up. About the time he realized something was wrong, Aaron and Jack were up as well. Before they had fully opened their eyes, men in police uniforms were inside the motor home yelling at everyone in the back. It was the Mexican police, screaming and yelling, "*Arriba, arriba! Get up gringos!*" They were banging on the door with heavy clubs in one hand and pointing their guns at them with the other.

The police hauled them all outside where they saw Olive, in handcuffs, leaning against a police car. Before they could catch their breaths, they too were handcuffed and pushed towards the police car. The girls were crying and were placed in the back of an old van.

Bart yelled some questions at Olive, trying to figure out what was going on. Olive did not respond at first. He just looked at them with a blank stare. He finally growled out, "I'll get you out of this, just don't tell them anything."

Bart was confused and angry. "Don't tell them anything about what? What the hell is going on? I go to sleep everything is cool. I wake up and I'm in handcuffs. What the fuck have you gotten us into?"

Jack was in a total state of shock. He could not say a word and was staring at the ground. He appeared to be catatonic.

Aaron took it all in better. He viewed the whole thing as a big adventure. "*Hola,*" was all he said to anyone who walked by. He eventually learned some of the policemen's names. "*Hola, Tito! Hola, Juan!* My *nombre* is Aaron." For some reason he was getting a kick out of it all. But not for long.

As they were being shoved into the back of the police van they all saw what the problem was. The police had opened the hatches underneath the RV and were removing one bag of leafy substance after another. It was then that Aaron sobered up and realized that they were in deep shit.

The four of them had been crammed into a small Mexican jail cell with no windows. It was very hot in the cell, too. No one even thought about what had happened to the girls that had come along, but assumed they were in their own cell. They were not offered any food or water either. There was a small toilet in the corner. It was next to a little hole in the wall. Rats ran in and out of the hole all morning long. Jack thought he was going to be sick.

Over the course of the weekend, there was no real communication between them and the police. Olive was the only one who spoke any Spanish, and what he did know was not that much. Sometimes Olive and the guards would be talking. Sometimes they were yelling.

Bart wondered who he would have to call to get them out of this mess, then wondered how long it would take for his family to disown him. Bart never settled down. When Olive was not talking or yelling with the guards, Bart was constantly yelling at Olive. He inwardly yelled at himself, too. He was angry and scared at the same time.

The quarrelling between Bart and Olive had one benefit. Jack was so preoccupied trying to keep the two of them apart he had not really thought about himself or how he would get out of this mess. Jack had to separate the two men more than once. Olive made the mistake of trying to push Bart out of the way so he could sit where it was cooler. Bart put Olive in a headlock. The second time, Bart put Olive on the floor with his arm twisted behind his back. It was more than obvious that Bart had had enough of Olive. And it was obvious that Bart had not forgotten the Vegas incident. The third time Olive came after Bart, Olive got a broken nose out of it. That was the last time Olive physically accosted Bart, let alone looked at him. Olive also would not forget the fact that Bart had broken his nose, ruining his face.

On Monday morning, after speaking to one of the guards for a while, Olive was let out of the jail cell. He was allowed to make one phone call. That phone call was directly to the firm. One of the new secretaries answered. Olive calmly asked to speak to Cadillac Dan, and in his office. Once Dan was on the line Olive told him basically what was going on. Cadillac Dan quickly called the partners into his office and closed the door. Gage put the phone on speaker as he answered. "Hello."

"I need some help, Gage. I'm in a Mexican jail with some of the boys."

"What the hell are you doing there? Why are—" was all Gage could get out before he was interrupted by Olive.

"Don't worry. I have it all worked out, but I need you guys to come down here to get us."

Haynes broke in. "What do you mean you have it all worked out? Why are you in there in the first place?"

Gage then asked, "Do you have my RV, Olive?"

"Yea I have it down here. Well, I guess the police have it now. But I can get it back, too. Is Manikan still there?"

"I'm here. What the hell do you need me for?"

"I need three of your Cadillacs when you come down."

"I'm not going down there. And why do you need my Cadillacs? Get your own damn Cadillacs. You have some."

"Yea I do. And what are you going to tell my wife when you go to my house to get them? It's not like I can run out and buy a few of them right now. No one has time to. The deal I cut won't be on the table for long. I need three Cadillacs and twenty-thousand bucks in the trunk of each one. And they have to be here by midnight. I have that much in my safe at home, so I'll pay you back."

"What the hell? Is this a bribe? Do I get my motor home back? I put a lot of work into that thing. Why isn't the cash enough? Why do they want the cars?"

Olive was stressed out as it was and all these questions were starting to piss him off. "It's just part of the deal, okay, so get your asses down here or I'm fucked! And the boys will be, too."

Olive managed to tell them where they were before he was forced to get off the phone. In a jail just across the Mexican border in a town near Matamoros, Mexican justice could have been much harsher. This was a town where no one wanted to know anything and the police made almost no money, so there was a different kind of "justice."

Gage, Haynes, and Manikan drove down in three of Cadillac Dan's cars. Crossing the border into Mexico was not a problem with bags of cash. The problem was going to be getting back into the United States with bags of drugs.

The three arrived with plenty of time to spare. Except for the three officers who had arrested everyone in the RV, no one else knew they were there. The sixty-thousand dollars bought everyone's freedom. The three Cadillacs had bought the release of the stash of marijuana Olive had picked up.

"Are you crazy?" Gage responded when he found out what the cars had bought.

"You don't understand, I have to get this to someone in Houston."

"Not in my RV you don't. Especially with us in it. I suggest you dump the drugs and get your ass safely home."

"Not an option," Olive grunted.

"What the hell does that mean?" Haynes glared at Olive.

"Nothing. Besides, one of these amigos is going to escort me across the border. I just need enough cash to buy a piece-of-shit car and I'll take it across the border by myself."

"Do whatever dude, but we are not a part of this. You need to rethink your options," Gage said as he opened the door to his RV.

For an extra five-hundred dollar "tip", Olive bought the freedom of the girls and an old pickup truck for himself from the police. It was a truck that had been confiscated from some other drug trafficker. Probably just another mule, though one who didn't have the money to bribe his way out a mess.

The pickup had a false compartment below the entire bed of the truck. Olive hid the bags of drugs and started driving. He was escorted on a back dirt road in an area where there were no checkpoints. The dirt road took him into Texas and eventually led him to a state highway.

Olive arrived in Houston just before daybreak Tuesday morning. He made his delivery with enough time to shower and change into a suit before the market opened. He walked into the office with all the other employees, jumped on the phone and began pitching bonds. To those who were unaware of the weekend fiasco, it appeared to be just another day at the office, other than Olive's where Bart had broken his nose. Most assumed it was just another wild party that got out of hand. They often did.

After the incident in Mexico, the next few weeks were tough on Jack, Aaron, and Bart. No one else at the firm new about it, nor was anyone who did know about it allowed to speak of it. For someone like Bart, whose family included generations of law enforcement, being behind bars was a wake-up call. Bart's rigid moral code began to eat away at him. He was the type who helped little old ladies cross the street, always threw his trash in a dispenser, and always looked out for the little guy. Bart had no tolerance for criminals or others who broke the law. He especially had no more tolerance for Olive. Every time Bart looked at Olive all he wanted to do was rip his face off.

This tension kept growing and soon led to a few arguments between Bart and Strong about how Bart behaved towards Olive. Bart's conflicts with Olive were growing by the day. It was Haynes and Gage who had the cooler heads. It was also Haynes and Gage who continued to protect Bart's job. Haynes hoped Bart would eventually let go of his anger about what happened in Mexico. More importantly to them, Bart was a big producer now and the partners liked all that money, even Olive.

CHAPTER FIFTEEN

▼

Lately, Bart had begun to let Jack look at his clients' portfolios. Jack advised Bart as to what particular bonds he should buy and sell within the portfolios. Bart's business started to evolve as Jack helped Bart pick specific products for his clientele. Instead of selling whatever was on the chalkboard or pushed by the firm, he became particular about the investments for his clients.

During this particular week, the market was thin and there was not a lot of variety of product to sell. Mean Dean had been on Bart's ass because he was not making a lot of calls. Alex and Strong gave him lip for not selling what was listed on the boards. Even Haynes had to talk to him a few times.

But Bart would not sell just anything to his clients if Jack told him a listed product was not a good investment for his clients. Bart represented almost exclusively governmental entities. These clients were also family friends, and friends of friends. Bart was not going to risk their money, their jobs, or the people they represented, just to make a few dollars.

The partners did not realize that Bart was getting advice from Jack. All they knew was that Bart was not selling and that he also was not listening to them. The friction was obvious. Finally, even Haynes and Gage said he would be fired if he did not sell what they told him to sell.

Bart eventually sold some product to one of his clients. As he got off the phone and yelled to Alex, he found out that Olive had just sold the same bonds moments before, but had neglected to erase them off the board.

Bart wanted to call his client to inform him the bonds had already been traded. However, Alex stopped him. "Let me see if I can find some more of those bonds. Give me about thirty minutes."

When the thirty minutes came and went, Alex informed Bart he could not find any. "I did find some that are pretty close though. The price is the same, but the interest rate is little lower. Do you want to call and ask if

133

they'll take the bonds?" Bart didn't like the idea. "It's not a good deal for my client."

Olive, however, was looking for a fight. "No. Bart will just drop the bonds into their account. They'll never know the difference. They don't need to know."

Bart objected. "Absolutely not. Those are tax dollars and I'm going to be straight up with my clients."

Olive yelled over to Alex. "Do it. You have their delivery instructions already. Just do it or it's your ass, too!"

There was little Bart could do. Alex followed Olive's orders and wired the trade. Alex then tried to calm Bart down and reminded him of the commission he had just made. It didn't work. Bart pushed Alex out of his way as he headed back to his own desk.

Olive started in on Bart some more. "Quit your damn whining you big crybaby."

It was not long before they both were red-faced and yelling at each other, again. The two were cussing and screaming in each other's faces. Although everyone on the trading floor was watching, they were all on the phones pitching bonds as if nothing was going on.

It was obvious to those who knew the pair's history that it was not the trade that was the real reason or the real problem. It was the pure animosity Bart felt towards Olive, and had seriously begun after the trip to Vegas and the incident with Floyd. By now the entire floor knew what had happened. The fight between the two was about to get physical, and Bart probably would have been fired this time, but it quickly stopped since Fast Eddie was cussing louder than he ever had before. Everyone's attention immediately turned to Fast Eddie. He was frantic, screaming and yelling, "Fucking motherfucker! I'm fucked. It's fucking over. Fuck! Fuck me! Fuck him! I'm done in this business!"

Fast Eddie had been in the business long enough to know how to play the game. He sounded Caucasian when he needed to and black when he did not. On the phone he could be anyone. Face-to-face was another thing. One of the benefits of working on the phone was that brokers rarely met their clients. For a black man working in an industry run by white men it was perfect. Now one of his biggest clients wanted to meet him. Face-to-face. New Orleans was the host city for the next banker's convention scheduled for the upcoming weekend.

Eddie's client was a bank in the south. A banker from Mississippi. A banker from a state that had yet to even ratify the Thirteenth Amendment to the United States Constitution. Eddie was running from one end of the trading floor to the other in a frenzy. "The fucking guy made me commit.

Fucking said he wouldn't do any more business. That I fucking had to fucking be there." Eddie only stopped cussing for a moment when he noticed a dirty spot on one of his shoes. "Fuck." Off the phone, Eddie could never stop dropping "F" bombs. Especially when he was excited or angry. And, as it turned out, this client especially enjoyed Fast Eddie's racist jokes.

The firm was already prepared for the convention. As usual, weeks in advance, Gage had rented an extravagant suite in the hotel where the convention was located. He also spent thousands of dollars catering food and stocking the room with liquor.

Cadillac Dan would also be speaking at this convention. This time the firm also tapped Jack to speak as well. Jack's ideas on manipulating and segregating the different bonds were a unique marketing tool for the firm, and the partners knew that the bankers would eat it up.

Jack's presentation convinced many of the bankers to head up to Gage's suite in order to learn more. Jack pitched his ideas and bonds and the partners pitched the firm. Surprisingly, the banks that Jack had rejected for his new ideas were the first to show up to Gage's suite. Either their ego did not like being told "no," or they respected someone who cared enough about them to tell them "no." Either way, Jack made friends and the firm made money.

Fast Eddie had managed to avoid going to any of the previous conventions, and until now, the partners had let it go. They knew it was best if he stayed behind and only did business over the phone. But now he was forced to go, otherwise he'd lose his biggest client, and thus might get fired. So he did not want to go to this one either because he was afraid he would run into one of his racist clients. He knew mostly what went on at these conventions, but not all of it. But it did not take long for him to be reminded how the firm played on everyone's sinful indulgences.

For the moment he was acting like his usual, easy-going self. "I will never miss another one of these. Are you fucking kidding me? Look at her ass! Oh, you can count on my natural black ass being at the next one. Who wants to make me another gin and tonic?"

Aaron interrupted Eddie's excitement. "There's a guy at the far end of the bar who was asking about you."

Eddie's anxiety immediately returned. "Are you sure? Did he specifically ask for Edward McClendon? What did you say?"

Before Aaron could reply one of the girls sidled up to him and gave him "the look," so he only was able to blurt out, as he was leaving with her, "Relax, you'll be fine. Trust me." And at that, Aaron winked at Fast Eddie and was soon walking away.

Eddie slowly made his way through the crowd. He could feel the sweat running down his back. There was only one man standing at the end of the bar. A man wearing black dress pants with a white coat that matched his white beard. He whispered under his breath, "Fuck me. Look at this Colonel Sanders-looking motherfucker."

As he walked towards the bar, the bartender yelled out, "Hey Eddie, you ready for another gin and tonic?" Upon hearing this, the man in the white coat looked at Eddie, and then walked directly towards the exit. Eddie stopped in his tracks. He did not even attempt to follow him out the door. He just watched him leave. His view of, what he thought was his departing client was blocked by another man walking towards him. With a total look of confusion the man uttered, "You're Edward McClendon?"

The same confused look reflected off of Eddie's face. "Yes, and you are?"

The other man retorted rather quickly. "I'm the only other black man in this room."

Fast Eddie immediately recognized the voice. They both stood there for a moment, not saying a word. Neither knew what to say anyway.

Eddie's client then spoke up. "I initially came here to fire your ass. I just wanted to see the look on your face when you realized you were telling all of those racist jokes to a black man. Now I find myself trying to figure you out. Wondering why I should continue doing business with someone like you."

Eddie was swift to respond. "You know exactly why. We are both black men trying to make it in a white man's world. I did what I did to get where I am. And so did you. So here we are, face-to-face. Are you really going to fire me and give your money to some honky you've never even met?"

After a bit of a somewhat heated discussion, they both settled down, and began to talk and learn about each other. After all was said and done, and after a few more drinks, a handshake sealed their business friendship.

For Fast Eddie, meeting this client turned out to be the best thing for him. The client had a lot of other friends in powerful places. He referred all of them to Fast Eddie. Eddie's business nearly doubled within the next few weeks. The best part for Fast Eddie was that from then on he did not have to degrade himself, or any minority, in order to keep their business. Really caring about the future of his clients for the first time, Fast Eddie asked Jack for advice in managing their portfolios.

As the weeks passed, Bart's relationship with Olive never smoothed over, but the explosive arguments died down. Bart's relationship, though, with the other partners improved because of the money Bart was making, but mostly because of Gage. Gage and Bart spent a great deal of time in his garage working on cars, and they had formed a special kinship with one another. They became more than just boss and employee.

Bart had been working on a potential client for some time. There was a particular banker near Gatesville, Texas who Bart had been calling on for months, but he was getting nowhere with this man.

Part of the problem was that the guy was never at the office. He was actually a rancher who started his own bank when oil was discovered on his land. Horses were his passion, and running cattle on his five-thousand-acre ranch was his profession. The bank was just his hobby that was fueled by oil. Mr. Wes Cooper was his name and being a cowboy was his game.

Bart eventually learned, after a great many phone calls to Mr. Cooper, that he only worked at the bank for a few hours, two days a week. The rest of the time he tended to his ranch.

Mr. Cooper's CATTLEMEN'S BANK OF THE SOUTHWEST was quite successful. All of the ranchers and nearby farmers pushed their cattle funds and their oil money through his bank. In the middle of nowhere, sat a small bank stocked with tens of millions of dollars in assets. Bart had spoken with Mr. Cooper numerous times, but the talk was rarely about bonds. It was usually about his horses or his cattle.

One day he told Bart about how he had to deliver a calf. Another day he shared that his horse lost a shoe. Bart learned that Mr. Cooper had grown up in Texas, and as a young man, drove cattle through Nebraska into Montana. Afterwards, at the end of the season, he would ride the train to Tucson, Arizona before coming home. It was one of his favorite places to visit. Bart found all of the man's stories fascinating.

Bart's favorite story though was the time Mr. Cooper rode his horse to the bank, tying it up under a tree outside, like the bank was a saloon. He stopped doing it one summer when it got too hot one day, so he brought his horse inside the air-conditioned bank. When he walked his horse, Chief, through the lobby doors, all of the women made such a fuss that he decided it was best to just leave Chief at the ranch from then on.

Yet Bart had never made a sale with this banker. In fact, no one had. Bart felt he was building a relationship that would eventually give him the business he desired. One time, while visiting for a bit on the phone, Bart started in on his pitch.

Mr. Cooper interrupted in his strong Texas twang. "Bart, you seem like a nice fella, but I don't understand what a city slicker wants with my little bank. We're just country folk 'round here. All I really care about is my land and my stock."

Bart tried to calm his concerns. "You don't have to Mr. Cooper. All you need to know is that I want to help your bank grow with the right investments. Trust is earned, and if you give me the opportunity, you'll not be disappointed."

"I like you Bart, always have. But I just don't see a need for my bank to grow. I don't need any more money. And I don't need any headaches either. I get these calls all the time, but I don't want any bonds. I don't quite understand them, and don't really want to either. Plus, I got all these damn committees that want to approve everything I do."

Bart thought he had a way in. "Now, I know you don't have to run everything by a committee. It's your bank. You telling me you can't do what you want in your own bank?"

"That's a very good try son. But you're talking to a good ol' boy who's played that card once or twice himself. Please accept my apologies Bart. I shouldn't have wasted all your time. But if you're ever in town, stop by and see me and maybe we can go out riding. The best of luck to you, son."

The phone went dead before Bart had a chance to respond. Bart wanted this account. He wanted the account because he really liked Mr. Cooper. He was a man who shot from the hip and always said what he thought. And Mr. Cooper reminded Bart of his own granddad, which only made Bart want to help him earn even more money. Bart also wanted the account because it was virgin territory. The bank had a lot of money and not a single bond in its portfolio.

After lunch, Gage noticed the gloomy attitude Bart carried on his shoulders. "What's up, Fart?"

"Oh man, I just got shut down on an account I really thought I had."

"And? What's new? You haven't learned that's part of this business yet?"

"It's not that. I guess I just really wanted his business."

"Let's go to my office and you can tell me the story."

Bart started to explain this potential client. "This guy reminds me of my granddad in so many ways. And I feel close to him. My granddad has a small ranch outside of town and I used to keep a horse he gave me for my tenth birthday there. I used to spend almost all my weekends there." Bart then continued to explain the bank's assets.

Gage thought for a moment after Bart finished. "Well, did he give you a reason why he wouldn't trade with you? Was his brother-in-law a broker or something?"

"No, he just said that we were city and he was country. We are talking about a man who likes to ride his horse to the bank for God's sake."

"Wow." Gage thought for a bit longer. A little smile soon appeared on his face. "Will he be there tomorrow?"

"In the afternoon. Why?"

"For sure in the afternoon?"

"Certain. Why?"

"How long a drive you think it is to his town?"

"About four hours. Why?" A curious look was on Bart's face.

"Just meet me at my house at six in the morning, sharp. Don't be late or I'm not doing it. Better yet, make it five instead."

"Doing what?" Bart questioned.

Gage just smiled even more as he stood up from his desk. "Time to get back to the phones." Bart started to walk out of the office as Gage said one more thing. "And Bart, dress like you're going to the Houston Live Stock Show and Rodeo tomorrow."

Five in the morning came quick. Five was especially early when the Zeros did not end until after midnight. Bart left after the poker games took all of his cash. He showed up at Gage's house a few minutes before 5 a.m. Even though they had become friends, there was always a line between a partner and any associate, so Bart knew that there was no room for tardiness.

Bart did not know what to expect. He jumped out of his brand new jacked-up four-by-four pickup. Bart was dressed in starched jeans, a starched button down white shirt, custom-made boots, and a slightly worn Stetson cowboy hat. Gage walked up to him dressed in a solid black cowboy getup.

Gage waved at him. "Come around back with me Bart. I need your help loading the horses."

"Loading the horses?" was all Bart could say.

"Did you bring a change of clothes Bart? I thought about driving back tonight, but I think it would be too much for the horses. Plus, we can get in a few extra hours with your cowboy."

"I can always buy some clothes on the way. So what's the plan? We gonna put a noose around his neck and drag him behind a horse until he buys something?" Bart asked sarcastically.

Gage smirked, "Only if we have to. I don't think it really matters what we do. You've not been getting his business, so we have nothing to lose but a day on the phones. But I bet you a thousand bucks he invites us to spend the night at his home."

Bart shook his hand. "You're on cowboy."

It was not long before the horses were loaded into the trailer and they were heading out. Gage's big four-by-four dually towed a trailer with tack and three of his favorite horses. For once he drove carefully, and slowly. "Can't be causing my favorite filly any stress," he said with a smile.

After hours of driving, they reached Mr. Cooper's little town outside of Gatesville. Pickups, horse trailers, and cowboy hats were the norm.

Gage and Bart set up shop at a hotel at the edge of town but within sight of the bank. The hotel was established in the early 1800s along a western trail. The caretakers of the hotel intentionally kept the same look as when trail riders stayed the night before heading west. Around the back of the hotel was a large shady area suited perfectly to tie up the horses, and there was a small stable as well. The hotel even had livestock handlers who provided care and feed for the animals. The front of the hotel had a small restaurant that advertised the best chicken-fried steak in Texas. Gage and Bart staked out the bank until they saw Mr. Cooper arrive.

Bart casually asked Gage, "What's the plan?"

"He likes to ride, we'll take him for a ride. Just follow my lead."

Before Bart knew it, they were saddled up and riding down the street. Gage didn't hesitate a moment as they strolled to the bank's entrance. He didn't bother to get off his horse as he opened the door to the bank and motioned for Bart to head on in, both still on horseback. Gage followed, leading the third horse, which was harnessed to a rope.

Bart sat on his horse, inside the middle of the bank's lobby, feeling quite stupid, but trying not to show it. Everyone who was inside the bank, and a few outside, had stopped what they were doing as they all stared at Bart and Gage.

Gage rode up to the teller's window and said that they were looking for Mr. Cooper.

One older woman finally spoke up in a broken voice. "Who should I tell him is calling?"

Gage looked back at Bart to answer her question.

Bart spoke up in his own Texas twang, "Tell him we're here to run some cattle up to Montana."

It was clear from the teller's call to his office that Mr. Cooper had no idea what was going on. The teller put down the phone and said ever so calmly, "He said it's too late in the season."

Without any hesitation in his voice Bart sprang right back, "If you would, in that case, please tell him we'll just have to take the train straight to Tucson."

A moment later a door to an office opened so fast and hard that the doorknob slammed a hole in the wall. It made such a loud noise that Bart's horse was spooked. Mr. Cooper appeared and saw the commotion. Two cowboys. On horseback. Inside his bank.

Bart settled his horse and looked down at him. "You told me that if I was ever in town we'd go riding! Well, here we are."

A big smile came over the old cowboy's face. "Well I'll be. Now that's a sales call if I ever saw one." Mr. Cooper went back to his office to grab his hat, strolled over to the third horse, checked it out, gave a nod to Gage, mounted, and then was ready to go.

All three started to take off until Mr. Cooper yelled out, "Wait, wait!" He turned to one of his tellers. "Give me all the money in your cash drawer, and make it fast!" The teller, with a smile on her face, grabbed some cash, threw it into a bag and tossed it to him. Mr. Cooper waved his hat as they rode out of the bank. "Damn, I've always wanted to do that!"

Bart and Gage spent the rest of the day riding around Mr. Cooper's ranch. The three talked about horses and cattle drives. The next morning Gage stayed at the house while Bart helped Mr. Cooper herd some of his cattle. As it turned out, Cooper did invite both Bart and Gage to stay with him at his ten-thousand-square-foot "log cabin."

They played cards and drank whisky all night. There was never any mention of any bonds or his bank. Bart wanted to, but Gage would not let him. Later, as they were heading off to bed, Gage told him why. "You are not here to sell bonds. You are here to sell yourself. Business follows pleasure. Trust me on this one."

Sure enough, before Gage and Bart packed up to leave the next evening, Mr. Cooper said those magic words. "Bart, why don't you call me on Monday and maybe we can make a little bit of money together."

On the road back to Houston Gage reminded Bart of their wager. "You owe me a thousand dollars."

"Can I write you a check?"

Gage responded without hesitation. "I know our money says 'In God we Trust'. So heathens pay cash."

CHAPTER SIXTEEN

▼

The partners had learned early on that Jack was astute when it came to finance and economics. He was perceptive to the fluctuations in the bond market. He was insightful about what the bonds would do. He also enjoyed looking at the history of the stock and bond markets. It made him proficient and profitable, something the partners appreciated, and what had kept Jack from getting fired the first months after he was hired.

The firm, however, was more interested in chasing commissions than it was in managing portfolios. Most everyone at the firm though ignored Jack if it would prevent them from making any money.

Cadillac Dan had received a disturbing phone call one morning from one of his clients. After talking softly on the phone for a bit he placed the caller on hold. "Hey Strong, a friend of mine, Rod Ross, the president of Tri-County State Bank, just committed suicide two days ago. The bank couldn't afford those bonds I sold him for forward delivery a few months ago. I guess Jack was right about the market."

Strong was initially inquisitive. "What do you mean?"

"The new president just told me their potential loss is so great it could close the bank down if they don't get help from somewhere. What should I tell him?"

Strong paused for a moment then spoke without hesitation. "Tell him tough luck. Tell him you warned the old president. Better yet, tell the new president that Mr. Rod Ross purchased five-hundred-thousand Ginnie Mays three days ago and he needs to take delivery of them now before the Feds shut his bank down permanently. Charge them five percent on your commission. He'll never know."

Cadillac Dan liked the idea and made the new president purchase the five-hundred-thousand dollars worth of bonds. It was not like Dan was in trouble, or his company was going to fail. All he was interested in was getting the commission, and to hell with the other guy.

At the following Monday morning sales meeting most everyone strolled in half asleep at 7:25 a.m., their usual time of arrival. Jack and Aaron were still there from the night before however. Smelly, half drunk, drinking plenty of coffee, but ready to make their calls. Strong and Alex were up front starting the show. Alex went through his list of bonds and stated the prices, yields, and spread so the brokers would know how much profit could be made.

Strong took over, but only for an introduction to the next topic at hand. "I have asked Jack to find a way to help those of you whose clients are losing money and feeling screwed, by us, on the bonds you sold them months ago for current delivery. And everyone listen up because I think we can all make some money on this one, too."

Jack walked to the front of the room, next to Strong and Alex. "I know many of us have been selling Ginnie May's since March for forward delivery in the next couple of months—which is way beyond the time I said you could do this. The way it *should* have worked was that your bank would buy a few million for forward delivery, but only for a couple of months. Many of you tried to take advantage of the situation and have sold twenty-million Ginnie Mays for six and eight months forward delivery to clients with only ten-million in assets. Your clients can't possibly pay for the bonds now. And many of them won't be around much longer if you don't do something."

Cadillac Dan laughed as he broke into Jack's presentation. "They won't be around much longer in more ways than one."

Jack continued, ignoring Dan's comment and Strong's smirk. "As I was saying, I've figured out a way for your customers to reduce their loss to something they can manage. Tell your clients to stand by on the delivery of their bonds for a couple of more months. Simultaneously, we'll pull in another investor to take the bonds in a special account. For reasons greater than you can imagine, this will make the investor a hefty profit when he trades out of the bonds and they are delivered to your client."

Olive stood up for a brief moment and spoke. "I have investors to put enough money into the accounts for everyone here, so don't worry about that."

Jack looked towards Olive. "You have investors? Maybe I should talk to them first."

Olive was stern in his response. "I said I have investors. Don't worry about it. You're just a shitty little associate with a few more brain cells than the others. So don't act like you can just talk to my clients whenever you please. Now continue."

Jack responded. "Do your investors know this is a one-time deal? You can't do this forever with them either, or they'll lose money, too."

Olive was not pleased. "You are like an insubordinate little brat sometimes. I said I have it covered. Now get on with the show."

Jack turned his attention back to the trading floor. "In essence, after this whole transaction goes down, if the market corrects sufficiently, in theory, your clients will not lose as much money. And if the market spikes enough, then they won't lose anything. Likely though, they will still take it on the chin for about ten-thousand dollars for every million in bonds they purchased."

Strong spoke up. "We're calling this the Standby/Takeout. Now tell them the best part Jack."

"I presume you mean the commission? It's three points. I called it the Standby/Takeout because your clients are standing by on delivery of the bonds, and the investor is then taking them out of the bonds." Jack continued to explain the intricacies of the deal. He kept talking for the next few minutes but failed to notice the glassy eyes staring back at him.

After Jack was finished the room was silent for a moment, until Bart asked a question. "Jack, I have no idea what you are talking about. Looking around, I think I speak for all of us. Just what are you talking about?"

Jack paused to think how to best explain how it all worked. "Let's see," he said as he took a moment to think. "The most important thing to know is that everyone has got to stop selling new bonds for forward delivery. If you don't it will crush your clients and kill Olive's investors. Everyone will lose, and lose big."

Jack was immediately interrupted by Strong. "Bullshit. Everyone keep selling everything. Sell both deals. Put them in one then put them in the other. If you don't understand, get the fuck out of here. Now get on the phones and sell. Shove it down their throats or up their asses. Whatever is bigger!"

Strong then paused and looked around the room. "If you can't keep up, we don't need you. Let's go people, get to work! Let's make some money!" He pulled out a wad of cash and smelled it. "Ah, I love the smell of success."

Even though they had no idea what they were selling, everyone on the trading floor starting making the calls. Strong nodded his head to Jack. It was a nod that meant he better get on the phone right away, no questions asked.

Jack walked by Bart's desk. "Don't worry about it. Your clients are government entities and they didn't buy any bonds for forward delivery. This deal isn't for your clients."

Mean Dean then interrupted them and said to Jack, "Get your ass on the phone you little homo. That's not your call anyway. Who do you think you are?" He then looked at Bart. "You too, Bart the Fart. Get your ass on the phone. And don't listen to Jack." Jack just winked at Bart. Jack had said enough so Bart knew that he didn't need to sell Jack's idea to his clients.

Gage, as always, was the first to start making sales. In addition to somehow making one of his banks buy Jack's idea, he had sold ten-million bonds. "I just sold those airports at 96 with a seven-and-half-percent yield."

Alex turned and looked at the board where they were listed. "What? They're trading at 94 with an eight-and-quarter-percent yield. What are you doing?"

"Hell if I know. But I made an extra two points on my commission. What is that, an extra 200K for nothing? That guy is an asshole anyway." The whole trading floor starting cheering Gage on, so no one heard what Gage had said under his breath. "Screw him. He foreclosed on my daddy's farm."

As the weeks rolled by, Jack's idea was making the firm a lot of money. Unbeknownst to anyone though it started a series of events that eventually led to Bart's departure from the firm.

The Standby/Takeout caused a lot of friction between Bart and the partners. Bart refused to sell bonds for forward delivery because his clients did not need the Standby/Takeout. And since Bart did not represent any clients who needed the Standby/Takeout he did not feel the need to drag them into what he saw was a potential problem. It took a few explanations from Jack, but Bart finally got the basics of how it all worked.

The Standby/Takeout also caused friction between the partners and Jack. The trouble was not because of Bart, but because Jack was not selling the Standby/Takeout either. Alex realized this first and told the other partners. Cadillac Dan and Strong gave Jack the most trouble about it. "Sell your product! What's your problem?" And they were not so cordial about it either.

At first, Jack got away with it since his response was usually accepted. "I already pulled my guys out of those bonds and I never put them back into them. I don't need it, but your clients do. And I'm saving your ass, not mine. I only came up with this idea to save the firm's reputation and to keep everyone's clients from falling into bankruptcy. I told you a long time ago that the market might change and that this could happen."

It was not so easy for Bart. Bart did not have Jack's knowledge of the market and only knew a little about how it all worked. No one in the office really knew how it worked and dared not ask. They just did what they were told.

Olive was constantly riding Bart about this. "Make your clients buy the bonds for forward delivery. Then do the Standby/Takeout. You'll get commissions on all of it. What's your problem? Sell the damn bonds. It's the easiest sale you'll ever make. There's no risk."

Bart was always tense when he had to respond to Olive's threats. "I have government clients. Those are tax dollars that pay for parks, firemen's salaries, and pensions. I can't, and I won't, risk their money like that."

Bart's working environment steadily disintegrated. The incidents with Olive began to flare up again and were becoming more frequent. Haynes or Gage usually interceded before things got out of hand. Olive was on the cusp of firing Bart but Gage was there to stop Olive from doing so.

Whenever Gage or Haynes backed Bart up Olive would then just verbally berate Bart. "Who the hell do you think you are, some spokesman for the county or local union? Maybe you should be working for the government. Just like the rest of your stupid fuckin' family."

It was another busy Monday morning a week later. Haynes was out of the office, telling everyone that he was looking at land in Florida. Gage was in his office getting ready to head out to lunch when Olive and Bart had begun yelling at each other. Gage picked up his phone and called Olive's extension down on the floor.

"What's up Gage?"

"Oh, nothing. Just wondering what all the racket is about."

"Nothing. Just The Fart not doing his job. No need for you to get involved. I can handle it. You don't need to know what's going on anyway."

"Olive, I am the all-knowing, powerful god brought forth to make your life miserable." Gage sighed. "Enough already. We'll talk about this when I get back from lunch."

Olive hung up the phone without responding, said a few choice words about Gage, then turned his attention back to Bart, who was just trying to stay out of Olive's way. Thank goodness it was lunch, so he and a few others quickly left before Olive could start in on Bart all over again.

Lunch was taking longer than usual, and Bart was feeling nervous. "We need to get back. You know Olive is just waiting for any reason to fire my ass." Floyd replied, still only midway through his lunch. "Relax. He's just blowing off again. Being his usual asshole self. You're fine." But Bart was insistent. "I need to get back. We've been gone too long. And Strong is looking for every excuse to get rid of me now, too."

"All right, guys, the man wants to go back to work, then we'll go back to work. But I didn't get to finish my meal," Floyd whined. Bart was just happy to be out of there and heading back.

After returning, Bart called one of his sure-fire clients. He phoned the comptroller of a county near the capital who was a friend of his father and granddad's. He was someone who trusted Bart simply because he knew the family. They were on a first-name basis and saw each other now and then.

"Hey Kevin, it's Bart. Long time no see. Not since we went dove hunting with that Labrador of yours, Caesar. How's the misses doing?"

"Oh, Courtney's fine. I think she's out riding that damn horse of hers. What's up?"

"I've got some bonds that I think are just right for you."

"I already bought some bonds earlier."

"What? What bonds? And from who?"

"From you. Well, not from you. Your office. I called earlier looking for you because I had some money to place. Someone then called me right back telling me about some deal. He said I had to jump in now as there were only a few bonds left. He said that you asked him to call me back."

Bart was silent for a moment, fear boring a hole in his stomach. "Who was it?" Kevin struggled to remember. "Oh, it was one of the head guys, that I know. Oliver, or something like that." Bart was trying to remain calm. "Tony Olive?" Bart could feel his blood pressure rising. "What'd you buy?"

"I bought fifteen-million Ginnie Mays for delivery in a few months. What a sweet deal. By the time I have to pay for them the price will have increased and I'll drop them back into the market."

Bart ended the conversation with as much composure as he could and immediately told Jack what had happened. Jack did not give him any comforting news.

"Government entities shouldn't be buying those. In fact no one should be buying those anymore. Delivery in six months? Are you supposed to throw them into the Standby/Takeout? This is the government. It doesn't work that way. The Standby/Takeout is only to save those who are already in trouble. It's like a Hail Mary. It's just a way to save them if the market springs back. If a bank goes under then there's insurance on the accounts. But if a county goes under, policemen don't get paid. The garbage doesn't get picked up. If the market turns around in six months, you'll be fine. You may even be a hero."

Bart could see the look on Jack's face. He heard it in his voice. The market would not be kind to this client.

As the next few weeks passed, the bond market changed for the worse. Every client who had been sold bonds for future delivery had to take delivery of bonds they could not afford and could not sell without taking an incredible loss. Instead of making an easy profit as promised, clients were losing tens of millions of dollars.

To the untrained eye, Olive looked cool as a cucumber. On the inside, though, he was stressed. It was not just because of the market. It was not because some of his clients were about to take the same hit. It was because his investor was about to lose a lot of money. It was the investor he feared most.

And as it turned out, Olive and Cadillac Dan had been calling a few of Bart's clients without his knowledge for weeks. Olive and Cadillac Dan had sold tens of millions of dollars of bonds for future delivery, and to anyone they could get their hands on. And it was not just Bart's clients they did this to.

Bart's clients had purchased bonds they could not afford. Olive's investor, who fronted the money to delay the delivery of the bonds, was losing money, too. The Standby/Takeout had been abused and was used to earn the firm commissions only.

Since the market had turned, Olive's investor, along with everyone else, was about to lose huge sums of money.

There were a lot of phone calls Bart needed to make that morning. He did not want to make any of them, but he had to. Now he was answering blistering questions from frantic government employees.

The more clients he called the more stressed he became, so he went to Jack to see what he could do. Aaron was talking to Jack about the very same thing. Bart had just started to ask Jack what to do when Mean Dean started in with his regular routine.

"Get on the damn phones. You three homos are always making out over here. Hook 'em up baby shit!"

Bart was not in the mood. He had been pushed over the edge. He reached over Mean Dean's back and pulled his shirt over his head. He then dragged Dean down to the ground as if Dean weighed a buck-o-five.

Bart held Dean's head to the ground using Dean's shirt. "Could it be you are always calling us queers because in fact you like to take it up the ass? You're not even married and you never even talk about women. And no one's ever seen you check out the sweet little asses we have walking around this office either."

Strong came walking around the corner just in time to witness all of this. He was not pleased. He pushed Bart off of Mean Dean. "What the hell is this? Who the hell do you think you are?"

Olive dashed up from the front of the room and starting pushing Bart around, even taking a few swings at his head. They both were yelling and screaming in the middle of the trading floor. Every broker in the place was watching silently. All of the angst, anger, and frustration stemming from Olive's behavior towards Bart, and from the problems caused for his clients because of Olive, finally surfaced.

"My clients are going under because you sold them something they shouldn't have bought. They're more than just my clients. These are friends. Family friends. People who have dedicated their whole lives to serving the public. And because of you they are screwed. They're losing tax dollars, and probably their own jobs. They're looking to me for answers and I don't have any. They're blaming me and my family for this mess!"

Olive did not have any intention of listening to Bart's whining. "You have no one to blame but yourself for this. You weren't on the phones selling what we wanted you to sell like we told you to do. We should have fired your ass a long time ago. You were not making the sales, so I did. Big deal if they lose money. And it's not their money. It's only tax dollars."

Cadillac Dan added his two cents. "They'll just raise taxes to cover it, or they'll issue more bonds. They'll be fine. They'll make money, and we'll make even more money. Quit acting like the world is ending."

Bart interrupted. "You just don't get it, do you? You can't screw the government and get away with it. And none of you even give a shit what happens to a client."

By now Strong's face was beet red. "Fuck you. *You* don't get it. You sorry little crybaby." Strong's voice was stern as he pranced around mocking Bart. "You're all worried about the public and someone else's job. Worried about who will get fired. Who the fuck cares about them? You are a closet government employee, just like the rest of your family. You-no-money-making public-servant son-of-a-bitch. You know nothing. If you like the government so much, go work for them. I hear they have great benefits. You are fired. Get the hell out of here."

Except for a few brokers making calls, most of the trading floor was focused on Bart, including his two best friends in the office as they watched him walk off the trading floor and out the doors of the firm.

CHAPTER SEVENTEEN

▼

Gage was always into the latest toys and liked to show them off to everyone at the firm. One day, in the middle of the week, he made his way downstairs with a new toy in his hand. He handed it over to Olive.

Olive took the latest toy of Gage's, looked at him with a questioning expression on his face, and asked, "What the hell is this?"

"It's a hand-held financial calculator that can do anything, and every broker should have one." The whole office gathered around Gage to examine the fancy new tool of the trade.

Cadillac Dan was unimpressed. "That's a stupid idea. No one needs one of those. No way something like that will ever catch on. Talk about throwing your money away. By the way, how much did it cost?"

Gage just smiled back at him. "Oh yea, this coming from a guy who has bought three Cadillacs this month. And by the way, love the new baby blue color."

Dan's attitude did not stop the others. In fact, most of them saw the genius behind it. Jack was thinking out loud. "I could work from my hot tub with this thing."

Dan was now more convinced of its uselessness. And the comment about his baby blue Cadillac didn't help either. "Did you see what you started Gage? That's just great." Dan grabbed Gage's calculator. "Who'll give me one-thousand dollars to throw this thing against the wall?"

Alex was amused by it all and said, "I will." But before Alex could finish saying, "Just joking," Dan slammed Gage's calculator against the wall. Gage's shoulders fell as he cocked his head towards the floor. He turned and walked towards his desk as said one thing. "Assholes."

At lunchtime, Gage, and about ten other brokers, including Jack and Aaron, rushed out to buy their own calculators. No one ever wanted to be last to get the newest toy. Gage got his second one and then left the store.

After having spent a couple hours at the store with Gage, Aaron looked at his watch and noticed that by the time they returned to the office the market would nearly be closed, so he shared an idea with Jack. "Let's just go to my condo. We can make calls from the hot tub and throw down some brews."

Jack at first was hesitant. "I don't know," he said. "Maybe we should get back." Aaron was not going to be swayed though. He was quick-witted and knew exactly what to say to Jack. "Relax. We can call from there and make some sales and then phone them in to Alex. It'll be cool. We'll be fine. I know what bonds we can push. They don't care as long was we're on the phones."

Jack decided that he liked the idea, but not to go to Aaron's condo. "No way dude. That hot tub of yours is nasty, and so is your condo. Let's go to mine instead. I have a maid, and I have my hot tub cleaned out every now and then, too. It'll give us a real chance to use the calculators, too."

Jack and Aaron had each purchased a penthouse in a high-rise condominium community and only their two condos shared the top floor. Each had a large patio balcony where they had had hot tubs installed.

In no time at all they were soaking in the hot tub and had knocked back a few beers. Quite a few beers in fact. But it was now time to get down to business.

Aaron was talking to a client when Jack's dog started barking when a helicopter flew over. Without missing a beat, Aaron told his client it was the excitement of the other brokers on the trading floor making all the noise. He closed the deal, passed the phone to Jack, then opened another beer.

Jack had been working a huge trade for some time and was a little more aggressive than usual, especially as the beer was affecting his sobriety. It was a monster trade that his client had just agreed to, if Jack could locate the product at the right price.

Jack was on the phone with Alex when he asked him to hold while he lit a cigar. Jack then continued to speak with Alex. "I need forty-million Ginnie Mays, eight-percent coupon, priced at eight-six."

Alex was yelling on his end of the phone. "What? I can't hear you. Are you outside?"

"Oh, it's probably the jets in my hot tub. And this damn helicopter keeps flying by, too." He grabbed another beer.

Alex was now angry. "Get out of the damn hot tub so we can get this done."

"No. I will not get out of my hot tub. If I have to get out of my hot tub we are not doing this deal!"

"What bonds are you looking for again?" And so it went, from his hot tub, and quite drunk, Jack closed the biggest trade in the firm's history.

*   *   *   *

One morning Cadillac Dan pulled in to see Haynes getting out of a brand new Cadillac convertible. As usual, the rest of the parking lot was filled with exotic cars.

Haynes hadn't even closed the door to his car when Dan started yelling, "What the hell is this?"

Haynes smiled like a proud father. "I just picked her up last night. It's a brand new 1978 Cadillac…."

"I know it's a damn Cadillac. I was told the '78s wouldn't be out until next month. I can't believe this shit. I'm going to have someone's ass. I'm out of here. See you later."

Cadillac Dan tore out of the parking lot, a man on a mission. He returned about three hours later in his own beautiful 1978 convertible Cadillac. He rode up in the elevator to the first floor to see Haynes with extreme pride showing on his face, though it did not last for long. When the elevator doors opened, he barely had a chance to look up before a man in a dark suit quickly stepped into the elevator, almost knocking Dan over. There was a lot of yelling and cursing going on behind the man.

Cadillac Dan jumped out of the way as Olive grabbed the man's briefcase and threw it into the elevator. Strong was yelling at the top of his lungs. "I don't ever want to see you in here again! I don't give a shit who you think you are!"

Cadillac Dan slipped out of the elevator before the doors closed so he wouldn't get stuck with the man inside. He stared in amazement as he opened his mouth. "Who, and what, was that all about?"

Olive responded first. "It was the damn NASD. Sent over some rookie runt to ask questions. He said his name was Billy something. Can you believe that shit? Who the hell do they think they are?"

Strong was just as irritated. "I can't believe he came in here trying to ask questions."

"What did he want?" Cadillac Dan inquired.

"Hell if I know, but he was asking about you, too."

"Me? What for? I don't know any Billys. I think I fired a Billy one time though."

Strong had gotten a little winded and over-excited, so needed to catch his breath. "I don't know. He was only here for a few seconds. We made him leave as soon as he said where he was from." Cadillac Dan wanted more information, but there was nothing else to tell since the man had barely said who he was before he was told to leave.

The seasons were changing again. The leaves started to turn yellow as fall approached. Autumn was one of the best times of the year in Houston. Moderate temperatures and low humidity made perfect weather for convertibles, and motorcycles.

In honor of the nice weather, Gage had recently purchased a new motorcycle to just cruise around town on. He even rode it to work a few times, but often had to catch a ride home with someone else because of engine issues. He had tinkered with the motor, trying to increase its output. Of course, he also added a turbo charger to it. Although his bike was not responding well to his changes, Gage kept at it. He had ridden the bike to work, but ended up pushing it to the parking lot the last few blocks, as it had stalled out again.

Thanksgiving was right around the corner and Strong was totally focused on the holiday and put all his attention on the surprise dinner he and Haynes were planning for the entire office. With the help of the other partners, it would be a Thanksgiving dinner to remember.

Haynes ordered ten Peking ducks. Strong wanted a few turkeys. Gage contributed a couple of hams and some roast beef. Olive was in charge of the wine and various spirits. Manikan was responsible for the banquet room reservation at one of their favorite steakhouses. Rejecting Olive's desire to be in charge of invitations because of the previous invitation incident, Manikan had them ordered and delivered to his desk.

Even though the market did not close early the day before Thanksgiving, the partners decided to let the employees leave at noon that day. This allowed for the perfect office Thanksgiving dinner. All of the partners left even earlier to make sure everything was prepared to their specifications at the restaurant.

The restaurant had set up the tables perfectly. At two o'clock the waiters brought out all the traditional Thanksgiving food. They centered the dishes on two long tables. The waiters spaced the Peking ducks, turkeys, and hams perfectly on each table. And there was a roast beef station near the back wall sitting across from the fully stocked bar.

The partners sat and waited with childish joy so they could show their gratitude to everyone. They impatiently sipped on wine and munched on appetizers. Two o'clock turned into two-thirty. Two-thirty turned to three o'clock.

Haynes finally spoke up. "Where the hell is everyone? Someone call the office."

Gage called. There was no answer. It was the same response after a few more calls to different desks and offices at the firm. Finally someone answered.

"HAYNES, OLIVE, GAGE & STRONG, how may I help you?"

"Who is this? Maria?"

"Yes. Is this Gage?"

"Yea, it's me. Where is everyone? Are you coming over?"

"Coming over, where? Everyone's gone for the day."

"Hold on."

Gage looked at all of the partners for a moment while he thought. Finally, he questioned the group. "I'm talking with Maria and she says no one is there. Who was in charge of invitations?"

Manikan looked down and said a single word. "Shit."

He grabbed the phone from Gage. "Maria, will you go into my office please? Let me know if there are invitations for the company Thanksgiving dinner sitting on the corner of my desk."

After a few moments she returned to the phone. "Yes. There's a whole stack of invitations just sitting there."

"Crap. Do you want to come down here and take a turkey home or something?"

"Oh, thank you Mr. Manikan, but I'm on my way out to visit with my family, and there's always too much food there as it is. I'm sorry, I wish I had known."

Manikan hung up the phone and turned to the others. "Now what?"

Haynes and Gage spoke almost in unison. "We could take it to a shelter."

The idea was well received by all. "What about the liquor?" asked Olive. "We shouldn't give them all this booze should we? That's why half of them are there in the first place."

Gage spoke up. "The shelter can't take it."

Strong paused. "Screw it. We'll eat and drink as much as we can before we drop the food off, and we can leave the booze outside the shelter."

The boys first dove into the booze, then the food. More wine was consumed than food, leaving plenty to feed all of the poor souls in Houston, according to Olive. Soon they were sharing stories, laughing, and having a good time as the waiters packed up all the food. The partners were getting ready to leave as they complained about family members who would be arriving at their homes to stay for the holidays.

Gage had no immediate family in the area and usually spent most of his holidays at one of the homes of the partners, or invited brokers to his home for a feast. Gage thought that after they'd had their fill of alcohol maybe he could convince Olive into going to Vegas for the weekend. "Why don't we take off Friday afternoon and head to Las Vegas?"

It was a given that Olive would say yes. At least it should have been. Even on Thanksgiving. Olive was hesitant though. "Oh, I don't think I can this time. Probably not a good idea. Family and all."

Everyone got quiet and looked at Olive. They were not certain if he was joking or not since he never refused a trip to Vegas. They sat there waiting for him to say he was in. It never happened. An odd silence came over them, then each asked in unison, "What, are you serious?"

Thoughts of what could be wrong were soon replaced with worries about Olive's investor, and the fact that all knew that the investor was taking a huge hit along with everyone else. The look on Olive's face just added to their worries. They wondered the same thing. Gage finally asked. "Are you doing business with *them*?"

"With who?"

Strong chimed in also. "You know who. Are you trading bonds for Joey or the casino?"

Olive was convincing. "No, I swear. I haven't sold them any bonds. Not a single one."

Then something occurred to Gage. "Shit, is this about the whole Mexico thing? Do you owe them money?"

Olive tried to dismiss it. "It doesn't matter, I'm square. That deal turned out all right at the end of the day anyway."

Haynes had a stern look on his faced and asked, "Are they the ones fronting the money on the Standby/Takeout?"

Olive was not as convincing in his response to Haynes as he was to Gage. "No, I swear. Not a penny."

A warning could be heard in Haynes' response. "I know you know better than that Olive." The three stared at Olive for a moment, then decided it could wait until after the holiday.

It took a while to get all the food packed into the cars. Cadillac Dan's baby blue Cadillac was completely full, including the passenger's seat. There was not much room in the other cars to put in any food as the rest of them had arrived in two-seater sports cars.

Since it had been one of those perfect days, Gage had ridden in on his motorcycle, enjoying the beautiful weather. This turned out to be more of a hassle than he anticipated. The turbo charger he installed was still giving the motorcycle engine problems. His bike repetitively stalled without warning, so he had ridden to the restaurant with Cadillac Dan.

They were all fairly intoxicated by the time they eventually left. Cadillac Dan was the first to leave since his car had most of the food they were going to donate to the shelter. The others stood there finishing their cigarettes and giving him the bird.

Suddenly, Olive fell over, his face smacking on the sidewalk. It was not until that moment they realized that he was too intoxicated to drive. It dawned on Haynes and Strong that Gage would have to drive Olive's car to the shelter. Grins appeared on everyone's face except Gage's.

Gage who was usually full of words looked up at them. "No," was all he said.

Strong began the pitch. "Oh come on man, are you going to pass up a chance to drive a V-12 engine? Five gears. Tight suspension so you can take the corners at full speed."

Haynes chimed in, "Man, you haven't lived until you've driven a Ferrari at a hundred-and-fifty-miles-per-hour. And then there are the girls. Oh yea, the girls."

Gage was not amused. "I've been laid before. I've driven a hundred-and-fifty before also. This ain't my first rodeo."

Olive's too-drunken self started to get up from the pavement and he soon added in his two cents as he stumbled to the passenger door. "It's only like five miles to the office. And everyone's driving a Ferrari. Come on man, everyone's doing it. Be cool for once."

Gage stood there for a moment, then reluctantly agreed. He was convinced, but only because he was too tired to walk back to the office and too drunk to think about calling a cab. He got in and started her up. Strong and Haynes watched Gage slowly pull out of the parking lot and on to the street. As they got into their own cars they could hear Gage revving the engine. They turned and looked just in time to see Olive's red Ferrari take off like a bolt of lightening.

They took off after him with a rush of adrenaline pumping through their veins. They were flying down the street while hitting incredible speeds between the stoplights. They were weaving in and out of traffic on a six-lane highway trying to pass each other.

Gage discovered that he was thoroughly enjoying himself, and Olive knew it. Olive decided to turn on his radio for some extra flair. "I've got the greatest cassette tape here."

Gage looked at him with a curious look. "You listen to music in this car? The engine produces all the sound you need to hear."

"No man. You're going to dig this shit. Check it out. It's the Bee Gees."

"The Bee Gees? You've got to be kidding me."

"Listen, just listen, okay?"

Gage was irritated and raised his voice, "You can't listen to disco in a Ferrari!" But Olive had already put in the cassette.

"I so love this song! *Stayin' Alive, Stayin' Alive. Da da da da, Stayin' Alive.*" Olive was bouncing in his seat as he sang along.

They squabbled over the music. Gage just wanted the ridiculous music to stop. He was driving twice the posted speed limit. He was not paying attention to the road or to the stoplights. An upcoming light had turned red, but he kept going as the other cars slowed down. A big silver tanker began to enter the intersection.

All the weaving in and out of traffic and changing speeds all the time was not helping Olive's condition. Neither was all the bouncing around he had been doing. Within a matter of seconds all hell broke loose. Olive looked away from Gage, trying to roll down the window, but it was too late. He began to vomit inside the car. The booze, lobster tails, and the rest of the Thanksgiving dinner projected out of him like a bullet. Gage slowed down as he tried to open his window. When he finally looked back to the road he saw the truck and its tanker pulling into the intersection. Gage did what only an experienced racecar driver could do. He dropped the car down a gear and hit the gas.

As he entered the intersection he swung from the right lane to the left lane, trying to get around the front of the tanker as it entered the intersection. The vehicle performed like only a Ferrari could. The car squealed by the truck's headlights, narrowly missing the truck. Of course, this did not help Olive's condition again, and out came another round of that day's feast.

As soon as he could, Gage pulled into the next parking lot. Strong and Haynes pulled in behind him a minute later. Gage was standing next to the car. The vomit inside didn't seem to phase him. "That was close," was all he could say when Haynes and Strong walked towards him.

They all knew why Gage never drove a Ferrari. When Gage was a kid, his dad had spent all of his time, love, and money into building a prototype engine for a racing team. At the last minute, the racing team's sponsor chose an Italian-made motor. Gage's dad never financially recovered. He lost his ranch when the bank foreclosed on it. Depressed and broken, his father died a short time later. Thus, Gage developed a distain for all cars not made in America, and especially hated Italian cars.

Gage finally spoke up. "This is my daddy's way of speaking to me. I shouldn't be driving this car. I'll take Olive back to the office, then I'll just ride my bike home."

They went their separate ways. Strong and Haynes met up with Cadillac Dan at the shelter. The shelter greeted the partners with a warm welcome as they dropped off all the food. But not as much praise as when they dropped off the booze.

Gage took Olive back to the office without incident.

Olive looked at Gage. "I've got pajamas in the back of the car, so you don't need to worry about me. I'll just sleep here."

"No problem. See you later."

Gage left, jumped on his bike, and rode away towards his condo in town. He didn't want to take the risk of breaking down on his way out of town to get to his house. On his way home he came upon a group of younger guys riding bikes, too. They began a friendly game of cat and mouse through the streets of Houston.

Despite his near-death experience Gage couldn't help but stay on the edge. He was cruising over a hundred-miles-an-hour when he noticed a glow coming from the engine of his bike.

When he looked down to find his bike on fire his attention was taken off of the road ahead. A vehicle had stalled in the middle of the road. There was a flatbed tow truck stopped behind it with its yellow emergency lights flashing. The excessive amount of alcohol consumed at dinner had dulled Gage's usual razor sharp reaction time.

He never saw it coming.

CHAPTER EIGHTEEN

▼

The news of Gage's death came as a shock to everyone at the office, especially for the three other partners. No one thought anything was wrong that he was absent the following Monday. The partners had not heard from him, but thought that he was sleeping it off, with a young lady, at his house. That was until Monday afternoon, when a call came in from the coroner's office asking one of the partners to come and identify the body. It was Haynes who went down to identify the body of Gage.

Haynes and the other partners gathered everyone on to the trading floor to deliver the bad news. While the news was tragic, the office did not stop. The phones kept ringing. The brokers continued to make phone calls. Mean Dean supervised his wards with an iron fist. Today was to be no different.

At lunch that day Jack, Aaron, Floyd, and Fast Eddie were talking about Gage's death. Even Swamp-Ass was there. A rarity since he usually just kept to himself.

"*Li youn bon moun.*"

"What?" the other four asked in total surprise as they looked at Swamp-Ass.

"I said that he was a good man."

"You speak English?" asked Floyd, totally flabbergasted.

"I actually speak English, French, Creole and Cajun, and I even know Spanish."

"Holy fuckin' shit," was all Fast Eddie could sputter out.

"No wonder we never could understand you," said Aaron. "You were never speaking English."

"*Vwala.*"

"WHAT?" everyone said at once.

They all fell silent again.

After a few moments of silence Jack said, "You remember what he used to say now and then?"

"About what?" asked Eddie.

"About how the day he ever drove a Ferrari would be the day he died."

"Shit," replied Floyd.

"*Lanfe*," was Swamp-Ass' response.

"You fuckin' can fucking say that again," replied Fast Eddie.

And with that the five made a toast to Gage. Then it was back to the phones. Business as usual.

The Christmas holidays were soon upon them and everyone tried to make the best of it. It was customary for the brokers to send small gifts to their various clients. Because of NASD rules, the gifts had to be at a minimal cost. Anything over fifty dollars would be considered a bribe.

Jack tailored each of his gifts to his clients. For instance, his clients located in Colorado and New Mexico received new skiing gloves and hats. His clients who hunted received ammunition and small kerosene-powered heaters for their deer blinds.

Aaron was not so personal and decided on a theme. "Everyone's getting a ham from me. Easy as pie. Best of all, the evidence will be gone before New Year's Day. You boys should make a note of that."

Aaron loved his idea. He purchased almost a hundred hams for immediate delivery to his clients. A costly expense to him, but one that he hoped would pay for itself in a phone call that would result in a sale.

Days later he started receiving the first of many phone calls thanking him for the gift. One of the calls was from a client named Michael Abrams.

"Merry Christmas, Mr. Abrams. And how are you doing this fine morning?"

"I'm great Aaron. I received your ham. I'm sure it's very tasty."

"My pleasure Mr. Abrams. It's the least I could do."

"Aaron." There was a small pause. "You know this is the Jewish Federation Council right?"

"Of course Mr. Abrams. I knew that before we ever did our first trade."

"Aaron." There was another small pause. "You know that I'm Jewish then don't you?"

"Well I pretty much assumed that, but I never really thought about it much I guess."

"Aaron, you do know that Jews do not eat pork. It's against, well, it just is not eaten."

Aaron was silent for a moment before he finally spoke up. "Umm, I, oh no. I am so embarrassed Mr. Abrams. And I am so sorry. I didn't—"

"It's okay Aaron," Abrams quietly chuckled. And by the way, we don't celebrate Christmas either."

"Oh, that's right. So I'm not supposed to say Merry Christmas then either?" Aaron was starting to lose it, thinking he was going to lose this client. "Have you received my Christmas card yet? Oh, man. I just did it again!" Aaron was now getting upset, and Mr. Abrams could sense what was going on. "What am I supposed to say?"

"How about just 'Happy Holidays'? That works just fine."

"Can I say Happy Hanukkah?"

"That's fine also."

"Again, I am so sorry. It never even occurred to me."

"No apologies are needed Aaron. I just hope you didn't send any other hams out to any of your other Jewish clients. Some might not be as forgiving as I am. Have a good day."

As he hung up the phone, Aaron muttered, "Oh shit."

He was more prepared for the rest of his calls as he created a small fib to pass the buck. His damage control was a story about his new college student assistant who interned for him during the holidays and who was responsible for the hams. Aaron did not lose any clients, but he learned to never make that kind of mistake again.

*   *   *   *

It was a fairly normal day in the office. Other than the death of Gage, everything had been going well leading up to the Christmas holiday, until Strong pulled Jack aside into his office where Haynes was waiting. Olive and Cadillac Dan followed them in. Jack had no reason to suspect that there was any problem.

Strong opened his mouth. "It's been months and we can't help but notice that you are not selling your own creation."

"And...?" Jack responded.

"You have failed to sell even one Standby/Takeout. What the hell is your problem?"

Jack was feeling the pressure, but he knew he had been doing the right thing. "I haven't failed to do anything. I've chosen not to sell any."

This angered all of them, but it was Olive who was the first to respond. "What the fuck does that mean?"

Strong broke in sternly. "It means that he's trying to make fools of us, is what the fuck it means."

Jack knew his material and he spoke with conviction. "No, it means that none of my clients are suitable for this product. The market has changed, so it's not a good deal for them."

Haynes had a question. "What the hell do you mean the market has changed? I'm still selling these. All of us are. The whole damn office is. Are you screwing us over?"

"No, the product is fine for certain clients, just not mine. And not at this time. I told you this a long time ago. It's not for everyone."

Strong was visibly perturbed. "Bullshit. You need to start selling your own idea and start doing it now. It makes a lot of money for everyone, including the firm."

Jack stood his ground, not sure how the partners were going to respond to what he had to say next. "I'm not going to sell a product just because it makes us money. It needs to make money for the client as well."

Strong lowered his voice so Jack knew he meant business. "If you don't start acting like a team player then there is no room for you in this firm. You *will* sell the same fucking product we sell. This is more than just your loyalty. If this Standby/Takeout is some bullshit crackpot scheme, then you are going down with us."

Jack started to say something, but decided it was best to keep quiet for now. He just nodded his head in acknowledgement. On the inside, for the first time, he realized that the partners only cared about the next commission. He recognized that this was not just bending ethical rules; the partners had no qualms about doing fraudulent business as long as it made them a profit. Jack muttered to himself, "I can't do this anymore."

No one else said anything as they got up to walk out of the room. Haynes had one more thing to add though before Jack left. "And what's this shit I hear about you selling Treasuries. That's the most efficient market in the world. You can't make any money off of those."

Jack replied, looking directly at Haynes. "I know, but my client needed to park some money in a safe place for a rainy day." He thought it was a good and solid response to the question, but he was wrong.

"Don't waste the firm's resources on that ever again. Find something that doesn't trade on one-sixty-fourth of a point." Haynes was not visibly angry, and he rarely got mad, but he always meant business. If he said not to do something, then no one did it.

When Bart was still working at the firm, he and Aaron and Jack had developed a Saturday night ritual to go to the bars around town. They wouldn't drink much, if anything at all. They went from bar to bar, picking up a new woman at each stop.

The objective wasn't to get drunk, nor was it to take a girl home. Their hidden objective was to remain on the streets of Houston hours after all the bars closed. Of course, this objective was frequently not achieved as they usually succumbed to the booze and the women. If all went according to plan though, they would stop and meet at a particular "midnight" diner at 2:00 a.m. They enjoyed breakfast and coffee, waiting for the drunks to get home.

The hours between 3:00 a.m. and 6:00 a.m. on a Sunday morning were prime time in downtown Houston for street racing, as the roads were totally empty. And Bart's friendships and connections with half of the police force afforded them even more benefits. Sometimes they would get an escort for the price of a few donuts and a cup of coffee.

It had been months since Bart had been fired, and racing the streets just wasn't the same without him. Neither Aaron nor Jack had had any contact with him since the weekend after he was fired. All they knew was that he said he was heading to Virginia to get his "creds." It was not the fringe benefits that they missed; it was his company. As they had learned, it was surprisingly more intense having three sports cars racing down empty streets than just two.

It was a perfect summer-time night when Jack and Aaron stopped at their favorite diner to wait for the streets to empty. As they sat at their table, they noticed a Ferrari pulling into the parking lot. It was Bart.

They ate breakfast and drank coffee just like in the good old days. They learned that Bart, unlike everyone else, had saved a lot of the money he had made. Bart was now working in D.C. for a government agency. The FBI. Jack and Aaron were not surprised. He had completed his training and was an agent now, assigned to a veteran to learn, as Bart said, 'the ropes.' No one mentioned the firm until Bart brought it up.

"How's the firm doing by the way?"

Jack and Aaron responded in unison. "Same ole', same ole'."

"Still making money?"

Aaron responded as he sipped his cup of coffee. "Oh yea."

"Always on the phone. One call after another. Did you hear about Gage?" added Jack.

Bart turned somber. "I know more than I care to know about it. I was told he was going over a hundred when he slammed into the back of that truck. Did you know that he was decapitated?"

Shocked, Jack looked up from his cup of coffee, eyes wide. "No, I didn't know that."

Aaron was somewhat dry. "Why am I not surprised?"

Bart dropped another piece of information on them that totally dumbfounded them. "Did you know he had almost no money in the bank when he died? He had less than twenty-thousand dollars."

Jack was amazed. "Holy crap. Are you serious? How did that happen? And how do you even know this?"

"The court-appointed attorney for his estate is a former police officer. He's a good friend of my dad's. He found a Last Will and Testament in his safe deposit box. It wasn't fancy, but the court ruled it valid. He left everything he owned in trust to his neighbor's son, Ricky. Remember Ricky Too?"

Aaron thought for second. "Yea. RT. Too bad there wasn't any cash for the kid."

Bart responded in a soft voice. "Maybe not, but he owned outright a lot of stuff. Seven condos near downtown alone. It seems every time a new building went up he bought a condo in one. He also owned a beach house, a lake house, and some land in central Texas, Colorado, Tennessee, and Florida. He was actually buried in Tennessee. Right next to his dad. I was told it was the only piece of land from his dad's farm that the bank didn't foreclose on way back when."

They were all quiet for a moment as they each thought about Gage. Then Bart spoke up again. "Man you should have seen all the toys Gage had. All kinds of watercrafts, motorcycles, you name it. Then there were all of his cars. RT worshipped Gage. He's going to end up okay, though Gage had it in his will that the kid can't touch it until he gets a college degree. RT was always talking about starting up a performance parts auto store. Guess he'll get a business degree." Bart paused.

Aaron finally asked Bart what Jack had been thinking for the last few minutes. "How do you know all this crap?"

Bart shook his head. "In his Will & Testament he made me the trustee of all his property until RT can get his degree. You guys wouldn't believe how much work this has caused me. I think he bought everything that popped into his mind. He was like a salesman's wet dream. I'm still liquidating it all and putting it all into a trust fund for RT. But enough about him. You guys want to run the streets tonight or what? I already made some calls. I even have a route planned out for us."

Bart had barely asked the question when Jack yelled out, "Check please."

Aaron was about to get up when he noticed someone walking through the doors. "Son of a bitch, look what the cat just dragged in."

They looked up to see three of the firm's ex-secretaries walk in together. Samantha, Mandy, and Kate. Also known when they worked at the firm as

Sissi, Mitzi and Kitti. And all looking good. All looking a little tipsy, too. They walked over and sat down with the boys.

None of the girls worked at the firm anymore. All of them were in college getting their degrees. As it turned out, there was another reason why all of the firm's secretaries only lasted a year or so. The girls could make enough money at the Zeros over a period of about a year to pay for their entire college education.

All of the partners knew this and encouraged it. They always wanted "new meat" as they called it anyway. Each departing secretary was given a thousand-dollar bonus for bringing in any new applicant who was hired. And each new applicant knew what was expected before she was hired.

Jack spoke up after listening to the girls talk about the firm. "We had no idea that it worked that way. We just thought all of the girls either got sick of working there or sick of the guys, or something."

Mandy responded for all of them. "That's true, too. None of us really enjoyed all the guys grabbing us or even partying all that hard. But we made a lot of money in a very short amount of time, even if it meant some sacrifices."

Aaron and Mandy had always gotten along well, so they carried on their own private conversation.

Bart and Kate whispered back and forth, as they played footsies underneath the table. Bart finally spoke up real quick. "I think it's time we go. You girls want to run the streets with us?"

The three girls answered simultaneously. "Sure."

Paired up, they sped out of the parking lot. Three Ferraris followed and chased each other over the empty streets of Houston. Speed limit signs were ignored as they flew by them without a concern in the world as officers waved them on.

When their racing games came to an end they returned to the diner to drop off the girls. After kissing the girls goodnight the boys hung out in the parking lot for a while. Bart had some parting words as he walked back to his car.

"Have you guys thought about leaving and going to work for another firm or anything?"

"Why do you ask?" said Aaron.

Bart opened his car door. "Oh, I was just thinking out loud. It's time to start preparing for the future. Rumor has it that they've over exposed your Standby/Takeout product and sold it way past its prime. It's causing some major problems. You're lucky you have someone watching over you."

Bart's comment confused Aaron. "What the hell does that mean?" Are we in trouble, or something? What's going on?"

"No one in the agency is looking specifically at you two as culprits, but I can't say that about everyone."

"What are you talking about, Bart?" Aaron asked

Bart looked right at Jack. "Jack, you were right. The Standby/Takeout wasn't a product for everyone. There are quite a few heavy players who didn't fare too well with it, and they are very unhappy."

"Shit, that's not my fault. They have been stretching those things out past a year and assuming a drop in the yield, but I think the market is going to invert and create even more losses. I told them that—", but Jack stopped as he noticed the blank look on Bart's face. "You still don't understand what I'm talking about do you?" Jack paused, "I've seen some big names investing in this product. Do they think this is my fault?"

"I'm not talking about you. Some of the brokers at the firm lost a lot of money, and to the wrong people. Especially one of the partners. These players run on both sides of the law, but they have two things in common, money and contacts. They can clean up a mess with one phone call. We can't stop any of them from doing what they're going to do."

Bart got in his car and lowered the window. "Call me if you need me," he said, and handed Jack his business card.

As Bart drove away, Jack had an epiphany. "What are we doing anymore, Aaron? What took the Feds so long? I think we are hanging on by a thread here." It was the relief he had been waiting for. He'd call Bart to see if he could tell the Feds anything they didn't already know and to pry more information from Bart.

CHAPTER NINETEEN

▼

The bond market moved erratically for the next few weeks. Over this span of time, the yields on the bonds consistently moved upwards. This meant the prices consistently went down.

Jack's Book eagerly awaited him every day for him to make his phone calls. Almost daily one of the partners was on his back about selling his own product, but he was still able to come up with a good reason to keep them at bay. He just told them that they all said no. It showed that he was at least trying.

Aaron had been piggybacking on Jack for months so his clients were equally unaffected by the turn in the market. Both of them had sold most of the bonds out of their client's portfolios at high prices over the previous months. As a result, the portfolios had money to spend, and lots of it. As prices went down and yields went up, their clients were practically stealing the bonds. They were buying many of the same bonds that they had sold just weeks earlier at higher prices.

Not everyone in the office was doing as well as Jack and Aaron, other than Fast Eddie, Floyd, and Swamp-Ass. Each had gone to Jack for advice on their client's portfolios, so most of their clients were not losing out either. The five spoke often, but not without the notice of the partners, so they began to limit their talks to lunchtime, well away from the eyes and ears of the partners.

Many of the other brokers were cussing and yelling at each other on a regular basis more and more. Fistfights broke out numerous times. Many of the brokers were fired when they failed to keep their quota of sales. A new freshman class started on the phones with the hope it would eventually produce one or two huge successes. And it was expected that no one would miss the brokers who were so callously called over the intercom by Strong. "Joe. Kirk. Jim. Kenny. James. Call me on extension 355."

The partners had seen this happen in the market before. Even though they acted unaffected by the turmoil, they pushed the brokers harder and harder to sell. Mean Dean kept a steady warpath as he strolled persistently up and down the aisles, constantly yelling at the brokers. It got to the point that the new guys were afraid to even go to the bathroom.

Despite Jack's advice to many of the brokers, these men were still selling bonds for future delivery and attempting to sell the Standby/Takeout to anyone in order to gain the commission. Even the partners continued to do so. The Standby/Takeout was not the product for every investor, yet the brokers were pushed into selling it by the partners, and then pushed their clients into buying it. Stressed brokers lit one cigarette after another, nonstop, all day long. The tension in the air could be cut with a knife.

Jack was feeling the heat not just from the partners, but from the other brokers. Olive took a lot of heat from his clients and spent most of his time in his office yelling over the phone with someone. He even tried bringing Jack into his office for conference calls with his clients to calm them down. Twice in a row, Jack informed Olive's clients that they basically were screwed and would have to take the loss. When Jack said this, Olive chewed Jack's ass out and forcibly shoved him out of his office.

One morning, as Jack had just finished a call, he heard yelling coming from Olive's office. One of Olive's biggest clients was in his office. The rumor around the office was that Olive had placed $50,000,000 of this renowned Texas family's money into the equity side of the Standby/Takeout. Jack listened intensely. Every now and then he heard his name. The argument was only interrupted by the sound of shattering glass. Olive's client had thrown a chair through the office window.

Storming out of the office, the client threw another chair over the edge of second floor railing onto the trading floor. He paused, turned and looked back at Olive. With an eerie calmness, he said, "You told me this investment was safe and profitable. Jack is not my broker. You are. So who do you think should answer for my losses?" The man straightened his suit and exited the building.

The brokers on the trading floor turned their attention back to their phones. Alex yelled to Olive. "You-know-who is on the phone. He insists on speaking with you immediately." Olive was glaring at Jack, but finally retreated to his office.

Soon enough, Jack could again hear Olive yelling from the upstairs hallway. Olive was cussing and screaming Jack's name. Olive ran down the stairs with a clumsy intensity, lost his grip on the railing and almost fell.

Olive approached Jack with a rage that no one had ever seen before. Olive grabbed Jack and pushed him across the desk. Aaron quickly jumped up to break them apart as Olive grabbed Jack's tie. Olive yanked him around by the neck and repeatedly punched him in the stomach, sending Jack to the ground. It took Aaron, Mean Dean, and Swamp-Ass to separate them so that Jack could get away from Olive.

Olive stopped throwing punches, stood back a bit, and composed himself somewhat. As Jack stood up Olive yelled at him in a strong Chicago accent. "This ain't over you motherfucker! And you better be here when I get back. Don't you dare go home. I'll find you. Fucking forget about it you dirty fucking rat!" Olive stormed out of the building in a furious rage.

Mean Dean was quick to get everyone back to work after the incident. "Get your asses on the phone! Nothing to see here." He kicked the back of Jack's chair as he walked away. He turned his head and yelled out across the floor. "Hook 'em up baby shit!"

Jack was reluctant to return to the office the rest of the week for fear of Olive. Luckily, every morning at 7:25, Jack entered the building for work, but there was no sign of Olive. Olive had not yet returned to the office after the outburst of the other day. The more time that passed, the better Jack felt. So did everyone else. Jack was looking forward to the approaching weekend and figured that the more time that went by would allow Olive to cool off.

Jack arrived Monday morning to find Olive's car in its parking spot. Upon seeing his car, Jack began to sweat underneath his collar. He entered the building, hoping to avoid Olive. He walked quickly and discreetly to his desk.

Aaron arrived a minute later and sat down. He didn't say anything other than asking if Jack had seen Olive yet.

There was still a lot of tension in the office. Aaron felt it too, as none of his clients had any problems with the investments that appeared to be bringing everyone else down. Jack was not the only one who had the partners, and other brokers, giving him a dirty look. The anticipation of another encounter between Jack and Olive was lingering throughout the office, making everyone nervous and tense.

It was near lunchtime when Strong's voice came over the intercom. "Jack, call me on extension 355." Jack thought the words in his head as Aaron said them aloud. "What the hell? Is he serious? You're the best broker here. You bring in the most money." Jack just shrugged and picked up his phone. Without any hesitation Jack called the extension. "I'll be right there."

Jack walked into Strong's office. Cadillac Dan and Haynes were already there. Jack was told to take a seat.

Jack was curious as to Olive's whereabouts. "Are we waiting for Olive?"

Strong took the lead. "No we are not. Haven't seen him all morning as a matter of fact. But that doesn't matter. What does matter is the circus from last week."

Jack spoke quickly. "I didn't start the fight. He just came down and—" but he was interrupted by Strong's gaze, bearing down on him.

Strong spoke without any emotion. "Shut up Jack. Normally your ass would have been fired already. But we have a sensitive situation."

Haynes started to speak. "You created this product and we sold it. We sold the hell out of it. The firm has taken a big hit over the past couple of months. We can't help but think this is all your fault. It *was* your idea."

Jack defended himself again. "I told all of you that selling bonds for future delivery was only a short-term opportunity, and then I told you that it had to stop. I told you that only certain—" Jack was cut off again, but this time by Cadillac Dan.

Cadillac Dan's face was turning red. "Shut up Jack. Shut the fuck up! You piece of shit. We're losing our clients because of you! They'll all be gone before we know it. Do you have any idea how many times a client has threatened to call the NASD or the SEC on me in the last month?"

Again Jack tried to defend himself and started to speak. "I tried—." He did not get out his first word before Strong sprung up from his chair and quickly came out from behind his desk. Jack could see the intensity in Strong's face. Strong grabbed a stapler and smacked Jack across his face so hard that Jack fell out of the chair. As Jack stood up, his nose began to bleed and his eyes to water.

Strong started yelling at him. "Cry me a river you bitch! We are in this together. There is no way now that you are leaving this firm. If this ship sinks then you are going down with it. You think you're worried about Olive? You have no idea what's coming to you! We will burn your ass if the government walks through those doors."

A knock on the door interrupted Strong's tirade. Strong yelled out, "Who is it?"

The receptionist's soft voice faintly came from the other side of the door. "I know you said not to disturb you, but there is a man up front looking for you."

"Who?" Strong yelled.

"He said he was from the Securities and Exchange Commission."

Strong and Cadillac Dan hurried out the door and headed up front.

Haynes was more reserved. "Wait here Jack." Unlike the other two though, he walked casually out the door. Haynes opened the double doors into the reception area to see Strong and Cadillac Dan yelling at someone in the lobby. Haynes quietly turned and made his way towards the stairs at the back of the building.

Once Haynes had left Strong's office Jack did the same, and began to walk back to his desk.

Strong and Cadillac Dan had made it to the lobby and pushed the guy towards the elevator. The man said nothing, turned around, and faced the elevator doors.

The doors of the elevator opened, and five men exited. One of them was Bart. He then calmly spoke to Strong and Dan. "What seems to be the problem gentlemen?"

Cadillac Dan did not understand the seriousness of the situation. "Ah, look, it's Bart the Fart. Working for the government are you?"

Bart smiled. "That's Agent to you Daniel." Bart turned to one of the men standing next to him, his supervisor. "This is Daniel Manikan, also known as Cadillac Dan. He's on the list."

Bart turned and looked at Strong. "Where's Olive?"

Strong was not as cavalier as Dan. "Don't know. Haven't seen him. His car's here though, so he must be around somewhere."

Bart looked at another agent. "And this is Jordan S. Strong." Strong was placed into handcuffs and was then taken to stand next to Dan. Both men just stood there, looking down.

Bart then asked Strong, "Where's Haynes?"

"Last I saw him, he was in my office."

Bart and the other agents opened the double mahogany doors that led to the trading floor. Bart saw Jack with blood all over his face and shirt. Jack was surprised to see Bart. Bart was certainly surprised to see Jack covered in blood. They did not say a word to each other.

Another agent asked Bart, "What about him?"

"No. According to the SEC we're only looking for the partners and junior partners. Olive and Haynes are the other partners. The trader, Alex, is a junior partner, and is on the list. There's also another one, Dean Davidson. Everyone else is free to go."

Bart turned his attention to Jack. "If you have any personal effects, like pictures, or a *book* at your desk, you should grab them now."

While this was going on agents had gone to all the other offices and brought all the firm's employees down to the trading floor. One of the SEC officials then told them the news. "This office is sealed. You are to only take your personal belongings out of this building. You have ten minutes to vacate."

Another agent then said, "You will not be coming back. As of now the firm is out of business."

All of the employees quickly walked out of the building with their belongings to the parking lot. It was at that moment they understood the magnitude of the situation as FBI agents flooded the parking lot. Within minutes, everyone had left.

A few of the rookies expected to be back in the office the next day or so, not truly comprehending what was going on. However, the FBI agents standing in the parking lot informed everyone that this was their last day working at the firm. The brokers were happy to get out of there as fast as possible, afraid that they too might be arrested.

Even though they had been told to leave the premises, Jack and Aaron stayed around for a while hoping to speak to Bart. The mention of Bart's name, and the fact that Bart had talked about them to his boss, meant that they could stick around, but they had to stay out of the way. Agents had scoured the building looking for Haynes and Olive. They finally came outside empty-handed, but leading Strong, Alex, Dan, and Dean to a waiting van.

Bart approached Jack and Aaron. "Seen Olive?"

Jack shook his head as Aaron spoke up. "No. Not in almost a week either. Weird. His car is here though. It was here when we arrived this morning."

Bart did not say much else about it as he looked around the parking lot. "We'll find him. These guys are going down. Through an ongoing investigation we've been able to determine that the partners have been violating the 1933 and 1934 Acts for some time. Not to mention racketeering, bribery, fraud, corruption, and," as he snapped his fingers, "all that jazz. It seems all of the employees and brokers were unknowingly, and unlikely, aware of what had been going on here."

Jack and Aaron just stood there speechless. Finally Jack asked, "What about us?"

Bart shook his head. "The SEC and my department's investigation found nothing to pin on anyone here but the partners."

"What about our licenses? Will we be able to keep trading and working somewhere else?"

"You should be fine. The Agency appreciates the cooperation and documents you two provided to help build up the government's case. Otherwise, we'd still likely be investigating them. However, if you decide to start your own company, be careful. Despite your cooperation, the SEC will be watching you closely, along with every other broker who worked here, for a while."

Bart started to walk off. He paused and pointed over to the security guard. "You know, his name is not Willie. His name is Frank. Olive started calling him Willie for no reason and it stuck. You'd be surprised about how much he actually knew about what was going on in this building." Bart paused for a moment, thinking. And he's been going to college for the past few years, too. Gage used to give him a thousand dollars for every "A" he received. Paid for his education, and then some. If you two were thinking about opening a firm together you might want to speak with him."

"How do you know all this shit?" asked Aaron.

"FBI. We know everything," he said with a wink. "Next time we meet, I hope it's not to save your ass again," he said as he shook hands with Jack and Aaron.

Bart had started to walk away when a commotion began around Olive's car. A handful of agents ran to the car, along with Bart. Jack and Aaron stayed back, but slowly inched nearer to Olive's car to see and hear what was going on. They could hear one of the agents speak. "Agent Dover was checking out the car and noticed that it smelled pretty bad, especially in the back."

The agents popped the lock on the trunk of Olive's black Mercedes Benz. When the trunk opened, the smell punched all of them in the face. Jack and Aaron watched as the agents all turned their heads for fresh air. Olive was tied up inside the trunk of his own car. Three gunshot wounds to his head.

That day was the last time Jack and Aaron saw most of the other brokers at the firm. It was time to move on.

EPILOGUE

▼

1986

They arrived a few minutes before Strong's funeral service was scheduled to commence. They watched Cadillac Dan walk towards them from his unassuming vehicle. He looked and acknowledged both of them. "Gentlemen," he whispered with a tip of his head as he opened the large door to the church. Seeing Cadillac Dan walk into the church was a bit of a surprise for both of them.

Jack and Aaron spoke quietly to each other as they stood on the church steps and lit cigarettes. Each took a drag off their cigarette and watched in silence as others walked into the church. All of them strangers. No one caught their eyes or attention.

Except one. A single individual approached the building. They threw their cigarettes to the ground and stepped on them as they hurriedly walked towards Bart. They had not seen or spoken to him in years, but they all spoke as if they'd just had lunch last week.

Aaron stuck out his hand and shook Bart's. "Where have you been man? You don't call, you don't write. You don't love us anymore?"

Bart smiled. "Oh, you would like that wouldn't you?"

Jack gave Bart a hug. "What are you doing here? I would have bet that you would be the one person that we would not see here today."

Bart just raised his shoulders. "I don't know. I guess it's the least I could do. Maybe I feel guilty. I'll never forget his little loyalty speech he gave me when I interviewed with him. I made a lot of money because of him, and my life is better for it. I'll just sit in the back where no one will see me. What about you guys? What's new?"

Jack quipped back. "Better than ever. But I'm sure you know that. The FBI knows everything, remember?"

They began to walk up the stairs to the church as Aaron mentioned Dan Manikan. "Cadillac Dan just walked in a few minutes ago." He pointed to the car Dan had gotten out of. "He's driving that piece of shit over there. Do you know his story?"

Bart's knowledge was a commodity now. "As far as I know he's still working at a bookstore as an assistant manager. He wasn't actually a full partner at the firm, so the Attorney General's office wasn't looking to crucify him. He served his four years like a good boy and has been quiet ever since. I know he tried to get a teaching job, but there's not much room in the education system for a convicted felon. The government seized all his assets and what little cash he had for reparations to some of his clients. I bet he still lives paycheck to paycheck."

Jack's response was simple. "Wow. The more things change, the more they stay the same. What about Strong?"

"Ten years is what the judge gave him. He got out a little early and tried selling cars. You would think he would have succeeded at it. I've been told that he just never recovered from his prison term. His wife divorced him while he was locked up, too. He apparently just slowly melted away the past couple of years."

"What about Olive? What was his story?"

"We still don't know. We know he lost a lot of money for some very rich and powerful people. It could have been anyone. He knew so many you know. We have a few suspicions, but no solid evidence. There was no trail to follow."

They were quiet as they opened the doors to the church. Bart then whispered something to them. "I'm surprised y'all haven't asked about Haynes."

"Oh, that's right. Whatever happened to that dude?"

"Not sure. He somehow managed to get out of the building the day of the bust. Haven't seen him since. We did hear that he had been in the Caribbean for a while. There was a story that he bought an island down near the northern tip of South America. But we have also heard he was living in a small town in Chile outside of a city called Rancagua. We don't have any extradition treaties with any of the places we think he might be, so it doesn't matter anyway."

Like insubordinate little kids, the three of them whispered in the back of the church throughout the entire service. Sometimes even squirming around trying to hold in their laughter. It was probably as inappropriate as it was fitting. Then Jack dropped the bomb that Swamp-Ass was working for them.

"I thought no one understood a word he said," replied Bart.

"Oh, no," said Aaron with conviction. He speaks about a zillion languages." And get this. He comes from money."

"What?"

"Yep," Jack said. "And are you ready for a good laugh?"

"Always," said Bart.

"His full name is Francois Thibault Beauchamp Yves St. Clair, the Fourth!"

At that, the three of them burst out laughing, causing a short interruption in the services and a few heads to turn to look back at them. Bart about slid out of the pew he was laughing so hard.

"We still can't understand a word he says, though," said Aaron. "And he refused to get caught up in all the politics at the firm. That's why he never hung out with any of us. And he still sells a lot to his family."

They got up to leave before the end of the service. As an afterthought Bart asked Jack, "What about One-Trade Maye? She used to open a lot of accounts."

"That whore? I don't think so. Aaron and I didn't think it was wise to have someone turning tricks at our company. But I'm sure the FBI already knew that." Bart seemed surprised. "Uh, actually no. It never even crossed my mind."

"But we did hire a few from the firm besides Swamp-Ass," said Jack. "Fast Eddie, Floyd, and Maria. Maria makes sure everything runs smoothly. Couldn't live without her. And Fast Eddie is making a ton of money, as usual. I don't know what it is with that guy."

"Must be all the "F" bombs he uses," replied Bart.

They all laughed again, remembering that there were some good times when they had all worked at the firm.

They walked out of the church saying their good-byes, knowing sooner or later they would run into each other again.

"If you ever get tired of working for the FBI, give us a call. You can always come and work for us. We'll find a desk and a phone for you."

Bart smiled and turned to leave, but then turned back and looked at Aaron and Jack. "I might be eating breakfast around midnight this weekend at this place I used to fancy."

Aaron smiled. "I think we know the place."

Jack smiled, too. "Maybe we could take a little stroll around town afterwards. I hear the streets are empty early in the morning."

Bart smiled as he walked away. "I could make a few calls."

LaVergne, TN USA
23 April 2010
180360LV00003B/8/P